# Shopping for a CEO's Fiancée

## JULIA KENT

# Shopping for a CEO's Fiancee

## SHOPPING FOR A BILLIONAIRE
### BOOK FIVE

JULIA KENT

Shopping for a CEO's Fiancée

BY JULIA KENT

**We skipped right over the whole fiancée thing and went straight from girlfriend to wife.**

At least, I think that's what happened. I wake up after my brother's Vegas wedding reception with my luscious girlfriend in bed with me. We're both wearing wedding rings.

So is her coworker, Josh.

And our Vegas chauffeur, Geordi.

Who the hell am I married to?

Unraveling this mystery will be as difficult as figuring out why Amanda and I are having panic attacks over the thought of being husband and wife.

Or whoever we're actually married to.

Oh, ^%$#.

It's true that what happens in Vegas stays in Vegas, with one exception:

If she's my wife, we'll make it work.

If she's not?

I'll make it happen.

*Listen to the audiobook, narrated by Audie award winner Sebastian York!*

2023 cover: Qamber Designs

Read my newsletter at juliakent.substack.com

# Reader Reviews and Emails

"You can see that he really loves Shannon to the very core of his soul, and it's beyond interesting to watch how that love can bring a strong, confident, alpha male like Declan to his knees."

"Wonderful laugh out loud story of a family that reminds me of my own. I'm a sucker for good 'how they met' stories, and this is is by far the most creative. I wholeheartedly recommend you read the series."

"Every chapter made my heart beat faster in anticipation. Julia Kent once again pulls at our emotions and allows us to fall in love with the characters all over again.... Very well worth my heart palpitations."

"If I could describe this book in a word, it would be, 'EVERYTHING'.

It has everything you want in a romance.

It has those witty and sometimes downright hysterical situations that you can't help but laugh at.

It has those hot, sexy moments that make a romance book a, well, hot and sexy romance book.

It has all those quirky, fun characters we've all come to enjoy through this series.

But better than all that, it has what I loved best about this book: those sweet, tender expressions of love that are written so beautifully and artistically."

"As an avid reader I have to say there is nothing better than an author that can combine romance and humor. Julia never disappoints, and is one of the best at creating stories that suck you in and keep you laughing."

"I just can't imagine how you come up with this stuff, but am so glad you do!"

"I finally had to write to you and tell you that you are simply one of the most amazing authors. Your humor is perfect. I really do bust out laughing out loud. My family thinks that I am crazy when I do it but I can count on a good read from you especially when it has been a rough day. There hasn't been a single thing that you have written that I haven't fallen in love with the characters. They become real and some of your lines have become a part of our family language. Thank you for sharing your amazing gift."

"Having another fantastic evening as I just finished your latest book and now the fam can go to sleep since the laughing/screaming out loud has stopped... Stomach muscles are sore. Better than sit-ups! :-)"

# Chapter One

Waking up naked with your face between your girlfriend's legs is the *best* way to start your morning in Vegas.

With your brother screaming at you from the other side of the covers? Not so much.

Amanda's thighs make great pillows that muffle out my brother bellowing, "What the hell happened in here?" His outrage makes the mattress vibrate, like those beds in seedy motels on television shows. In a pinch, Declan's yell is worth a quarter. Maybe fifty cents.

I sit up and scream back, "WHAT THE FUCK?"

Because that is a perfect example of executive mastery and grace under pressure.

It's the morning after my brother's wedding. I am in my hotel suite here at Litraeon, the Las Vegas Strip resort owned by my company, Anterdec. My girlfriend, Amanda, is with me. We're both naked. We should be alone.

We're *not*.

That needs to be rectified.

My head fills with metal shavings masquerading as lightning bolts that run through my veins. I flop back, eyes closed.

The world needs to stop spinning. Now.

I reach for Amanda. Her soft, creamy skin anchors me to the world. She's mine again. Mine. All mine. She moans, the sound unrecognizable. It's nothing like the little gasp I elicit during intimate moments. She sounds like Gloria Steinem at a Ted Cruz rally.

If I ignore Declan, he'll go away. Maybe this is a nightmare.

"ANDREW!"

Nope.

I lift my arm to rub my eyes and ask Declan why the hell he's barging in on Amanda and me. Who keyed him into my suite? Someone on our security team is getting fired. Besides, it's the first day of his honeymoon. Doesn't he have something better to do right now?

Something deep in my core stirs, a discontent that is both familiar and exasperating.

I start to rub my eyes in a weak attempt to wake up and—

Wait. What's that weight on my left hand?

And when the hell did Declan start to look so much like my dad? My vision clears and there's Dec, standing next to Shannon, who is watching Amanda with an intensity I've only seen in one other woman, ever.

Jessica Coffin.

"Is that a wedding ring on your left hand?" Declan shouts, like I'm Gollum and he's Sauron. What ring? What the hell is he talking about?

I check my hands. Right hand clear. Left hand—

Uh, oh. How did *that* get there?

Amanda screams. My sister-in-law's cat, Chuckles, is on the bed. He's wearing a veterinarian's surgical cone with the words "WILL SLEEP WITH PUSSY FOR FOOD" written in Sharpie.

The handwriting is familiar.

*Too* familiar.

Chuckles claws Amanda, yielding a wild shriek from both. Declan gets the cat off her and she sits up and—

She's Gollum, too. Yep.

My precious has the Ring.

Amanda starts saying something about a tuba, and then her friend Josh pops up from the floor. He looks like a really whiny ninja with no body fat. He's fully dressed, fastidiously so.

I clear my throat and start to stand, ready to resume control over this mess. The stirring inside me has taken more breaths and awakens, assessing, observing. Time to exert authority over these people. The cacophony is too much. I can't take it. They need to do exactly what I tell them, which means *leave*.

I stand.

I'm naked. Damn.

Unlike my brother, I don't believe in parading my junk for the world to see. Only people with something to prove need to do that.

You know. Like guys who aren't CEOs of Fortune 500 companies.

I clutch the covers. My stomach twists. I feel like a victim in a Dexter episode, except there's been a mistake. Amanda's pinning her head in place with her palms, and a weird ringing fills my head. Josh has his hand in the air, a strange glare of sunlight on—

Oh, shit. A ring.

What the hell *happened* last night?

Rainbows explode all over the other side of the bed. Rainbows and chocolate penises. A chocolate penis the size of a baseball bat is in the hands of a guy wearing a tie-dyed shirt and a head made of rainbow hair.

This is all a dream, right? The rainbow is wearing a wedding ring, but no underwear, and a sudden, cold clarity hits me as I look around the room.

I have a wedding ring.

Amanda has a wedding ring.

Josh has a wedding ring.

Rainbow chocolate-dong-holding dude has a wedding ring.

One of the hallmarks of my moving up the ranks so quickly at Anterdec has been my split-second decision-making ability, and my willingness to take business risks that scare the hell out of anyone else. Puzzle pieces fall in place in seconds when I observe, analyze and act. No wishy-washy wondering.

Intuition kicks in. Judgment is based on the gut. Decisions rest on data points and an ambiguous collection of—

Hold on. Sunlight passes over Amanda's left hand.

"Who the hell is *she* married to?" I ask Declan, pointing at Amanda. Her skin is so luscious in this morning light. A lovely, healthy glow that reminds me of sunsets on the ocean.

Then I narrow my eyes and realize her breasts are orange.

Day-glo orange. The nipples are paler than the rest, like eyes.

Shannon's damn cat pees all over the really nice giant teddy bear I bought Amanda, prances over, and leaps into Declan's arms. I want to ask how my brother trained the cat to do that, but Amanda's screaming in my ear.

"Who am *I* married to? What? What kind of question is that?" she snaps. I liked her better when she moaned like Rachel Maddow interviewing the Zodiac Killer at a presidential primary.

"There are three men in here with wedding rings on!" I shout back. Only one of us should be her husband, of course. *Me*.

I pause. Why did I think that? I don't want to marry Amanda. Not yet, at least.

Not *yet*. Not...what? What am I thinking?

"That's riiiiiiigggght," Josh says. "And the Supreme Court declared last year that I can marry anyone I want, too." He wiggles his eyebrows at me like I'm a dessert buffet. "You could be my hubby!"

Guys have hit on me before. It's cool. Signals get crossed.

But hold on, here.

Josh is not my type.

If I had a guy type, I mean.

Oh, hell.

Declan's voice cuts through it all. "Little bro, the more important question is: who the hell are *you* married to?"

My brother has this way of looking at me that combines disgust, amusement, determination and just enough abuse to make me jump off the bed, nakedness be damned, and tackle him around the waist.

And right into the giant teddy bear.

"Ooooo! Cat pee! Cat pee!" Shannon squeals.

"Cat fight! Cat fight!" Josh shouts, clapping. "My bet's on my hubby, Andrew!"

"I am not your husband!" I shout, my cheek against Declan's belt.

"You don't knoooooooow that," Josh calls back.

"Why is Andrew's mouth orange?" someone asks.

"I'm *Shannon's* husband, you dumbass!" Dec grunts. "Speaking of which—hey! Shannon! Get a spray bottle!" Dec calls out.

"Why? Just wrestle him off you. He's drunk and in pain. You can take him," she replies.

Shannon has a hidden dark side.

"I don't know where to put my hands!" Dec confesses. "His junk is everywhere!"

"That—*grunt*—is because—*grunt*—my junk is so big —*grunt*," I groan.

"YOU BOYS STOP RIGHT NOW."

As if this couldn't get any worse. Just did.

That's my dad.

We ignore him.

Like hell I'm giving up.

"You are such a little shit," Declan hisses, as he tries to fight me without actually touching my bare skin.

I am winning.

And then Dad shouts to Shannon, she tosses something at him, and I hear:

"This is remarkably satisfying, Shannon! You're on to something," he says with a tone of admiration, as I get a face full of water mist. Declan lets go.

"For the record," I say, wiping my cheeks, "you let go first. I win."

"Dad sprayed us like dogs!"

I rush him again, but he stops me with arms of steel.

Mine, however, are titanium. We lock grips and wait, poised.

"Andrew James McCormick, you just blew off a two-hour meeting with the Sultan of Al-Massi. The damage control on this is incalculable. I didn't build this company just so you could tear it down because you were on a bender in Vegas!" Dad roars, his body tense and immobile, but his voice carefully calculated to intimidate.

That doesn't work on me, though. It makes me let go of Declan, who casually hands me something from the floor to cover my groin. It's brown and plush but it makes me respectable.

*Ish.*

"I'll fix it," I snap.

Amanda gives me an odd look, then goes back to fighting her inner tubas.

"No time." Dad turns to Declan and looks him over. Dec is dressed in a bespoke suit from a tailor I discovered and referred him to. "Your brother, unlike you, looks professional enough for a meeting with the Sultan."

"Or a Moroccan stripper," Shannon whispers in a weirdly bitter tone that makes Declan's eyebrow arch.

Declan's demeanor changes instantly, his stance uncomfortable. Shannon averts her eyes and the two look like teenagers at a dance in *Napoleon Dynamite*, trying to figure out how to fit in.

"How," Josh asks, peering intently at my crotch, "did you turn your love pole into a Wookiee?"

"Love pole?" The entire room says the phrase in unison, and in the *exact* tone I'm thinking.

I look down. Dec handed me a Chewbacca stuffed toy as my junk cover.

"Maybe he just wants a little Chewie down there," Rainbow dude notes, as he starts to back out of the room, taking Josh with him. Self-preservation is a strong instinct.

Rainbow dude finally covers himself. I hold one finger up to Dad, like I'm pausing him.

Dad doesn't handle being paused well.

"Well," Josh says slowly, giving Rainbow dude, who I realize is one of the chauffeurs (George? Geoff?) a series of nervous looks. "We snuck back in to find Geordi's pants sometime after three a.m., I think."

Geordi. That's right.

"And my dong." Geordi holds up the item in question. The chocolate is starting to melt in his hand.

"So you didn't sleep in the room all night? You weren't, er...." Shannon grimaces, looking at Dec, who gets an *aha!* expression on his face.

"This wasn't a foursome?" Dec asks bluntly.

"What a ridiculous question!" Dad shouts, exploding on the spot.

"Oh, no!" Josh squeals, flailing his hands. "No, no, no! I don't sleep with—" He breaks off the sentence and looks at me, biting his lower lip, eyes filled with the kind of panic usually reserved for contestants on *Hell's Kitchen* who move a basil leaf counterclockwise as Gordon Ramsay's coming over.

"You don't sleep with...what?" I ask.

"I don't sleep with *women*!" He points at Amanda like she's wearing a scarlet letter on her chest.

A scarlet W.

"And I don't sleep with gay guys!" Amanda moans back.

"Aside from that hook-up our freshman year," Shannon whispers.

"You pinkie promised never to talk about him!" Amanda hisses.

Declan and Dad start hooting.

"Trust me," Josh says in an acid tone. "The only two people in this room who had sex last night were you and Amanda." He looks down with a forlorn look.

Declan thumbs toward Shannon. "Actually, we did, too."

Josh's turn for a raised eyebrow. "In this room? Kinky."

Declan shuts him up with a glare. Josh and Geordi wisely leave.

"Now that we've gone into more detail about my sons' sex lives than an IRS audit, could we please get back to the fact that the CEO of the company I built from scratch is currently wearing a Star Wars action figure as a penis cozy and can't perform his job!"

You can guess who said that.

"Technically," I correct him, looking down, "this isn't a Star Wars action figure. That would be far too small to cover my—"

7

"Are you really arguing with the semantics about a stuffed Chewbacca toy?" Dad snaps.

"Declan can't take that meeting with the Sultan, Dad," I grind out, trying to take the heat off me.

"Why not? You're here, Dec. Delay the honeymoon by a few hours." Dad's hand does the familiar dismissal gesture. "The jet can wait."

"No, Dad," I explain, trying to catch Declan's eye. He won't give it to me.

"Andrew, you smell like a distillery and—" he sniffs the air. "And oddly enough, cat urine. You're standing in a disgusting room filled with people who are staring at your naked body while you use Disney merchandise in a decidedly unconventional manner. You're hardly in any position to argue with me over whether Declan is a better fit for representing Anterdec in a high-level meeting for a multi-*billion* dollar deal."

I try. Declan has a chance to cough it up on his own. Instinct makes me pause. Or maybe that's nausea, roiling in my gut. What the hell did I drink last night? Normally, I can hold my own with liquor. I go up to the line, and even cross it by a single, regrettable drink, but I don't do what I've clearly done to my body.

Mustering clarity, I give Declan a hard look. Silence.

Huh.

Looks like he isn't going to step up, after all.

"Declan resigned from Anterdec last night, Dad. He bought a coffee chain for Shannon and he's declared himself the CEO of the new company. He can't represent Anterdec because he doesn't work for us anymore."

Declan flinches at the word *us*.

If I had any muscles to spare, I would, too. It sounds really awful coming out of my mouth, and a part of me wishes I could take it back.

But not a big part.

Declan clears his throat and does the unexpected. He reaches into his breast pocket and pulls out another resignation letter. I had to lead the way. Big brother follows.

Does this really have to happen *now*?

8

Dad looks at me with disgust, then turns his attention to Declan, brow turned down, the lower half of his face blank. He starts reading the letter just as Amanda's mother, Pam, appears behind him, stepping gingerly through the mess on the floor, her eyes catching mine, briefly stopping at the beast I'm pressing over my groin to hide my...beast.

Her teacup Chihuahua, Spritzy, jumps out of her little handbag and sniffs the area around the giant teddy bear. Then he lifts his leg and does what any self-respecting male would do.

Claims his territory.

"You *resigned*?" Dad's words scream in my head, echoing off the walls of my skull like—

Like a tuba. Amanda's got a point.

Dec squares his shoulders and faces Dad, and now I smile.

Achievement unlocked: deflection complete.

"Yes." Declan's voice is forceful. He won't take crap from Dad. Shannon moves closer, her fingers wrapping around Declan's elbow, and for the first time in my life, I think Declan has a shot at truly taking on Dad. In a game of tennis, this would be *Point*.

"You can't resign!"

"Just did."

"I won't allow it."

Oh, big mistake. Big mistake, Dad. When we were kids, the worst phrase you could utter to Declan was "You can't."

"Allow?" Declan's across the room in a flash, right in Dad's face, making Pam take a step back. Spritzy rushes across the room, collar jangling like he's Quasimodo the serial killer, destroying me and Amanda with that gong of a collar.

"That's right." Dad won't back down.

"I do not need your permission to buy my own company and to resign from yours."

I flinch at the word *yours*.

*Set*.

When my mother died, I woke up in the hospital to a life that was someone else's. Nothing made sense. Dad was angry, Declan was shut down, and Terry was off at college. He came back for the funeral and disappeared again. Mom was gone.

One arena made sense, though: business. Joining Dad in running Anterdec was the only way to get his attention.

And now Dec is leaving.

Sharing Dad's attention is one thing. Being the top dog and edging Dec out just slightly is enough.

Having the full fire hose of James McCormick's expectations aimed at your face is more than enough.

I have a beast inside me. No, not the flesh stick between my legs.

This creature has no name. It thrives on control and vigilance. It needs to know all. Complete control is not its goal. Oddly enough, it defers at times. Rare times.

*Very* rare moments.

This is not one of them.

"ENOUGH!" I bellow, dropping the Chewbacca pillow, because why not? I have nothing to lose.

I bend down and find the first piece of clothing that will cover my body. It's the pink robe I bought Amanda when we arrived. The one with lace at the breasts. I'm not picky. I'm not one of those guys whose masculinity is threatened by feminine attire.

Not that I have a history with that. It's just that pink lace is an upgrade from Peter Mayhew.

True to form, Dad doesn't budge, Declan shifts his weight to one hip and thinks he can give me a blank, intimidating look and that will work, and the rest of the interlopers actually do move toward the doorway.

Amanda starts to crawl out of bed.

"Not you. *Them*."

"But I need to pee. And quit staring at my breasts. You always stare at my breasts."

"That's because they're luscious."

"Oh, brother," Dad and Dec say at the same time, finally moving toward the door.

"So firm and supple," I continue.

Declan glares. Pam looks like she's starting to faint. Dad grabs her arm and escorts her out of the bedroom.

Ordering them out of the room doesn't work, but talking about Amanda's naked body does? Fine. I take a deep breath and ignore the nine-member funk band in my head and start to talk about my favorite subject.

She looks down and screams bloody murder.

"I look like a human Cheeto!"

And then she faints.

"OUT!" I shout.

They listen to me. People do. I have a voice that makes it clear that not following my command is not an option.

Though I'm guessing that the Chewbacca crotch had something do with their exit.

I join Amanda under the covers and pass out.

*Match.*

# Chapter Two

Hours pass. I don't *know* that hours pass, because my consciousness is filled with dreams about Sultans in Dubai with rainbow penises having sex with — "

"Andrew," someone says. Someone with a creamy, sexy voice.

"Look at my hands," I mutter. "Can someone with hands like this have a short chocolate dong?"

"What?" The creamy voice curdles.

I startle. It's dark in the bedroom, and Amanda's sitting up in bed, her lap covered by the bedspread, her breasts still orange. The way her eyes catch mine makes the room feel warm and sweet. Protectiveness kicks in even more. She's tenting the covers and looking at her midsection. Her dark hair spills over her shoulder, but it's matted with something white and gooey.

No, not *that*. I lean toward her and sniff. Her hair smells like lemon and salt. For a moment, I close my eyes, trying to regroup. Five days ago, we were broken up. Irrevocably split for one simple reason:

I had a moment of stupendous idiocy. I'll own it.

More than a moment, too. I'm man enough to admit it. I let risk aversion nearly destroy my best hope for love.

Which meant that I simply miscalculated the risks.

Hence the stupendous, *temporary* idiocy.

We reunited only five days ago. Five damn days. The bandages on her arms are a stark reminder that the wedding in Boston was less than a week ago.

We're back together, but there's still so much left to learn about each other.

Little things, like which side of the bed each prefers. Favorite colors. Food preferences.

Or, you know, like whether we're *married* or not.

"How did I get Cheeto coochie?" she asks, pointing to her breasts, which look at me like Sirens on an island in the ocean. *Andrew*, they croon. *Come play with us....*

My mouth is cotton. Fermented cotton. And salt. Something salty. "What?"

She peers at me. "Your mouth matches my coochie. It's orange, too."

"Coochie?" We've only been back together for less than a week. I didn't know "coochie" was part of her personal vocabulary. "Cheeto coochie" sounds like the name of a tapas dish at a low-end restaurant.

Or a stripper name.

"You know." She peers down. "If your mouth is orange, and my breasts and, ahem," she points down, "are orange, then we committed some kinky acts with snack foods last night."

"You're the one with the Cheeto-marshmallow fetish."

She covers her mouth with her hand. "Don't mention food."

I wave my ringed hand. "Too much talk. Basics first." I force myself to stand and walk into the mini-kitchen. Water. I need water. Water and half a jar of ibuprofen-flavored beer.

And my memory.

*Bzzzz.*

"Your phone!"

"Probably Gina."

"Who is *Gina*?" The arch tone gets my attention and makes me smile. Now I know something new about Amanda.

She gets jealous. I grin and smother it with my hand.

"My new admin," I say, muffled by my palm.

She lets out a cute little huff of relief. "What happened to...Bethany?"

"She was *three* admins ago."

"Lucy's gone, too?" Amanda asks, incredulous.

"She was overly rigid." I can hear the defensiveness creep into my voice.

"She was great!"

"She lasted ten days."

"You have an admin problem, Andrew."

"No, I don't." I ignore my phone. If I can keep a Sultan waiting, I can defer my admin back in Boston, the new young woman the temp agency sent me a few weeks ago. What I need right now is water. Water and Amanda. In that order.

"Your admins have an *Andrew* problem."

"I'm a great boss!" Irritation sets in. We've spent five days trying not to talk about any topic more intense than whether to add cinnamon to our breves, how to handle all the sex chafing, or debating whether jalapeno-flavored aioli is better than bacon-horseradish mayo.

After rescuing her from the pool at Dec and Shannon's wedding in Boston, we became so wrapped up in the Vegas chaos that we settled into a pattern.

A pattern of sex, food, gifts, and...sex.

That's right.

Guy nirvana.

Now she wants to *talk*?

Guy hell.

My slow walk to the kitchen should be filmed by a documentary crew with the soundtrack to *Apocalypse Now* in the background. The bedroom looks tame compared to the living room and kitchen. No cat. No dog. No giant pee-covered teddy bear, which means the living room should be an improvement.

I gag. Why does it smell like a distillery in here? A quick push of buttons on the wall and the curtains part, filling the room with light and, as the windows vent, some air.

Then I see the pile of glow-in-the-dark sex toys on the coffee table.

And a giant yoga ball.

That is buzzing.

"And soon you'll be *my* boss," Amanda tosses off.

I don't answer that, because the buzzing comes from a glowing appendage attached to the yoga ball. The tip curves to the left and if I squint, I can read some words on the shaft.

Yo! G-spot Ah.... An acronym for YOGA.

That's a brand name? I'd fire the person who pushed that to market. No focus group on the planet would approve *that*.

I solve the problem by grabbing a throw blanket and covering everything. If I pretend it doesn't exist, then it doesn't. That's how Dad handles emotions in other people, and if it works for him, I can apply it to errant piles of sex toys.

"Oh, my God. I don't understand. What really *did* happen last night?"

*You and me both, babe.*

Amanda's words float through the air with a tempo they're not supposed to possess. I flatten my palms against the granite countertop in the small kitchen of our suite and take a deep breath. My shoulders rise up and expand out. I feel my soles against the marble tile. Emotion washes over me like the shame my father was trying to instill. He failed, but the attempt lingers.

My eyes catch the glint of gold against the polished granite.

Husband? Wife? Josh and that rainbow chocolate dong dude skedaddled along with the rest of them earlier. I breathe, inhaling and exhaling, counting to four, then eight, using every technique that I normally don't need to use.

It's not anxiousness. It's overwhelm. And when I get overwhelmed, there's only one solution.

Control.

Actually, now there are two. The new one is sex.

I like *new*.

Instead of going back for my cell phone, I reach for the corded one and dial a special code that takes me straight to my number one here at Litraeon.

"Mr. McCormick? How may I help you?" It's Brona Jordan, vice president of operations. Her voice has that smooth, cultured

15

tone with an accent that you can't quite pinpoint. European? Central Asian? Boston Brahmin? Brona's been with Litraeon for the past five years, and profits have gone sky high since she brought on a new line of chefs and stores to the attached mall. While she isn't the top dog, she's best at meeting delicate situations.

I am the poster child for *delicate*.

"I need a suite."

"You already have a suite. You require a *second* suite?"

"I want one of the presidential suites instead."

Silence. I know what I'm asking. Declan, Dad and I settled for these second-tier suites because of the last-minute nature of the wedding mess. The cream of the crop should be mine again. I'm done playing second fiddle. Sunlight flashes off the ring on my left hand.

Funny. I haven't taken it off yet.

"Yes," she says slowly, "we can accommodate that, of course. You realize we will need to relocate the Sultan."

The Sultan?

"He's *here*?"

"Yes."

My mind races and clears at the same time, as if my gray matter were being pressure washed of toxins and left gleaming and renewed.

"And that's the meeting I missed." Dad's fury connects with Brona's observation. Anterdec is in final negotiations to expand our resort network into Dubai. We have two smaller properties there, but this would be an enormous capital investment, with a fifty-story tower, massive water park, private airport and all that goes with the definition of luxury among the ultra-wealthy.

And I blew off a meeting with the Sultan because of—

"Cheeto coochie!" Amanda moans from the next room.

"Excuse me?" Brona asks. "Did you say something, Andrew?"

And then there's that.

Brona's shift from formality tells me even more. Dad's

already gotten to her and let her know why I'm missing the meeting.

I've lost control here.

Time to gain it back.

"Get me into a presidential suite within thirty minutes."

"I need sixty, and permission to relocate anywhere they ask."

"What does that mean?"

"They might want to go next door if you kick them out."

Next door. We're competing with the owners of that resort for the Dubai deal.

"Damn it," I mutter.

She merely clears her throat and waits. I chug half a gallon of water and sigh.

Control. I need—

"May I make a suggestion?" Brona's words are soothing. "What if you reserve a royal suite next door?"

"Me? Why would *I* move out of my own property?" And when the hell did the place next door create *royal* suites?

"To throw them off." She sighs. "And yes, we're working on creating our own royal suites. Already in development."

Tumblers click in my head. Gears sync. I have a naked mystery shopper in my bedroom. Brona's suggestion sets off a firestorm of connected thoughts, lighting my CEO brain up like a thunderball.

"Perfect. Do it. We'll take their best."

"Nothing but," she croons. "Anything else?"

"No—wait. Yes. Check the security video for the hallway in front of my suite. Copy it from about eight o'clock last night until right now. I'd like to review it with Jed." Jed is our head of security here at this Vegas Strip resort, Litraeon.

*Click.*

"We're moving," I announce, carrying a glass of water for Amanda back to the bed, handing it to her.

She immediately pours it down her front, starting with the collarbone, the water cascading down her torso, pearling on her nipples, rolling down the slope of her breasts like something out of really high-quality porn.

"That's *not* how you drink water," I explain. How drunk is she?

"I cannot have this all over my breasts!" She takes a corner of a sheet and rubs furiously at her chest, her tits bouncing. It's a delightful sight. I start to tent my pink silk bathrobe.

"Who were you talking to?" she asks as she rubs. I imagine her rubbing hand on a part of me that loves to be rubbed.

And I'm hard.

"Brona. My main person here at Litraeon. We're moving."

Amanda pauses. "We're what?"

"In an hour. We're getting a better suite."

"Why?"

"Because this one is a mess."

*Because I can't handle being surrounded by signs that I lost control last night and holy hell are we really married?*

Keeping my mouth shut is my primary business skill. I don't speak that random thought. I'm not stupid.

"Then get someone to clean it."

"No."

"Why not?"

"I can't stand to wait that long."

"You'd rather move?"

"It's easier."

"Where are we going?"

"Next door."

"Next door? Why?"

"So we can do some corporate espionage."

"You're not making sense."

"You're *orange* and you're judging me?"

"You're orange too, buddy. Go look in the mirror."

She points to the bathroom.

Every bit of the room goes into soft focus, my eyes only on her. In the craziness of this morning, I haven't really looked at her. For five days she's been all I touch, all I see, all I feel and want to feel. We've spent these days in Vegas in a vortex of sex and damage control. Shannon and Declan's wedding damage control. Between media reports and PR tracking and press inquiries and thousands of personal and professional messages that have eaten up nearly every waking hour of my time, the stolen moments with Amanda have been entirely about sex.

Not that I'm complaining.

I cross my arms over my chest. The cold metal ring registers against my ribs.

Being orange is the least of our worries.

"Amanda."

The grin she gives me is part pain, part jaunty. "You can't even look because you know I'm right."

"Amanda."

This time, her grin falters, her eyes tip up, looking at me. I take in the bandages on her arms, the curve of one breast against the pillow, the disorienting range of her chest, and the wild hair.

I love every inch of what I see.

"Amanda," I say again, across the room in a flash, one knee on the bed, then the other, and my mouth is on hers before I realize what I'm doing. The wet sheets twist between us and her hands are under the damn pink silk robe I'm wearing, on my back, flat and imploring, pulling me to her. I wiggle out of the frock. We're reeling from waking up married. Maybe. We're half-drunk and hungover and embarrassed and confused.

At least, *I* am. I suppose I should ask her how she feels, but based on the little moans and sighs coming out of her, I'm guessing she's not suffering right now.

Sex is easier than talking. Sex is better than working.

Kissing her is better than—

"Coffee," she whispers.

"Sex is better than coffee?"

"Who said that?"

"You did."

"No, I didn't!" She pushes me off her and stands, holding her head between her palms. "I mean, it is. Normally. But not right now."

*Bzzzz.*

I grab my phone. Gina.

"Is that a resignation letter from your new admin?" Amanda

wanders out into the living room. "Holy shit!" she says, reacting to the mess out there. "Why doesn't this hotel room have a coffee maker? You own the resort! Make them add coffee makers!"

I thought she was panicking about the sex toy cemetery out there.

"You don't need to mystery shop our room."

"I do when your company is so barbaric that they don't provide *coffee makers*. You have complimentary bathrobes and you can't manage coffee?"

*Tap tap tap.*

Amanda lets out a tiny scream of surprise. "Who the hell is that?" She half-shuffles, half-sprints back into the bedroom, a Cheeto-marshmallow treat in one hand, a glass of water in the other.

"Probably the coffee." I set my phone on the nightstand and grab a white robe from the closet, shrugging into it. Amanda does the same, only this time she's wearing the pink robe I left on the bed. She looks exhausted and sweet, all at the same time.

Her face softens. "You ordered me a breve?"

"Of course." I don't mention that Brona probably did.

I'm right. Room service appears with a rolling table filled with all of our favorites. Two pre-made breves, a small pot of espresso, a small pitcher of frothed light cream, fruits and baked goods, and scrambled eggs and bacon.

"Coffee's all I need." Amanda turns green, which is a good color to go with orange. I motion for the staff person to push the rolling table closer to the door and grab Amanda's breve. All deliveries to our room come with built-in tips, so within seconds, he's gone. I sit on the couch and Amanda curls up in front of me, her back to my chest, her long sigh gratifying. As she melts into me, I drink my own fortification and all the thoughts I've held at bay come rushing in.

Dad.

The Sultan.

Declan's resignation.

Acquiring Greg's mystery shopping company.

A merger in—

"Stop," she says suddenly.

"Stop what?"

"Worrying about work."

"How did you know?"

"You roll your shoulders when you're tense and it's work-related."

"You've catalogued *that*?"

"I'm perceptive."

"Amanda." Her name trips off my tongue so easily. She snuggles in, draining her breve and setting the empty cup on the end table.

"Yes?"

"A week ago," I begin. She stills. Her hair's matted and wet at the ends, and her soft pink lacy bathrobe only half-covers her orange-stained skin. Her eyelashes flutter against her cheekbones and I can hear the soft rasp of her breath as she waits for me.

Talk about control.

"A week ago," I say more firmly, wondering how to convey the last week's tumult through the inadequacy of language. "A week ago, I refused to let you love me."

"You failed," she says under her breath.

Dark laughter pours out of me, making me choke. She isn't making this easy.

And yet she is.

"We haven't really talked." Isn't that the woman's line?

"No. We haven't. When were we supposed to talk?" She reaches up with her left hand and touches mine.

Our rings clink against each other.

"And then there's that." My voice drops as the sentence ends.

Along with my stomach.

"We're not—you don't really—we can't be—"

"Married?"

She laughs, but it's a brittle sound. "Come on. We didn't actually have a wedding last night."

"We didn't? You're sure?" I perk up. Great. *She* remembers last night. I squeeze my eyes and try to recall something—

anything—that happened after Declan and Shannon said their goodbyes at the reception last night.

"I'm, well, I mean..." Twisting in my arms, she looks at me with those big, wide, trusting eyes, her left hand splayed against my bare chest, digging in where the robe has separated. "You don't remember what happened?"

My voice drops with uncertainty.

Hers goes up.

"No."

"Quit joking."

"Not joking."

"We both can't remember any part of last night?"

"When does your memory end?" I ask.

Mascara is streaked along the corner of her eye, and any makeup she wore last night currently resides somewhere on my skin or on the bedsheets. I can only imagine what I look like.

Amanda, though, is gorgeous. In my arms and looking at me with a perplexed expression, biting her lower lip while she flips through the filing cabinets of memory in her mind, and—

"I don't know."

I sit up. "You're the fixer."

"I know! But I remember saying goodnight to Shannon, hugging Declan, and then—*poof!* Nothing."

Poof.

"That's when my memory ends, too," I say, my skin beginning to crawl. "I know one thing: we did not have a foursome."

"And I soooooo did not sleep with Josh. He's gay. The man can't handle watching a birth video. A real-life vagina would send him into cardiac arrest."

"I know my heart pounds whenever I see yours," I whisper. She gives me a reluctant smile, in spite of her hangover.

"That was baaaaaad," she groans.

"All signs point to the sex question being put to rest. Worst case, all we did was sleep with each other," I note.

"*Worst* case? Buddy, sleeping with me is *best* case. Best case. Always *best*."

That was an unfortunate choice of words on my part. Before I can do damage control, she speaks.

"What if we are?" she hisses.

"Are what?"

Her eyes dart to mine.

"Married."

# Chapter Three

*Tap tap tap.*

"Who the hell is that?"

*Bzzzzz.*

"And that?" Amanda jumps off me and walks slowly to the door. I find my phone. It's Brona.

"Yes?"

"We're moving you. Just change into whatever you need, Andrew, and the rest is done."

"Fine."

"Security reports that your current room will need some conditioning."

*Conditioning* is hotel code for a complete overhaul because of crazy partying.

"It's not that bad."

"Why is there a nest of baby gerbils in the bathtub?" Amanda screams from the bathroom.

"Ahem," Brona says.

"Fine. Conditioning."

"Do I need to call the Humane Society?"

I peer into the bedroom. "Do they take six-foot teddy bears?"

"Excuse me?"

"Yes. Call them." I hang up. Who knows what else the staff will find?

Amanda has let a group of staff inside the room, and with brief nods and blank faces, they pack our belongings.

Ten minutes, fourteen gerbils, one bearded dragon, an unopened five-pound bag of sugar-free gummy penises and twelve half-eaten chocolate dongs later, they leave us with a change of clothes and promise to return shortly to finish.

*Tap tap tap.*

"That better not be my dad," I mutter, opening the door.

Worse.

It's Declan and Shannon.

"Back for more abuse?"

"To receive it or hand it out?"

"Both."

"Where's Amanda?" Shannon asks, peering around, her nose wrinkled.

I point to the kitchen. Shannon makes a hasty retreat.

"This is your biggest screw-up yet," Declan says drolly.

"How was the meeting with the Sultan?"

"There was no meeting. He was kicked out of his suite here and is on his way back to Dubai. Said you ordered him out."

"WHAT?" Damn it. Brona sent out feelers and signals got crossed.

"Dad says it's a stroke of genius," Declan says pleasantly.

"What?"

"Has your vocabulary devolved into the word *what?*"

"Huh?"

"That's an improvement. Variety is the spice of life."

"Says the man who just tied himself to one woman for the rest of his life."

Dec yanks my hand. I steel myself. He can't move me an inch.

"People who live in glass wedding rings shouldn't throw stones, Andrew."

"That doesn't even make sense."

He laughs. "But it's funny."

"What do you mean, Dad thinks accidentally kicking the Sultan out of the Presidential Suite was a stroke of genius?"

"The Sultan's had too much power in all the negotiations. Being an asshole to him helps reset the balance."

You have got to be kidding me. Only Dad could take this situation and turn it into a positive.

"Do we get the deal?"

"You figure it out. Dad wants you in Dubai next week." His eyes land on my ring finger. "Unless you'll be too busy on your honeymoon."

"Honeymoon? Why would I—"

He yanks on my ring finger.

"Oh, screw off," I grumble.

"You've always been jealous of me, Andrew, but upstaging my wedding?"

"Upstaging? You think I did this on *purpose*?" None of this involved volition.

Not mine, anyway.

"Who, exactly, are you married to?"

I go silent.

"You still don't know?"

More silence.

"What do you remember about last night?"

"Nothing."

"You drank so much you blacked out?"

I shrug. "If I did, so did Amanda. We can't remember a damn thing after you and Shannon left your reception."

"You don't remember *marrying* someone?"

"We're just piecing it all together."

He shakes his head in disgust. "You partied in college, but nothing like this. It's not like you."

We both frown. The staffers return, moving swiftly around us as they pack the rest of our belongings, and I let his words sink in. He's right. This isn't like me. I don't do this. I don't black out, and I don't party hard to the point of marrying someone.

Especially potentially marrying one of three different people.

Deeply disturbing thoughts begin to surface inside me. What if we didn't get drunk last night? What if—

"Amanda seems to be taking this in stride." Declan tips his

chin toward the kitchen, where Amanda is whispering in Shannon's ear. "And you're too blasé. How can you both be so calm?"

"Because being calm is my job, Dec."

He snorts. "Showing up for business meetings is, too."

"And then there's that whole Cheeto coochie condition."

"Cheeto *what*?"

I wave around my crotch. "You know. She keeps calling it Cheeto coochie."

"The right drugs can cure that."

"Don't talk about my girlfriend's sweet cave."

"Her *what*?" He grabs my jaw and peers at my mouth. "You have Cheeto mouth."

"I do?" Amanda wasn't joking.

"Cheeto coochie is contagious." His eyes drop to my junk.

Reflexively, I cover my crotch with my hands. "My junk is not orange."

"Oh yeah?"

"What—you want me to show you?"

"Are you two having a penis contest again? Can you just measure and be done with it?" Shannon keeps making this joke. It's not funny. But if I roll my eyes in front of Declan, he'll yell at me, and my hangover headache is still in that precarious zone where yelling makes me want to stab my eye with a chopstick.

"Depends. Does Cheeto dust add an unfair advantage to length?" I mutter.

"Cheeto *what*? Is that a kink?"

"Ask Andrew!"

The sound of running water interrupts the argument. Amanda must be in the shower. I grit my teeth. If the suite were empty, I'd be in there right now. Talking might be awkward, but I can express an incredible amount of emotion in other ways.

And by *incredible*, I mean—

"Excuse me, Mr. McCormick?"

"Yes?" Declan and I answer in unison as a staffer comes back down the hallway.

"We found this among the gerbils."

"Gerbils?" Dec's eyebrows go up.

The staffer holds out his cupped hands, which contain a baby chick.

"I can't believe this, Andrew."

Shannon cranes around Declan, trying to get a look. "No kidding!" she chirps. "Where was that?"

"In the bathtub, with the gerbils and the—"

"Security has a report of an unattended fainting goat that is loose in the building as well, sir."

"A *what*?" I snap.

"A fainting goat."

"How do you know it *faints*?"

"Guests continue to report a dead goat. Surveillance footage shows that it's just fainting."

"What a relief," Dec says. "Because a fainting goat is so much better than a dead one." He turns to me. "When did your suite become a petting zoo?"

"Shut up."

I've had enough. More than enough. I'm still dehydrated, and there's not enough headache medicine in the world to take care of my hangover. Add in my brother, the Sultan mess, and a menagerie of animals that are relics from a night I can't even remember—plus these damn wedding rings—and I've had it.

"OUT!"

"That's not going to work this time," Declan informs me.

Fine. "Then be useful."

"How?"

"Meet us for coffee next door."

He brightens. "At my new chain?"

"At your new—oh, damn it." I forgot he bought the place. He's going to be insufferable for a while.

And by "for a while" I mean *forever*.

"Glad to see you're admitting it's better than this place." He sniffs.

Shannon gapes at him. "You are such a cocky bastard."

I knew I liked her for a reason.

The carpet is littered with feathers, Cheeto dust, empty liquor bottles, candy wrappers, and small piles of detritus that could be dissected, but are better left untouched. I can't stand the mess. It distracts me, like an itch. A visual itch that can only be scratched by leaving.

And then I hear it.

Over the noise of the shower running, there's another sound. Since I was a small child, I've had the kind of hearing that drives parents batty. Mom used to say that if working in the family business didn't pan out for me, I could find a career as a human hearing aid.

And right now, I hear Amanda, sobbing, in the bathroom.

"Out," I repeat, this time with a deadly growl, turning away from Declan and entering the bathroom, holding the door open just enough to slide in sideways.

Where I discover, to my chagrin, that I am right.

This is one of those rare moments when I do not want to be right.

She is sitting on the edge of the tub, crying softly, fingers buried in her hair, the room completely overtaken by steam.

"Hey."

She sniffs but says nothing.

"It's not that bad," I say, bending in front of her.

"Are you insane? It's not that bad? If this isn't that bad, how the hell do you define *bad*?"

I let that sink in.

"Bad," I finally reply, "is when your brother has to choose between you and your mother."

She gasps.

"Bad is when your mother thinks the father of her child has killed her in a drunk-driving accident."

She sobs.

"This? This is a situation, Amanda. This can be managed."

"You have a very stark way of putting things in perspective."

"That's my job."

"I might be married to one of three men! One of whom faints at the sight of vaginas!"

"I'd like to be very clear that I am *not* that man," I say, clearing my throat.

"A fainting goat would have a better chance of remaining conscious than Josh looking at some pink."

"Or orange."

She gives me a weak smile. "Ha ha. We have no memory. How do we manage this?"

"One shower at a time."

Unexpectedly, she reaches down to her left forearm with her right hand and *riiiiiiip*!

"What are you doing?"

In one smooth move, she grimaces and tears the worn bandage off her left forearm, revealing a network of animal claw scratches. Amanda does the same with her right forearm, leaving me stunned.

"I'm ripping off the Band-aid," she says, her voice filled with pain.

"You still need to see a doctor."

"No. I need a shower, a gallon of ibuprofen, more coffee, and you."

"Me?"

"You."

We stand and I pull her into my arms, her naked body soft and sticky against my skin and open robe.

"If I have to be married to anyone, I hope it's you," I whisper, before kissing her softly. My blood pounds against my skin, my breathing slow, as the scent of her fills me. Her shoulder is so soft against my chin. She relaxes against me, so delicate, yet strong. Less than a week ago, I watched her nearly drown, a part of me dying as seconds ticked by underwater and I couldn't free her fast enough. Sheer determination got her to the surface in time.

Overriding instinct takes a terrible toll on the body.

And it's even worse on the heart.

"Considering the options, I'm not sure whether to be flattered or to hit you."

"Trust me. It's a compliment. Besides, I'm not sure I can handle any more pain right now."

Steam surrounds us, making my lungs fill slowly. The warmth helps, but being alone, upright, with her in my arms is the best medicine right now. So much remains unspoken between us. The vocabulary just isn't there.

I wonder if that's the whole point of committing to one person: you have the rest of your lives to figure out how to say what you feel. You build a language for two. Fluency isn't optional.

While the rest of the world ticks on, and my workload piles up, I can ignore my mistakes and the puzzling circumstances of our possible marriage if I just kiss her again.

So I do.

And in that kiss, the first dangerous thought of the day slams through me.

Would it be so bad if I *am* her husband after all?

# Chapter Four

"This really is the best coffee I've ever had," Amanda says, with a sigh that women usually reserve for guys like me.

"Best in Vegas!" Declan crows. He's arrogant enough as it is, but now all I'm going to hear is nonstop chatter about his superlative coffee empire.

I wonder if Dad was like this, circa 1981.

"Litraeon has great coffee," I argue.

Shannon, Declan and Amanda all snicker.

"Once we're up and running, we can work on getting Grind It Fresh! in Anterdec properties," Dec says, suddenly serious. "It'll be win-win."

Business talk. I might be married to one of three different people and all Declan can talk about is his damn coffee chain.

"We have bigger fish to fry."

"We have to unwind last night," Amanda explains, looking at Shannon. "I texted Josh and Geordi. They're on their way." She glances at me. "I hope you don't mind."

"Mind? I texted them, too. We need to get to the bottom of this ASAP. If we keep this quiet, then we can figure this out with a minimal amount of spillage."

"Spillage?"

"Unnecessary word getting out."

"I'm here to help!" Shannon's mom appears with her dad, Jason.

Great. So much for spillage. Marie is the equivalent of a tractor-trailer accident involving a honey truck crashing into a hot-fudge-filled semi.

"You bought my daughter a fabulous wedding present, because the coffee here is orgasmic!" Marie says to Declan. She and Jason are carrying Grind It Fresh! to-go cups.

"Litraeon coffee is just fine."

Everyone ignores me.

"You two were hilarious last night. I had no idea you had such a wild side, Andrew!" Marie plucks a pink macaron from a tray filled with them as Jason settles into a seat next to her, giving me an evaluative look.

"What does that mean?" I ask slowly.

"You did a fantastic job emceeing the stripper finals at the adult products trade show!"

Declan grins and gives me a look.

"I *what*?"

"Here. We caught part of it on video."

Video? "How did you get video? Amanda and I checked our phones and we have nothing. No pictures, no videos, no evidence of anything from last night."

Marie shrugs. "You were too busy." She slides her phone over to me.

I'm shirtless and oiled up, hair soaked with sweat, and I have a Sharpie marker in my hand.

"Are you the one who wrote on Chuckles?" Amanda gasps. "He's never going to forgive you."

"A cat with a grudge is the least of my worries," I whisper.

"That's what you think," she says cryptically.

"Let me see that!" Declan says, trying to snatch the phone out of my hands. He may have the advantage of surprise, but my will is stronger. And I'm in better shape, so I leap up and vault away.

He doesn't chase.

"No." I cover the screen with my hand and watch.

Apparently, last night, I didn't just emcee a men's stripper final competition.

I decided to *join* it.

"Can I watch?" Amanda asks, her head peeking over my shoulder. I relent and tilt the screen.

Slightly.

"Why can she watch but not me?" Declan protests.

"Because I have a vested interest in Andrew's naked body."

Dec and I just stare at Amanda.

"Point taken," he says, backing away slowly.

Amanda takes the phone from me, mesmerized by the scene unfolding on the screen.

As my own very drunk, increasingly naked form gyrates on the video, I can only watch *her*.

My humiliation unfolds before us, second by second, but a parallel experience is taking place inside me. Her mouth curls up on one side, her smile coy and suppressed. She's as enchanting as she was more than two years ago, that day she stormed into my office to demand I help her reunite Declan and Shannon.

A man could do worse than being married to her.

"WHAT THE HELL IS THAT, ANDREW?" Amanda screams, flinging the phone at me.

It clatters to the floor and I look, dumbstruck.

Because I am kissing Jessica Coffin on the phone screen.

Declan bends down, retrieves the phone, and rewinds by a few seconds. He watches.

"Whoa."

"Jessica Coffin is here?" Shannon gasps, turning to Marie with a glare.

Marie's hands go up. "Don't blame me! I swear I didn't invite her!"

"Then what's she doing here?' Shannon whines.

"Who cares why she's here?" Amanda hisses, looking at me the entire time. "I want to know why my husband is kissing Jessica Coffin on video in front of a bunch of naked male strippers."

"They're not naked," I argue. I let the "my husband"

SHOPPING FOR A CEO'S FIANCEE

comment go unchallenged. The sound of it makes me grin.

"No, but you are, bro," Declan adds helpfully, handing me the phone.

I close my eyes. I can't look. I just can't—

Dec lets out a low whistle. "Turnabout's fair play, huh?" he says to Amanda. I open my eyes to see him wink.

"WHAT THE HELL IS THAT SUPPOSED TO MEAN?" Amanda yells at him.

Declan arches one eyebrow, hits rewind, and hands her the phone.

I watch as my maybe-wife kisses...

Jessica Coffin.

"EWWWWWWWW," Shannon and Amanda squeal.

"I thought you were only pretend gay," Marie says, clearly confused. "Mystery shop gay. You said—"

"That's kind of hot," Dec mutters.

"Oh, God," Amanda moans. "I would never, *ever*, kiss Jessica Coffin!"

"I think you owe me an apology," I inform Amanda.

"For what?"

"For being outraged that I kissed someone else."

"But you did!"

"So did you!" I note.

"We both cheated."

"Real cheating, too. Not just coffee cheating," Shannon adds, giving Declan the side-eye.

"That's not helping," Amanda snaps. She reaches up to her lips. "I kissed Jessica Coffin!"

"Is that some tongue I see in there?" Marie asks, pulling a pair of reading glasses out of her purse and peering at the phone. She pauses the video, reaches into her purse, and adds a second set of glasses on top of the first.

We have *lots* of help, don't we?

"Mom!"

"Amanda got to first base with Jessica," Marie says in a mournful tone. "Maybe even second base. What's your hand doing there?" she asks, pointing to the screen.

"Wait a minute," Shannon says, taking the phone from her mother and making the picture bigger. "Hold on. That's not Jessica Coffin."

"It looks just like her," Marie protests.

"But look. She has huge feet. And she's taller than Andrew."

I'm 6' 3."

"Even in heels, Jessica isn't taller than me," I note.

"And does Jessica have a shoulder tattoo?" Shannon asks, pointing.

"No," I respond quickly.

Amanda frowns. "You know an awful lot about Jessica Coffin's body."

Declan shifts uncomfortably.

I give him a look that says, *Don't say a word.*

My oldest brother, Terry appears. We might as well recreate the reception at this point. Jason stands and moves another table over to our crowd and I notice the big, white to-go cup in Terry's hand.

Grind It Fresh!

Traitor.

"Amazing coffee, Dec! You've got a winner on your hands." Coming from Terry's deep voice, it sounds like an announcer at a sporting event.

He turns to me and says, "You were hilarious last night, Andrew. How late did you party with the drag queens?" Terry's wearing a tie-dye shirt, shorts, and Birkenstocks. It's like he's trying to piss off Dad just by *being.*

"Drag queens? I kissed a drag queen?"

"You kissed about eight of them."

"Maybe that explains your orange face?" Shannon asks. "Makeup?"

"No, we know the source of the orange," Amanda mutters, then whispers in Shannon's ear.

Shannon reels back. "Not drag queen makeup. Got it." She stares intently at my mouth, then says to Amanda, "But wouldn't it hurt, putting them inside you?"

Amanda pales.

"This video has gone viral by now, right?"

"Not this exact video, but—"

My phone buzzes.

It's Dad.

"Oh, hell." I ignore it.

"He'll just have security track you down," Declan chides.

I go cold.

"So what?" I jut my chin up in defiance. I am five years old. Damn it. Dec makes me feel like the helpless little brother, mercilessly under his thumb.

You cage someone too many times and they become feral in anticipation of being caged again.

Declan scoffs. "Don't try that *so what* crap on me. You know damn well you care about Dad's opinion. A little too much, Mr. CEO."

"Is that what this is about? You're jealous?" I snap.

"Jealous? Of you? Jealous of a guy who can't break away from the one and only world he knows? Jealous of a guy who lives in fear of—"

"Of what?"

"Of everything."

He's such an asshole most of the time, but he's also my best friend.

Which is the definition of *brother* for most guys.

"You are out of your mind! I'm not afraid of anything!"

Amanda and Shannon clear their throats simultaneously.

Feral, remember?

"Why would you be afraid of anything other than losing out on this fabulous time?" Terry asks, his voice in falsetto, waving my phone around, making Marie, Shannon, and Amanda giggle. I know what he's doing. Dec knows what he's doing. This is what Terry does.

Terry hates conflict.

Terry makes silly jokes.

"I remember seeing you at the gift table with Amanda, and you grabbed a bottle of homeopathic wine that was just sitting there," Terry says, eyes lit up with amusement. He looks so much like our mother for a moment that I have to look away.

Shannon's oldest sister, Carol, appears, smiling at Marie, carrying a coffee from—oh, hell, they're all just drinking coffees from Dec and Shannon's new chain.

Grind it in, why don't you.

Grind it nice and fresh.

"Where are Jeffrey and Tyler?" Marie asks. Carol's sons are ten and seven, I think. Not sure. Something like that. I'm not their uncle, and all kids look a lot alike to me. I assume that changes when you have your own. It's like buying a new car. You don't really notice all the identical makes and models until you have one you call *mine*.

And one you have to maintain to make it function properly.

Carol jerks her head toward the pastry case. "Deciding which sweets to get for the flight home." They share a tired smile.

"The wine. We asked Marie for permission!" Amanda interjects, looking at Shannon's mom. "You told us we could take the wine!"

"So you're the one who grabbed the bottle," Declan says.

"We're not pointing fingers." I'm defensive, suddenly, and want to protect Amanda. She reaches for my hand and squeezes it.

"Just locking down details," Dec replies, eyes narrowing as he thinks. "We had a few people give us bottles of wine as wedding gifts."

"Who?"

"Terry."

"I had mine sent to your wine cellar back in Boston," he clarifies.

"Okay," Dec says. "I think Jed gave us one."

"That was Champagne, and we drank it as the first reception toast," Amanda says. We share a look.

"I remember that," I say with a touch of acid. "I don't remember much after that, though."

"And then there was Lüq," Marie adds.

"Lüq?" Declan and Shannon look at her.

"You know. He runs the spa at Litraeon?"

"Mom," Shannon groans. "Hu. Not he. Hu is gender fluid."

"Yes. *Hu* came to the reception and delivered a lovely bottle of wine in a basket with some sort of herb designed to help Shannon's ovaries turn into blossoming wildflowers." Marie drinks the rest of her latte. Her eyes cross and she lets out an intimate moan I wish I could unhear.

"Why would I want flowers in my ovaries, Mom?"

"I don't know. But the basket was so pretty, and Lüq spent ten minutes reading my past lives. Hu said I ran a brothel in Paris during the Revolution!"

"What about the wine, Marie?" Dec asks.

"What about it?"

"What happened to the bottle?"

"I put it on the gift table after Lüq gave it to me. You and Shannon had just left when hu appeared."

"And I hope you enjoyed it," says a voice with an accent I can't put my finger on. We turn to find Lüq standing next to us, wearing a Scottish kilt, knee-high riding boots, and a dashiki-like dress thing. He has a goat on a leash.

No one says a word about the goat. I wonder if it faints.

In his other hand is a Grind It Fresh! to-go cup.

Declan hired Lüq a few years ago, sniping hu from one of the top Parisian salons. I've met Lüq twice before. You don't forget hu.

Dec stands. "Thank you for the wine," he says, gracious and smiling.

"You are most welcome." Hu holds up his coffee. "And the coffee company you gave to your wife is outstanding."

Dec gives me a look but says "Thanks" to Lüq.

"I hope that you enjoy the wine someday. It is my own blend."

"You're a vintner?" I ask.

"No, although I do perform cleansing ceremonies for the grapes from time to time in Napa. I blend my own vintage for those who need to explore the many layers of love that we leave untouched."

I frown. "What does that mean? Blend your own vintage?"

"I take the superior wine and enhance it."

"Enhance?" My eyes dart to catch Amanda's.

*Enhance?* she mouths.

"For centuries," hu intones, eyes going soft, voice taking on a dreamy quality, "mankind has—"

"Oh, brother," Dec mutters.

"—sacrificed the very best of the past for the short-term hustle bustle of the now. We forget that our bodies are etched with the scratchings of the past. Our relationships form layers of centuries that must be explored if we are to live in the here and now as full and complete lovers."

"What does any of that mean?" I mutter to Dec.

"Hell if I know, but hu gets people to pay $25 for a latte in the spa and the profit margins are insane."

"You put something in the wine?" Jason asks. It's the first time he's said a word. The guy is Marie's lapdog, but his question is the most cogent sentence I've heard since Lüq appeared.

"Of course."

I tense. "You put 'something' in that bottle of wine? A blend of more than one wine, you mean?"

"*Non non non*. I enhanced the transformative properties of the already sacred and made it more in touch with—"

"You spiked my daughter's wedding gift?" Marie hisses.

Lüq glares at her. "That was a special bottle of wine designed and made specifically for the bride and groom, for a ritual to bring their body-spirits together on a different plane of existence."

"It was Three Buck Chuck with a bow and some glitter paint on it," Marie says with an eye roll.

"I told you it was entheogenic!" he hisses. "Seventh-century druids died to make that wine."

"Did they die from disbelief?"

Entheogenic. *Entheogenic?* There's an SAT word if I've ever heard one. I dust off my ancient Latin lessons and start to dissect the word.

"I haven't heard that word since college!" Amanda says in a tone of marvel. "You added *hallucinogenic drugs* to the wine?"

She beat me to it.

"Oh, my," Marie whispers. "Thank God Shannon and Declan didn't drink it."

"But it's fine that *we* did?" Amanda snaps.

I turn to Marie, a dim flicker of memory stirring. "*You* told me it was *homeopathic*, which we assumed was a joke, and..."

"Entheogenic, homeopathic," she says in a sing-songy voice. "Same thing."

"It is NOT the same thing!" I roar.

"What the hell is homeopathic wine?" Declan sputters, "What do you do—put a drop of Merlot in a swimming pool and dip your wine glass in it and drink?"

"We're not talking about homeopathic wine!" I hiss, my tongue embedded in my cheek, my muscles turned to sheetrock.

"Actually, we are," he counters.

I turn to Lüq. "What the hell was really in that wine? Did you lace it with acid?"

"*Non non non*," Lüq protested. "It was infused with a mind-blossoming drop of the spirit world."

"What, *exactly*, was in that wine?" I try again. Declan is the brother with the temper, but...

"I can never tell, monsieur, for—"

"Tell me, or you're fired."

"It was mescaline," Lüq says quickly.

Never underestimate the power of being someone's boss.

"See! I knew you cared about keeping your job!" Marie crowed.

Never, *ever* underestimate the power of a woman who needs to meddle.

"Marie, this isn't about you," I growl as Lüq makes a hasty departure, diaphanous dress floating behind hu like a wedding train.

Marie's hand goes to her heart, eyes wide, lips trembling. "I am just trying to help you and Amanda! Amanda is like the daughter I never had!"

Shannon and Carol turn on their mother like a pack of feral dingoes.

You know what else you can never underestimate?

The ability of meddlers to get themselves into trouble on their own. All you have to do is let them talk without interruption.

I see two little kids in my peripheral vision, and without looking I know they're Carol's sons. If they're carrying coffee cups with the Grind It Fresh! logo on it, I'm done.

Declan's phone buzzes. He looks at it, face closing like a fist. "Time to go."

He pulls Shannon to her feet. She clings to her latte.

"Where are you going?" I ask, my voice making it clear he does not have my buy-in.

"On my honeymoon," he says slowly, one lip curling up in a sneer that says, *Dare you to stop me.*

"We can't leave Amanda now!" Shannon gasps.

"She can't come with us," he declares, staring at me. "Unlike *some* people, we only marry one person."

"Can't we stay—" Her face changes expression as Declan whispers something in her ear, cheeks flushing. She readjusts her purse on her shoulder and gives everyone a kiss.

"Bye! See you in—"

Declan's pulling on Shannon so hard we can't hear the rest of her sentence. Carol and Marie follow, like a chattering batch of fishwives following a thief at a market. Jason sighs, shakes his head, and follows slowly, clearly accustomed to cleaning up emotional messes.

The sound level at our table drops by seventy-five percent, although it's hard to be accurate given the constant ringing in my ears.

"So much for needing to be here for me," Amanda mutters.

I nuzzle her ear. "You would have insisted she go anyhow."

She huffs. "How do you know me so well?"

Amused by her tone, I slide my left hand over hers, threading the fingers. "Because I'm your husband."

# Chapter Five

"We don't know that!" says an arch voice from behind us.

Josh.

Of course. Who better to interrupt this lovely, heartwarming moment than a man who can't do Lamaze breathing exercises without a paper bag, and who is carrying a cat wearing a cone on its head, which he drops instantly as Chuckles makes a sound like he's Dracula's undead feline with a three-hundred-year-old hairball to cough up.

I would not marry him even if I *were* into dudes.

Josh, I mean.

"Let's just get this out of the way right up front, though," Josh says with a long sigh appended to the end. His hand is outstretched, palm facing me, and his mouth is tight. The guy is the cleanest man I have ever seen. Slightly balding in the way that Prince William is getting thin up top, Josh wears rimless glasses, and has not a single stray facial hair. Does the guy wax his face?

He's pale, like a desk jockey, and Rainbow Brite is with him, sporting a leather vest, no shirt underneath, and Bruce Springsteen jeans, complete with the red bandana in the back pocket. He is also wearing a Yankees cap.

And one more minor detail: he's now dragging Shannon's cat on a leash.

And by dragging, I mean *dragging*. The cat is on its side,

stubbornly refusing to walk. Putting a cat on a leash is stupid. Might as well get a Bernie Sanders supporter to talk about how much they love Hillary.

"I," Josh says dramatically, "am not married to you." His eye contact would be unnerving if his words weren't exactly what I wanted to hear. The look he gives me makes me feel like he's patented a new technology for peeling off clothing with eyeballs. "I know this is sad news, but—"

"Thank God," Amanda mutters.

I clap my hands once, then rub them together. "Great news."

"For some," he says sourly.

"How do you know you aren't married to Andrew?" Amanda asks, then winces. Her headache's still lingering.

"Unlike *some* people who can't hold their liquor, I metabolize very quickly. My liver is pristine. It's probably because of the wheat grass juice and goat colostrum protocol I started, along with my daily supply of Soylent," Josh says, giving Geordi a wide smile.

Amanda gapes at him. "You mix your Soylent in with Diet Mountain Dew! You make chocolate fudge with Velveeta!"

"Liar!" he screeches, pointing at her, giving Geordi the side eye. "Velveeta is the tool of Satan. Do you have any idea what it does to the microbiome of the gut?"

"Is that a food hack?" Geordi asks. "I've heard the plastic in Velveeta can actually help to break down biofilms."

"Really?" Josh's eyes go wide.

Is this what public school does to people?

"Can we get back to who I'm married to?" I ask, as Geordi and Josh debate the merits of adding Kava to a mixture of CBD oil and Velveeta. I don't get foodie geeks. Then again, my girl-friend—*wife?*—is a Cheeto-marshmallow freak.

"No one," says a woman's voice. We turn in unison.

I've never seen hackles rise. The room fills with ozone, the tiny hairs that dot my arms rising up slowly, like little tension boners.

"Kari," hisses Amanda. Her eyes narrow, fingers curling into claws, and her face morphs. Gone is the sweet, open woman I love, who approaches the world with an attitude of possibility and trust.

She is replaced by Katniss facing off against Clove.

A tall blonde with brown eyes and a friendly, open expression looks at me. She's wearing a red and white flower-patterned dress that hugs some very nice hips. Unlike Amanda this morning, she does not look like she was the unwilling drumhead for a bongo last night.

When her eyes flick to Amanda, they narrow, her expression guarded and suspicious. The change almost makes me laugh. Whatever the battle between these two, the stakes are low.

Which makes me wonder why they're fighting in the first place.

"Andrew McCormick," I say, reaching out for a handshake, introducing myself. Amanda's hand immediately goes to my other arm, her grasp primitive and protective. She shuffles closer, her soft warmth radiating from my calf to shoulder, her cheek hovering above my shoulder, her chin defiant.

*Mine*, she says with her body.

I stand taller, a predatory creep making my skin buzz.

Who in the hell is this Kari person?

"Kari Whitevelt. I'm a colleague of Amanda's." She takes my hand, her eyes shifting between mine and Amanda's. Nothing special about her handshake, other than she's not one of those limp-wristed women who give you their hand like it's a wet, crumpled napkin they just sneezed in.

"Colleague?"

"She's foked," Amanda adds helpfully.

"I work for Fokused Shoprite," Kari says through gritted teeth.

"Nice to meet you. I'm—"

She laughs, showing perfectly straight teeth, her smile making the skin beneath her eyes wrinkle in a friendly way. "I know who you are. Can't work in Boston and not know who the McCormicks are. So nice to finally meet you." A quick glance at both our left hands and she smirks. "You're in much better shape today compared to last night."

45

I tighten my grip on Kari's hand. Amanda sinks her fingers into my bicep, like a claw.

"You saw us last night?"

"Saw you? You crashed my wedding!" Kari exclaims, eyebrows up to her hairline, her laughter a weird mix.

"Your *wedding*?"

"My work wedding."

"What's a work wedding?"

"It's like a work date," Amanda says with a sigh, as if I'm supposed to have this vocabulary.

"You're evaluating DoggieDate, too? You married a dog?" These mystery shopping companies are hard core.

"Ewwww, no." She gives Amanda an odd, smug look. "I am getting married fifteen times this week. You crashed wedding number eight. You insisted that the twenty-four-hour drive-up Elvis shop take your order before they finished my wedding. You appeared at the window and asked for a Venti mocha half-caf with cinnamon and peppermint, a twenty-pack of chicken nuggets with marmalade packets, and proceeded to shove marriage licenses through the window."

"Marriage licenses!" Our first factual clue. I look at Amanda. "We had *marriage licenses* made?"

Plural. She's saying this in plural. My gut tightens. If I'm going to be a bigamist, being married to two guys isn't exactly how I'd envision this.

Four people. Two to the power of four. Sixteen possible marriage combinations.

Wait! Not exponential. Factorial.

Screw it. I can't *math* right now.

Exactly how many of those combinations happened last night?

Hold on. I latch onto hope for the null set. Zero. Best case scenario, *zero* marriages happened last night.

Kari nods. "They made you come inside because you tried to have too many weddings done at the same time at the drive-thru. And they were out of chicken nuggets."

"Too many? There really was more than one?" Amanda gasps, looking at her ring, loosening her grip on me.

"You two don't remember any of this?" She looks at Josh. "You don't remember hitting on me?"

Josh goes from pale to the color of fresh snow.

Amanda folds in half with laughter, then begins moaning with pain, holding her head. "Josh *hit on* you? Josh can't look at a vagina without doing an Exorcist imitation! He would never hit on a woman!"

"His exact words were, 'Hey, baby, I'd love to see your vagina dentata. Show Daddy some teeth.'"

Josh faints. Drops to the floor like a sack of bones and Velveeta, resting quietly next to Chuckles, who stands up, still on the leash, and begins head butting Josh with his cone.

Which still says "WILL SLEEP WITH PUSSY FOR FOOD" on the side in Sharpie. My stomach chooses this moment to growl.

At that exact moment, a goat walks by, sees Josh, and faints. Now we know Josh's spirit animal.

I grab my phone and text Jed, the head of security at Litraeon.

I text: *Goat located next door. Send goat retrieval crew.*

Geordi bends to help Josh, while Amanda tries to laugh and manage her headache.

"Josh is part goat!" Amanda declares, snickering and groaning in alternating currents.

Kari and I are the only two reasonably functional people in the room.

*Bzzzz.*

Jed texts back: *Sir, we don't have a goat retrieval crew. Suggestions?*

I reply: *Ask Brona.*

There. Done. See? Being CEO is easy. You make everyone else do all the work you don't want to do. That's leadership.

"What was the name of the place? Where are the marriage licenses?" Amanda asks.

The goat stands up and wanders off toward the macaron case.

JULIA KENT

Josh is still on the floor, but he sits up, revived by Geordi, who is
feeding him sips of coffee.

"Love Me Tenderly was the chapel. Some strange woman
with auburn hair mumbling about bagpipes and $700,000 was
the one in charge of your paperwork."

"Marie!" Amanda hisses.

"She wouldn't be crazy enough to file them, would she?" Josh
asks, his voice faint.

Amanda and I give him twin looks that make him add
quickly, "Okay, okay, I know she's more than crazy enough. I
mean—she didn't go to the license bureau and really file them.
Right?"

"And did we—" he points between himself and Amanda—
"have a marriage license drawn up?"

"The woman only had one in her hand, but a bunch sticking
out of her purse. *You* had two ceremonies, actually." Kari looks at
Amanda with suspicion. "I didn't marry a dog, but you married a
cat."

"I *what*?"

"You insisted on marrying a cat you kept calling Charles
Kulls. Said his nickname was Chuck." She looks down at Shannon's cat and wrinkles her nose, reading the Cone of Shame. "Is
this the cat? Because you could do better. He looks like he has
mange."

Chuckles glares at her like Hannibal Lecter staring at Clarice
through the bars.

Josh stands, blinking hard, looking like a white owl. Geordi's
next to him, their fingers threaded, holding hands. Even if I am
married to Josh, I think he has other romantic prospects.

"Chuck Kulls?" I can't keep the snicker out of my voice.
Amanda punches me, hard, in the breastbone. I deserve it.

"First you married him—" Kari points to Josh, "and then
good old Chuck."

"I did not marry a cat," Amanda says flatly.

"She can't marry Chuckles," Josh adds. "He's neutered."

"Why would that stop someone from getting married?"

48

"We're talking about a human-cat marriage, people," I say, exasperated.

"Not because of that," he says pointedly. "Because Amanda wants kids. Four, to be exact. Two boys and two girls. She's talked about it forever and—"

Amanda's sucker punch folds him in half.

"Four kids!" I choke out as I watch Josh with a detached awareness. "*Four?*" I look at her hips, assessing. They're nice and wide. She could produce plenty of McCormick children. Big heads tend to run in our family.

Case in point: Declan.

She shrugs. "That was before I married a cat. A girl can dream, right?"

"You plan to have them in litters?"

Her eyes meet mine. For the first time in this madcap race to figure out whether we're married, who we're married to, and what happened last night and this morning, I feel a sense of peace.

"Injured husband over here!" Josh rasps.

"You're not my husband!" Amanda and I shout in unison.

Kari gives us a series of looks that make her face shift, like she's living in stop-action animation. Maybe my brain creates the effect. What's the half-life of illicitly-slipped-in-wedding-wine mescaline?

"He's mine, anyhow," Geordi hisses. Rainbow Brite bares his teeth at me. Not only is he wearing a lip ring, but he appears to have his *gums* pierced.

"Isn't he your boss?" Josh says out of the side of his mouth.

Geordi tips his chin up. "I don't care. Love means sacrifice."

"Love?" Josh gasps, looking down at Geordi with wide, emotion-filled eyes. "You love me? How can you love me? We only met last night!"

"I didn't say I'm *in* love with you. Just that there's, you know —" Geordi reaches for Josh's hand and watches it, suddenly shy. "A spark."

"A spark?" Josh's voice goes low.

Chuckles stands up and begins head-butting Geordi's shin,

looking at Kari. If Chuckles had fingers, two would be pointed at Kari in an *I see you* gesture.

"Let's get going. We need to find Marie," I say to Amanda, wrapping my arm around her waist. Kari cocks one eyebrow.

"'We need to find Marie' is not part of your vocabulary, Andrew," Amanda says.

"It is now."

Chapter Six

I've never been inside the spa here at Litraeon. I have my hairstylist and groomer back home. My treatments are done in my office, away from prying eyes. Yes, men get aesthetic treatments, too. When you're a CEO and the paparazzi *click click click*, one stray hair becomes fodder for negative media.

The only reason I let Amanda drag me downstairs is because our security detail keeps the press out of Litraeon. Being this hungover means that no amount of lighting can save us from bad pictures.

"My God! You look like Lucifer himself took you home and chained you to a wall, with tentacles entering every orifice!" shouts an accented voice.

I look at Amanda, whose face is surprisingly angelic, ethereal and captive, as she searches the room for the source of that statement.

"Lüq?" she whispers, enraptured. I straighten.

She's never said *my* name with that kind of reverence. She's come damn close a few times in bed, but I think calling me *God* was justified then.

I have zero desire to see Lüq again, and the idea of a conversation with hu and Marie at the same time makes me want to rip my hair out, strand by strand.

Which would reduce the need for any grooming treatments for a while, but leave me looking like The Rock, muscles and all.

"Entheogenic Twins! How are you, Le Hawk?"

My fingers curl into fists as Amanda embraces Lüq, hu's face calm and appreciative as hu's hands sink into Amanda's body, caressing and touching her like hu has a right to do so. Lüq's got to be my dad's age, right? Hu isn't my competition.

"You are the most beautiful creature in this resort," Lüq says to her, pulling back and stroking her hair.

"That's my line," I say. I'm not joking.

"You are *orange*," hu declares, examining my face under the bright lights next to a fountain that has a strange, salty musk scent. "Evangi! Gagai!" *Snap snap.* "Get Mr. McCormick in the hot seat immediately!"

Hot seat?

A tiny little pixie of a girl with enormous eyes brings me a latte and we follow Amanda and Lüq. I take a sip. Not bad. a little watery, and the milk tastes sweet. Must be skim. I take a bigger gulp and wonder if Declan and Shannon are right.

Is the coffee next door better?

I hold out my palms in protest. "I'm not here for a treatment. We're looking for Marie."

"Marie?" Hu shudders. "That vile woman who is poor Mr. Declan McCormick's mother-in-law? She is not here, but let us delight you with a surprise of self-care and compassion for your poor little pores!" Hu's fingers flutter to my jaw. I stiffen, but let hu, wanting to gauge how far hu will go.

Studying people is a crucial part of being a CEO. In fact, it's quality #1. You have to be able to map out people and understand their motivations and needs in any given situation so that you can exert authority.

"What did you do to them? They cry out in pain, my ears hearing them, the torture too much." Hu's voice goes falsetto. "Help us, Lüq! We are so dry and cramped, we need to be scratched smooth!"

He's talking about my pores like they're balls.

If he's hearing my pores screaming in agony, then the

entheogenic wine makes more sense. I look around for an empty bottle.

"Just go with it. Trust me. But don't drink the hot spring water," Amanda whispers in my ear, right before a tall, lithe woman wearing eye jewelry yanks me into another room.

"What?" I look through the threshold between the rooms.

Amanda gives me a little wave as Lüq undresses her.

*Undresses.*

"Hold on!" Definitely time to exert authority. Maybe I've underestimated hu. Lüq's hands are on Amanda's creamy, bare shoulders, and as her shirt slides down around her waist, she stands in the doorway wearing only a bra, the mist from what looks like a pool behind her curling around her, making her look like a Siren from Greek mythology.

I've got a siren going off in my own body all right. In my pants.

Which are being stripped off me by a woman who is wearing eye jewelry.

"Whoa, there! That's my girlfriend's job!" I choke out.

"Americans," she mutters.

As I bat at her hands and try to maintain some sense of control and dignity, Amanda's bra comes off. She's half naked, twenty feet from me, and Lüq is helping her finish.

The same woman whose worst fear was being naked in public is undressing willingly in front of my spa manager.

Did we just have an entheogenic latte? Because this cannot be happening.

Pushing the *Blade Runner* chick's hands aside, I march over to Amanda, my pants undone and belt clicking as it hits my fly. My hands are on her shoulders, brushing Lüq's aside, as I turn my head and look at her.

She is enchanted by the pool before us, a hot spring designed to look like a rainforest.

And I am enchanted.

By her.

"Get out," I say through gritted teeth. Lüq leaves instantly, abandoning Amanda to me.

As it should be.

"Marie's not here, Amanda. Let's go." My mouth says *let's get out of here*, but my hands say *breasts*.

Just...breasts.

Beautiful, slightly orange breasts that are bare in front of me, the hot spring mist wafting into the space between us, which I remove the second my hands find the soft, slight weight of her deliciously bare skin. They rest in my palms, a little larger than the span of my fingers, abundant and ripe.

Her sigh makes me glad my belt is undone, my zipper lowered, because I have room for the growing need that blooms when she sighs like that.

"Isn't it beautiful here?" she asks, looking out at the lagoon-like pool. We've designed this part of Litraeon to be an oasis, a hothouse for orchids and stress relief, a place where women can hide from the cares of the world.

I stare at her chest, the rosy nipples tightening under my touch. "Yes."

"I meant the hot spring."

"I've got something hot that's about to spring on you."

"You make everything so porny."

I frown. "Your point is..."

"This is bliss."

I squeeze. "Sure is."

"Not my breasts!"

"I beg to differ."

"I mean....this. This place. It's enchanted and magical. You can float and relax, crawl into a part of yourself where no one needs anything from you."

"Like sex."

"That's how sex feels for you?"

"Yes."

She frowns, eyes clouding with confusion as she looks up at me. Both of my hands are planted on her breasts like her nipples are magnets and I am the Iron Giant.

One part of me certainly is.

"But during sex, you do want and need something from the other person. Isn't that the point of sex?"

"Not the same as being in the world. With sex, you give so much that eventually you get back what you need."

"That's really how you view sex?" She moves closer, my fingertips grazing up. Her skin is wet and yielding, the room's heat making her glow.

"With you, I do."

She sinks against me, our lips meeting, and I take a step back to catch my balance as she pushes against me, my hard-on pressing against her hip, her bare breasts crushed between my chest and my palms.

And then we tip.

That's not a metaphor for a deep, layered kiss that transports us emotionally.

We literally tip over, falling into the water half clothed, the wrenching difference between being incredibly aroused by her words and breasts and the sudden onslaught of wet, buoyant water jarring.

A mouthful enters me and I find my footing, pushing up and spitting at the same time.

"Oh, no! You swallowed! How awful!"

Said no guy, ever.

"Andrew, do you know what's in this water?"

I roll my tongue around in my mouth. "Salt water?"

"Semen!"

"I haven't even come yet!"

"Not *your* semen!" she shouts, sputtering, wiping her face, displaying those gorgeous globes. "There is whale sperm in the water."

Huh?

"Whale sperm?"

"It's supposed to have anti-aging properties."

"Says who?" I ask, eyes crawling over her face, taking her in. We're in three feet of water, and her knees are bent, arms under water. Those breasts bob like two little tugboats waiting for a big boat to come along and get pulled into harbor.

She may have a point.

I am a little porny.

"Says Lüq. Just like the breast milk latte."

At the word *breast*, I defer to my inner pervert, eyes back to her tits. "Breast milk?"

"Lüq says—"

"Lüq was indirectly responsible for getting us high as kites and for your cat wedding."

"I did not marry Chuckles!"

"As far as we know."

She splashes me.

I lunge.

Water is my second home. Swimming twice a week keeps me sane. Lap after lap, stroke after stroke, I disappear into the pool at Declan's place, the one in my apartment building too warm for miles of swimming. You fade into nothing but the differentiated cells of the body when you turn into a machine that reaches, kicks, breathes—and repeats *ad infinitum*.

So I reach, I kick, I breathe—and I kiss her until I disappear into the water and Amanda, my own name fading as I become nothing but water and love, tongue and heat, fingertips and pulse. We kiss in the water, my arms steel bands that cage her, our bodies melting in the humid heat of a fake rainforest that contains too much real love.

Releasing her, I wriggle out of my wet pants, kick off my shoes, and swim away, letting the water take me, a simple crawl speeding me to the end of the meandering pool. Designed to look like a naturally-shaped pond, there is no true side, and I misjudge, whacking my hand on the green-painted cement edge.

I can't do an underwater flip, so I pivot, returning to her, roaring up with a few butterfly strokes designed to cover her with a giant wave of foam.

She's laughing when I surface, her hair covering her like wet ribbons, her mouth open with joy, eyes wide and amused. I hope her headache's gone. I hope her hangover has dissolved. I hope we can capture this moment for a few more seconds and laugh together, because it's the first time in my life that I've felt like infinite good exists in the world, and I'm only touching a tiny grain of sand in a vast ocean of it.

"You swim like Michael Phelps!" she gasps.

"Michael Phelps swims like *me.*"

A fit of giggles overcomes her and I watch, cocking my head to catch her at an odd angle, the tiny perspective change an order of magnitude in difference. Luminous and winsome, Amanda's eyes catch mine, darting between them, as if she's trying to look at me forever.

I grab her and the brush of her breasts against my bare, wet chest takes my breath away.

"You have the body of a swimmer," she says, her voice rumbling, making me groan as she nips my earlobe.

"And you have the body of a goddess." I reach for her and she pulls away, giggling.

"Not here!"

"Why not?"

"We can't have sex in public!"

I look around. "No one else is here. I own the resort." I bridge the gap between us and watch her react to my words. Lust and restraint fight for dominance in those lush brown eyes, warm and tempted, her pupils big and open.

"It's not like we can just lock the door."

I walk out of the zero-gravity pool and grab the corded phone by the door. Two sentences later, it's done. A red light on a control panel pops on. Locked.

"Yes," I say, turning to her with a grin. "We can."

It's good to be the king.

I can't get back to her fast enough, the water welcoming me, the knowledge that we're alone and will not be disturbed a titillating, erotic secret that makes me so hard I ache. She's in my arms and I'm kissing her, bare, wet skin dominating every second, and if I can't get inside her soon, I'm going to die.

*Bang bang bang*

"Amanda?" shouts a familiar voice. "Amanda? I heard you and Andrew are looking for me?"

Marie.

"Oh, God," Amanda groans, the sound hot and tortured against my mouth, her tone matching my erection's voice. If it had one, it would sound exactly like Amanda, and why not?

Her mouth is pretty much where I'd want it to learn how to talk.

"Ignore her," I hiss.

*Bang bang bang*

"Amanda! Chuckles is here and he really misses you, and Pam's worried about you. She's in her hotel room and doesn't feel well. If you're in there, it's okay. I've seen you naked plenty of times before. It's nothing special."

Amanda rolls her eyes.

"It's everything special," I rumble in her ear, my hands all over her as goosebumps pop up where my touch lands.

"I am about as aroused as a woman at a gynecologist's appointment."

I'm confused. "Give me a sense of where that falls on the arousal spectrum."

"Unless you're a fetishist, it means I'm about as dry the Sahara now, Andrew. Having Marie pounding on the door while you pound me isn't my idea of *sensual*."

And that single sentence makes me go soft.

"Okay, then. Arousal spectrum calibrated."

Damn it.

"Go away, Marie!" I shout.

"But you said you wanted your marriage licenses!"

I'm up in a flash, across the room, opening the door. I'm wearing wet boxer briefs, but no worries. It's not like anything's being outlined right now, other than a package of unfulfilled expectations.

"Did you file all those marriage licenses last night?" I demand, in her face, furious and self-righteous. They say hell hath no fury like a woman scorned, but hell *really* hath no fury like a guy with a boner untapped.

The hell drains into the balls and turns blue. All those pictures of a red devil? Nope. Should be blue.

"Did I...what?"

Amanda picks up her wet shirt and wraps it around her chest like a bandage. "Hi, Marie. Did I really marry Chuckles last night?"

She sounds so defeated. I become angrier.

"No, honey. The people at the Love Me Tenderly drive-thru wedding chapel said even *they* had standards."

Amanda's sigh of relief goes straight to the root of my heart.

"Did you seriously think that you married that damn cat?" I ask, unable to keep the outrage out of my voice. This should be funny. It would be funnier if I weren't standing in a misty hot spring wearing wet underwear, skin screaming and body buzzing, my ring catching on the elastic waistband of my briefs while I plant my hands on my hips and glare at everyone.

"I didn't really think so, but it doesn't hurt to know I'm not Mrs. Charles Kulls!" She looks wounded, but a bitter beast inside me sets that aside. I'm spiraling through rage that needs to be expressed, frustration at being out of control, like a monster that has discovered the bolt attached to his chain is loose in the stone wall.

"Didn't the Supreme Court make inter-species marriage legal last year?" Marie asks.

"Shut up!" Amanda and I shout in unison.

Marie cowers. Good.

"Where are the marriage licenses?" I demand.

Her eyes go wide and shifty at the same time.

"How would I know? Is that why you're looking for me?" She laughs nervously.

"Kari told us she saw you holding one of them, and the rest were in your purse."

Marie's eyes land on my left hand, then jump to Amanda's. "You want to know if you're married to each other."

"Or anyone else," I snap.

Her throat moves as she swallows. She's in her fifties and done to the nines, all makeup and hair product and style. Unlike most of the older women I associate with, Marie doesn't broker in aloofness, using sophistication as leverage against a world that quietly dismisses them as washed up.

She's bold and weird, flighty and unpredictable, and that combination makes me seethe.

She's cagey. This does not add up.

"I did exactly what you asked of me last night," she says slowly, backing out the door.

I rush her, planting one palm on the doorjamb, stopping her from exiting. Water from my legs drips on her shoes.

"Define that."

"Define what?"

"What did we ask of you last night?"

Her eyes ping between me and Amanda, who has her back turned to us, her arms like noodles as she tries to dress.

Silence.

"Damn it, Marie, are we married to each other?"

Marie's eyes narrow, then soften, telescoping as she focuses on my face, then on Amanda, over my shoulder.

"Do you want to be?"

"That's not the question!" Amanda shrieks, turning around, her shirt buttons in a crooked line between her breasts. "What did you do with those marriage licenses, Marie? Were they real?"

"Oh, yes. We all went down to the Regional Justice Center downtown and you pulled them." Marie has sidestepped the real question here, and I give her just enough rope to hang herself. Intuition plays a major role in business, and right now she's setting off every alarm bell inside me. But for what reason?

"We really *did* have a marriage license made up?" Amanda squeaks, pointing between us.

"Yes."

Marie's not the one-word-answer type. I approach her slowly, chin down, eyes up, sending every intimidating signal I can.

"Start from the beginning."

"What?"

"Tell us exactly what happened last night, from beginning to end."

"I don't have time! Jason's waiting for me back in our room. Our flight leaves in less than an hour. Carol and the boys are already boarding!"

"Are you taking the Anterdec jet?"

"Yes."

I reach for the phone. "Easy. I'll have them hold it."

"But Jason needs to get to work tonight! So does Carol! And Jeffrey and Tyler have missed school."

I smile.

Leverage. Ah. That's so much better.

She sees it, too, her shoulders slumping, her breath let go in a long sigh. "Fine. I confess."

"You *did* file the marriage licenses?" Amanda says with a groan.

Tears fill Marie's overdone eyes. She palms away one rolling drop. "I'm so sorry."

"Are we married to each other?" I ask, pointing to Amanda.

Marie shakes her head.

"Shit!" The word's out of my mouth before I can stop it.

"Am I married to Josh?" Amanda asks.

Marie shakes her head.

Amanda fist bumps me, then freezes. "Is Andrew married to...Josh?"

Marie shakes her head. She's being way, *way* too quiet.

"Am I married to Rainbow Brite?" I ask.

Marie shakes her head.

"Marie, who is married to whom?" I ask tightly.

Her hands cover her eyes and she says, "I'm so sorry! I'm so sorry!" over and over, rocking against the bamboo-covered wall.

Amanda and I exchange a look. I convey, through a single glare and a sudden eye tic, the message that dragging the truth out of Marie is Amanda's territory.

"Marie, what did you do?" she asks.

"It's what I *didn't* do! You clearly wanted me to file those marriage licenses, but it was late and I was tired, and I'm so sorry!" She reaches into her enormous purse and pulls out a sheaf of thick papers, mangled and stained with reddish-purple wine rings.

I snatch them up, rifling through them. I learn something new.

When drunk on entheogenic wine, I spell my name *Ayndrough*. That's my handwriting. No denying it.

Amanda correctly spelled her entire name, but saw fit to draw pictures of butterflies with enormous, anatomically-correct penises and balls attached.

"The state of Nevada issued these?"

We have licenses for:


*Amanda and Ayndrough*
    *Josh and Geordi*
    *Amanda and Charles Kulls*
    *Josh and Ayndrough*
    *Geordi and Josh*
    *Josh and David Gandy*


"Pfft. Right. Like David Gandy would ever marry *him*," Amanda says.

I laugh.

"Because if anyone's marrying David Gandy, it's me."

I stop laughing.

"I'm so sorry!" Marie cries.

"Why are you sorry?" Amanda asks.

"Because I didn't file any of these!"

I frown at her, completely stymied. "You think we're upset at you for *not* filing these marriage licenses?"

She grabs them back. "If I rush, I can get there in time for—"

Amanda yanks them out of her hands and flings them into the hot spring.

"You're our hero, Marie!" she shouts, pulling Marie into a tight hug.

I blink over and over, staring at the papers on the water as the saltwater soaks in, turning them to wet, sopping messes.

Which one is ours?

Not that it matters.

I wade in, mop up the useless pieces of paper, and wade back out, marching to a trash can and throwing them in. Staring at the clump of paper, I sigh.

We're not married.

I'm not married to anyone.

Great.

My eyes land on an animated Amanda, who smiles and frowns in alternating patterns as Marie chatters away. My right index finger finds my left hand, the metal of my wedding band warm from the room's ambient temperature. The ring is smooth and unyielding, an infinite loop.

Amanda hugs Marie again, who looks at me with a shaky smile.

"I didn't mess up? You *didn't* want me to file the marriage licenses?"

"Did you really think Amanda wanted to marry Chuckles?"

"No. But I'm getting the feeling you really wanted to marry her, Andrew."

Laughter rips through the room as Amanda reacts.

I just run my finger around the ring, over and over, silent.

# Chapter Seven

"So no one's married to anyone?" Josh asks, his voice peaking on a high note, turning to give Geordi a pouty look. Geordi seems to have fewer facial muscles than the rest of us, because he just broods.

"Nope," Amanda says with a grin, taking a sip of her mango cucumber kale monstrosity that someone in the casino made for her. We're sitting on purple velvet couches in a sunken pit near the High Value baccarat room where Jason won all that money yesterday.

And gave it right back to my casino.

I like Jason. Men who give back that kind of money after winning are guaranteed a comped room for the rest of their lives.

After interrupting us back at the spa, Marie needed concierge service to shoo her and her crew out of the state, which meant Brona intervened and sent a message to my admin, Gina.

Who urged me to answer the three hundred texts queued up in my phone.

Instead of having luscious sex with my once-maybe-wife in a rainforest hot spring, I've spent the last ninety minutes perusing spreadsheets, giving one-sentence up-or-down decisions, and listening to a very pissed off Sultan rant in my ear.

While drinking substandard coffee.

Damn Declan. He's right—Grind It Fresh! coffee is better.

"We're free! No one married anyone! Then we don't need these!" Josh slides his wedding ring off his finger. Geordi does the same. Amanda tries to pull hers off and can't.

"Ugh! I'm too swollen and bloated!" she complains. "Must be from all the drinking and the Cheetos last night."

My heart soars. I slide my left hand around her and give her shoulder a squeeze. Good for bloat. I can't stop my gaze from jumping between our respective rings.

"We need to let Dec and Shannon and James know that no one's married to anyone," she says, snuggling in. Ten more minutes of conversation and we can excuse ourselves and go back to my suite.

Even if we're not married, we can pretend it's our honeymoon.

"Hi!" Pam appears behind Amanda, holding her teacup Chihuahua in her handbag.

These mothers have impeccably bad timing.

Spritzy pokes his head up and sticks his tongue out, panting. If dogs could smile, he'd be grinning.

"Mom! Where have you been?"

Pam takes a few steps toward Amanda and winces.

"Flare," she says simply.

Geordi looks at some pins on his leather shirt. "Are not!"

"Not 'flair,' Geordi," Josh says with a laugh.

Amanda peels out of my arms and gives Pam a gentle hug. "I'm so sorry."

"I hear you married three men while I was resting."

"And a cat," Josh adds helpfully.

"Everyone needs a little pussy for a companion sometimes," Pam says unironically. "They're so nice to stroke."

Amanda squeezes her eyes in a nonverbal tip I pick up instantly.

Josh shouts, "Why is everyone talking about vaginas so much?"

Josh clearly struggles with social cues.

Pam pales. She matches Josh. Amanda helps her sit.

"Va- va- va-" Pam sputters.

"Speaking of vaginas," Josh asks, "where's Marie?"

*Non sequitur* of the century.

"She left. Took Jason, Carol and the boys home on the jet." Dad insisted. Said that after what Jason did, returning $700,000 of his winnings in the high-stakes baccarat room, the man gets *everything* comped. I agree.

"Did Amy ever make it?" Pam asks, clearly thrilled by the topic change.

So am I.

"No," Amanda says with a pout. "Her new internship took longer than expected." Amy is Shannon's younger sister, and was part of the wedding party. She's the type of young woman Anterdec would have in our intern program if Amy didn't insist that she wasn't "into nepotism," whatever that means.

"Who knew that venture capitalist work could be so invasive for an intern," Pam says with a sigh.

"Oh," Amanda says brightly. "She loves it. And she would have missed the wedding anyhow. She'll be there for the presents, though!"

"Presents?" I ask.

"Shannon and Declan have more than six hundred presents waiting for them back home. Grace has them in storage. Marie's inviting everyone to go to a party at Shannon and Declan's place to open everything when we all get back home."

Parse that.

And your brain burns.

Dec has no idea what he's coming home to.

I grin.

"Great!" My word makes Pam frown.

"Six hundred gifts? It will take a week to open them all."

"All the more reason for Dec and Shannon to host a big, sprawling party!" I say, trying on enthusiasm, liking the idea that Dec will come home to a pre-arranged wedding-gift party in his apartment he has no choice but to throw.

Pam's scrutinizing me. The woman appears to be able to sniff out irony like an IRS agent searching for a fake home office deduction.

She's my girlfriend's mother, so I need to shift. Play it cool. Make a better impression.

"How's your room, Pam? Is the staff giving you everything you need?"

"Your father sure is!"

Josh leers. "You and James—*ahem*?" He clears his throat meaningfully.

Pam is either clueless or very, very sly, because she answers Josh as if he were asking the question straight. "Yes, James. He's been so pleasant."

"You're sure we're talking about my father, James McCormick? Hair the color of ash, with an ego the size of Texas?"

"He can be a bit gruff at times, but he's taken a liking to Spritzy."

"Hope that's all he's taken a liking to," Amanda mutters.

"What did you learn?" Pam asks. "I assume no one is married to anyone."

We gape at her.

"How did you know?"

"Easy. First of all, Amanda's a mystery shopper. She engages in behaviors that are crazy on the surface, but perfectly logical at heart. Second, you can't legally marry a cat, and I knew that Chuckles didn't have any ID and therefore couldn't even try to get a marriage license."

"But—"

"And third, Marie called me from a local strip club and asked me what to do about all of you standing at the bar shoving marriage licenses at the poor bartender. Apparently, you were quite intimidating, Andrew. You pushed a few hundred-dollar bills at him, insisting he sign the government documents and make them official."

Everyone slowly cranes their necks, looking at me.

"What," I ask her with as much dignity as a man can muster under the circumstances, "did you tell her?"

"I contacted the concierge at Litraeon and they made fake

documents for us. By the time those were done and 'signed,' you were both beyond reason. Accepted the papers."

"Both?" Amanda peeps. "Both? MOM! You've known the entire time that those were fakes?"

"Didn't Marie tell you?" Pam seems genuinely horrified.

"And *I* told the staff to stock the corporate jet with our finest Champagne for the trip home," I grumble.

"It wasn't entheogenic by any chance, was it?"

"Not even homeopathic."

"Whew!" Geordi says, smiling at everyone. "It's settled, then. We know what happened. No one actually legally married anyone. We've unraveled all the mysteries."

Not quite.

Brona. I wonder if she was in charge of generating the fake documents.

"Pam, did you tell my father all about the fake marriage licenses, by any chance?"

She grins. "It was his idea."

# Chapter Eight

"What?" Dad shouts into the phone as I call him from the corporate jet the next morning. Amanda and I are alone, and I intend to keep it that way. "It made perfect sense!"

We escaped the fracas of the Vegas clan, leaving them to finish packing, sorting out their goodbyes and work schedules. Dad, Pam, Josh, Terry and Spritzy will follow on a different jet. We are on the lesser of Anterdec's jets. Dec and Shannon stole the one with the bedroom, damn it, leaving us with one that requires a certain level of discretion to fit in sex.

My middle name is discretion.

But at Amanda's urging, I've made a huge mistake.

I called my father to find out what the hell he was thinking when he had all these fake marriage licenses created.

"Dad, you told the staff at my resort—"

"*My* resort—"

I ignore that. "To create fake marriage licenses."

"It was brilliant! Shannon and Declan's wedding escapades only dominated the media airwaves for five days. We needed something new! Fresh!"

"And getting a marriage license for my girlfriend to marry a *cat* was part of that strategy?"

"You have to admit it was clever."

"It was stupid. And you made me look like I might have married a guy." *Or two.*

"I thought you were enlightened." His voice has a mock-chiding tone.

"I'm fine with guys marrying guys. Just not marrying *me*."

"Gay CEOs test well, Andrew." His pregnant pause makes me groan.

"I'm not changing my sexual orientation to get free PR, Dad."

I am very, very done with this day. My three hundred text messages are starting to look like the most relaxing part of my life.

"There's something to this technique, Andrew. Using the 24/7 media to boost our corporate image. All those free logos plastered all over the news. The helicopter lifting away from Farmington Country Club was even on BuzzBuzz and The Garlic!"

"*Buzzfeed. The Onion.*" My head starts to hurt again.

Amanda motions for me to put the phone on speaker. I do. Might as well share the pain.

"I'm pretty sure Johnny Carson came very close to covering it." What's next? Did Dad use his slide rule to calculate the value of all this free press?

She frantically waves her hands at the phone in a gesture that I assume means, *Turn off the speakerphone.*

I snicker.

"All right, Dad. Got it. Point made." It's not worth correcting him.

"Any chance Shannon's pregnant right now? Because that would—"

Amanda's eyes bug out of her head.

"DAD! Stop!"

"When you're back, let's have a conference about ways we can leverage our personal lives for this kind of coverage."

"You sound like Marie."

A grunt comes across the phone. "That was low. Your brother said that, too."

"You know you're on the wrong track when Declan and I agree on something."

Another grunt.

I look at the ring on my hand. Amanda's still wearing hers, too.

"You've spent most of my life teaching me how to remain private. How not to let the media use me."

"I was wrong."

I burst out laughing. "Good one, Dad." Never heard those words out of his mouth.

"Andrew, I—"

I cut him off. "We're about to take off. I just found out I'm not married to three different potential candidates. My girlfriend almost married a cat because of you. I have three hundred text messages waiting for my attention, and my new admin is about as polished as a piece of coal. Worse: it turns out Declan's new coffee chain *does* have better coffee than Litraeon. Goodbye, Dad."

*Click.*

Amanda laughs softly through her nose. "He's a piece of work."

I do not want to talk about my dad.

"Want to join the Mile High Club?" I inhale slowly as I reach for her delicate wrist, my ringed hand gliding up, her skin so soft and smooth.

"Holy topic change, Batman!"

I shrug.

"Really? Here? Now? After everything we've been through?"

If I just sit here in silence, the idea will grow on her, right? Something on me is growing.

"That's not going to work."

"What's not going to work?"

"Thinking you can wait me out and I'll magically throw myself at you and we'll join the Mile High Club."

We? I start to correct her, then shut my mouth. Fast. The past is the past, and bringing it up now is about as safe as stealing in North Korea.

She glares at me.

"Fine. *Me*."

Oh, hell. She reads minds. Mine, at least. The funny part? It's as if I have no past. No other woman has imprinted herself so thoroughly on me as Amanda. No other woman evokes more of me—the true Andrew—than this very pissed, extremely angry, deeply simmering woman sitting next to me on a plane, a day after learning we're not married.

Why are we *not* married?

I squeeze her hand, careful around her wounds. It's only been six days since she rescued the animals in the pool at Dec and Shannon's wedding. Six days.

We're been back together for six days, and this is the first time we've had an extended stretch of time to just talk.

Mile High Club, or deep discussion? C'mon. Which one would most guys pick?

I pick deep discussion.

No, really. Seriously. I do.

*I do.*

Those words have too many meanings. Too bad they're so loaded. A wall has formed between Amanda and me, an instant barrier between us, as if erected by the impossibility of true love. People aren't supposed to find their one like this.

It's a pipe dream.

We're drunk with pheromones and adrenaline, still a little off-kilter from psychotropic hallucinogens we never intended to consume, and maybe Amanda's right.

Maybe I really am an asshole for suggesting sex mid-air.

And maybe I just don't deserve her.

See that? Those bricks? The seconds that tick by are like little time masons, adding to the wall.

Faces change when emotions churn under the surface. You have to watch carefully. Dispassionately. Most people let other people's emotions trigger their own. Back and forth, they lob their inner states like a game of high-stakes Hot Potato.

If you watch someone morph through their own reconfiguration, it is heartbreaking.

It's also revealing.

Revelations bring power.

Declan deals with other people's emotions by turning his own off.

I just watch.

And learn.

But there's one thing I don't do: reveal.

Because when you reveal, you cede. There's a reason why poker is such a popular game. The money is an afterthought.

Poker faces reveal nothing, but that doesn't mean they don't reflect the truth.

And the truth is that there's a roiling boil beneath the surface, waiting to come out if you give it the smallest chance.

Amanda doesn't play games, though.

Which means the stakes are that much higher.

We're playing for keeps.

At least, I think I am. And it terrifies me to think she's not.

I open my mouth to say something smooth. Suave. Caring and articulate, hot and emotional. The perfect words to make her know how authentically I love her, and that makes up for the craziness of these past few days.

"I dated Jessica Coffin."

See? The perfect words.

For a man on death row.

Her breath catches in her throat, and she blinks, over and over, as if trying to clear her vision. I expect her to yell. Shout. Turn red with anger. Snap at me, incredulous.

Instead, she nods slowly and says, "I wondered."

Oh, hell.

I'd rather have her yelling.

"You *wondered*?"

"The race."

"Race?"

"Oh, come on. The race? The one I volunteered at and Anterdec sponsored, two years ago, when Declan was being such a jerk to Shannon?"

"What does some charity we support have to do with my dating Jessica?"

"I saw you talking to her and—" She pauses and looks at me. Her face is impassive, a sheet of glass with two enormous, closed-off eyes that blink slowly, methodically. Unnerved, I watch her watching me. Amanda generally shows all her feelings in a big pile of emotion in her eyes, which now narrow.

"Did you sleep with her?"

And here we go.

"No."

Amanda just blinks.

"You don't have to lie."

"I've never lied to you before. I wouldn't start now."

"Why are you telling me this, Andrew? If you're trying to have a Mile High experience with me, this isn't the best form of foreplay."

"It's not? Because *Men's Health* magazine says that spilling your guts about your past girlfriends is the best aphrodisiac."

"Girlfriend? She was your *girlfriend*? You told me you never had a serious girlfriend!"

"Part of my junior year of high school, yes. For about a month."

"Oh."

"Right. Doesn't count."

"Who broke up with whom?"

"I dumped her."

"Why?"

"Does it matter?"

She shrugs. "Probably not, but it will kill me not to know. You can't just blurt out that you dated my best friend's nemesis and not expect the Spanish Inquisition."

"Ready for takeoff," the pilot announces. "Estimated flight time five hours and twenty minutes."

This is going to be the longest flight of my life, isn't it? Longer than that Boston to Hong Kong leg.

"Who was the first guy you ever slept with?"

Her mouth drops open.

I actually don't want to know the answer. In fact, the minute she spills the name, I'll have Gina create a hot sheet on him and he'll find himself signed up for every nasty porn site and political volunteer list in the U.S.

But I ask because I need her to stop looking at me like that. Like my past is ruining my future.

She smiles.

"You."

*My* mouth drops open. My balls fall through my seat cushion and dangle with the fuselage.

"Ha! Gotcha!" She sighs. "Fine. Don't tell me why you broke up with her." She wiggles in her seat, her head turned away from me, tilted down for a nap. "I don't need to know." She yawns. "I love you no matter what."

This is the difference between men and women. Not the ovaries vs. the balls. Not the breasts vs. the pecs. Not even the up-down toilet seat controversy or the Period Errand vs. the Morning Wood.

Oh, no.

She cannot settle in for a nap while my brain burns with the need to know the name of the guy who deflowered her.

"She didn't like the way I kissed," I say with a sigh.

Amanda sits up fast, like someone's pulled her up by her hair. "What? Is she crazy?"

"We were sixteen. She went to a different school. We had three dates. We texted with flip phones. She was shallow and said I kissed like a sloth with an overproductive salivary gland."

"She said that?"

"Worse. She texted it. There was no Twitter back then. Do you know how determined she must have been to take the time to text all that on a flip phone?"

One corner of Amanda's mouth curls up. Her nostrils flare as she purses her lips, trying not to laugh.

"Quit shining me on."

"I'm not!" I stick my tongue out at her and loll it to one side. "See? Wet-tongued sloth."

"Andrew."

I pretend to snore, tongue hanging out.

"You are impossible."

"What's his name?"

"Who?"

"The first guy you slept with."

"You really want to know?"

"No. But yes."

"Fine." She thinks about it for a few seconds, just long enough to make my brain turn into ribbons of pain.

"And?"

"Charlie."

"Charlie? You date him for long?" The thought of some gawky teen slobbering all over Amanda awkwardly makes my gut hurt.

"We never really dated. Just hung out a lot."

"He didn't take you out? Buy you dinner? Go to the movies?"

"No. He was more of a stay-in kind of guy."

"Bastard."

"He did have this kink."

I freeze and close my eyes.

"What?"

"He liked to pee on shoes with laces."

I open one eye. "Charlie, huh? Last name wouldn't happen to be Kulls?"

"How'd you guess?"

I snort.

She laces her fingers through mine. "It's okay. Just never, ever tell Shannon you dated Jessica."

"Why would I?"

"It could slip out."

"That's not the kind of statement that just slips out."

She cocks one eyebrow at me. Huh. She has a point.

It just did.

"Telling you is different."

"Why?"

"Why did I tell you, or why is telling you different?"

"Both."

"You always say both!"

"I always want to know as much as possible."

"So do I. Tell me his name, Amanda."

We're at a standoff. I crack first. And that's okay, because relationship negotiations are different from business negotiations. In business, if you crack first, you lose.

In relationships, if you don't crack first, you lose out on sex.

I hate losing.

"I told you because it felt dishonest not to."

She just nods.

"And telling you is different from telling Shannon because she doesn't need to know."

"And I do?"

"I think so. Otherwise, there's too much power to the information."

"Did you love her?"

"Hell, no!"

"She was just a fling?"

"It was high school. She was a schemer then, just like she is now. Our parents were in the same circles."

"And she's easy on the eyes."

"No." My answer precedes thought. "She's not. Not anymore."

"She's gorgeous, Andrew. Don't patronize me."

"I'm not. Swear."

"But back then?"

"Back then I thought that surface looks were a clue to the inside of people. Before I learned better." I reach over and stroke her cheek with the back of my hand.

She falters. "Am I supposed to be flattered by that?"

I chuckle. "You're beautiful inside and out. Jessica is a Barbie doll on the outside, and nothing but molded fakery on the inside."

"Why did you break up with her?"

"Tell me his name."

She dips her head and smiles. "Al Barkin. Senior year of high school. Prom night. We were in school band together. Clichéd, I know."

I can't breathe for a moment. Amanda's look says, *I showed you mine. Show me yours.*

My turn. "I dumped her because she went after Declan."

"And that," Amanda says in an arch tone, "is why Shannon can't know any of this. Wow. Jessica tried to date Declan while she was your girlfriend?"

"Ambition. Why date a Milton guy when he had a Harvard brother?"

Amanda frowns, the skin between her eyes crinkling, the expression adorable. "Your junior year. That was Declan's freshman year?"

I know where she's going with this.

"Yes."

"Right after your mother died."

"About six months later, yes."

"That sleazy little psycho bitch."

"Don't hold back, honey. Tell me how you really feel."

Rising up out of her seat, Amanda starts to stand, her fingers curled into claws, as if she's about to go find Jessica and cut a bitch. I push her down gently by the shoulder.

She is a live wire, eyes bulging, her fight response primed.

This is *so* hot.

"How can you even talk to her now? Anterdec does charity work with her family's foundation! I see you chatting with her at events. She's gone after Shannon in such a distorted way, and now you're telling me she used you to get to Declan?"

I shrug. "She has no actual power."

"She can ruin someone with one tweet!"

"You consider that to be power?"

"Yes."

"No. Wrong. Let's stop right there." A flash of insight. "Jessica has no intrinsic power."

"Intrinsic power?"

"The only influence she has comes from other people. It's basic popularity, which is a mirage on top of an optical illusion."

"Huh?"

"Popularity comes from getting enough people to say you're

a hot item that others believe it. Critical mass and all that. It's fleeting, and relies on the masses propping up your influence. That's all Jessica has. She's a paper tiger."

"But she's so powerful on the social scene."

"I think you give her way more sway than she really possesses. Stop reacting to her. Stop reinforcing her with others."

"She made fun of Shannon's *poop*."

"She is just a paper tiger."

"Was she always like this?"

I have to think about that one. "Yeah. I guess so. I never really got to know her."

"Didn't date long enough?"

"No. She just wouldn't let me in."

"I didn't mean sexually."

"I didn't either. She was tight as a drum emotionally. Our month of dating was mostly focused on my getting her into big parties at Milton so she could social climb. Then taking her to Harvard to visit Dec. All it took was one Cambridge party and *bam*—I found her on his lap."

"Whoa."

"He was shoving her off it." I remember it perfectly. *'These things happen'* was all Jessica said, as if that explained everything.

"Why are we in a private jet, finally truly alone for the first time since the wedding, and we're talking about Jessica Coffin?"

"You brought her up."

"Actually, you did, Andrew."

I restrain myself from replying immediately. In the space of a few breaths, I find a more authentic answer.

"I wanted to give you a piece of me. That means sharing more with you."

"What do you mean?"

My inner life is a spiral staircase that ascends and descends to infinity. I brace myself and confess, "I don't know how to do this."

"Share?"

I shrug.

"How to be in a relationship?"

"Any of it."

"It's new to me, too."

"Not the newness. Being new is the easy part. I get that. I don't know how to lose myself in you without losing all of myself. How do I let go and trust that you'll give me the freedom to figure out who I am and at the same time trust that you'll be right there with me?"

"*That's* your idea of a relationship?"

"It's wrong, isn't it? Jesus, Amanda, I don't even know how to describe my own confusion properly."

"It's not wrong," she says slowly. "Just interesting."

"Interesting how?"

"I never thought of it that way. Guaranteed freedom and guaranteed company. That's such a paradox."

"Which means it can't exist."

"Can't it? Why not? Says who?"

I don't have an answer to that.

"We both know how to manage systems, Andrew. We're experts at looking at processes and understanding how to make a process work. How to use systems to serve people—with an end goal in mind."

"So?"

"Isn't a relationship just a series of emotional processes?"

"You sound like Declan."

That's not a compliment, and she knows it.

"I'm not wrong."

I make a derisive sound that I cut off, because I suddenly sound like my father.

"This is a lot to take in after the insanity of the last week." She looks at her ring finger.

"That doesn't make any of this less real."

"You're right. We broke all the rules. Took all the steps and shook them up."

"There's so much more to relationships and love than a nested list of steps and procedures."

"Are you sure?"

I grab her, hard, and kiss her, the impulse driven by something that does not appear anywhere on my personal Gantt chart. This kiss holds the world together. My hands on her soft, yielding shoulders are pillars, meant to hold up the next layer of emotion. We are the moon and stars, her eyes are the atmosphere, her breath the air I breathe.

Laws of attraction keep atoms together, electrons and neutrons repelling and migrating closer, forming differentiated objects that serve our purposes.

Feelings shouldn't follow the same pattern.

And yet they do. The heart may be a muscle, but it's also a vessel that pumps blood and magic through cells that I'm kissing with yearning, cells that kiss me right back, with heat and warmth and wetness that curves into me, our skin attracted to skin by nothing more than emotion attached to biological processes.

That feel damn good.

So damn fine.

The earth jolts. I knew we compounded energy, but—

"Sorry about that, Mr. McCormick and Ms. Warrick. Problem with turbulence."

Amanda gives me a weak smile and asks, "What if that were more than turbulence?"

"Excuse me?"

"What if we had five minutes before the plane crashed. What would you do if you knew we only had five minutes left before we died?"

I give her a look.

"I know it's silly," she says. Her expression says it's anything but.

"I would regret not *really* marrying you."

Her eyes move down, unfocused suddenly, her blinking in time to the beat of my heart. I know she's processing what I just said, integrating the implications, trying to decide whether to believe it or not, shock wearing off.

What fills in the spaces once the surprise is gone?

"You're wrong."

"Wrong about wanting to marry you?"

"Wrong about not knowing how to reveal yourself to someone, Andrew."

What the hell am I supposed to say to that?

My turn to look away. Stare out the window. Pretend I'm thinking through her words when all I'm really doing is trying to hold it together. How can I stare down a Sultan during intense business negotiations but a simple question from my girlfriend shatters me?

Love.

Right?

Cotton and warmth take over, my lungs inhaling Amanda, exhaling confusion. She's next to me, her eyes guarded yet hopeful, trying to understand me from the outside in. That's all we can do. Look and listen, touch and hear, filled with the infusion of our lover's scent and their very essence, until we know them as well as you can know someone whose flesh isn't yours.

And if you're really fortunate, you uncover parts of yourself through them that would otherwise remain buried under that outer shell that you present to the world as *you*.

"What about you?" I challenge. "Five minutes. You have five minutes left before dying. What would *you* do?"

Her kiss is my response.

And wetness on my cheek.

Alarmed, I reach up, cupping her face with both hands, not breaking the connection our mouths make. Deepening the kiss, I sweep my tongue between her lips, sucking, her sweet teeth nipping at my lip, the softness turning urgent. More tears, and I'm torn. I want to pull back and say all the right words to make her stop crying, but instinct makes me search for an answer with my mouth, my lips, my hands and tongue.

I turn in my seat, seeking her soft curves, wanting her heat against me, needing her.

"We're not married," she whispers against my mouth, our foreheads pressed together.

"I know," I rasp, ready to tell her how much I want to propose, how she's the one, the only one, and how that feeling makes my chest collapse.

Clarity is so rare. Certainty is slippery. As I kiss her again, my hands integrate with her space, our bodies no longer separate from each other, hearts fusing. She is becoming me and I am becoming her and by God, this is such a familiar feeling. The curve of her spine against my fingers, the tickle of her hair against my nose, the way she inhales as if she's whispering my name through centuries—it's already in me.

This is déjà vu through touch.

She's already mine.

The stupid ritual of getting married, of rings and parties and vows and commitment, is just dressing. She's right: we're not married.

And I need to confess how sorry I am for that.

More than that, I need to correct this.

"Thank God," she adds, laughing softly. "Can you imagine how ridiculous that would be?"

I go cold. I am a wall at my company's ice bar. I am an iceberg. I become liquid nitrogen.

Ridiculous.

Right.

I can't breathe. My throat closes, mind a whirl of all the business work Gina has texted and emailed to me, a helicopter cutting through the perfect familiarity of two seconds ago and shredding it with blades that become claws.

"Andrew?" she asks, snuggling against my shoulder, the angle awkward, her ear over my heart.

Can she hear it break?

"Right," I choke out, plastering on a smile. I force a low rumble of a laugh. "Ridiculous."

She lifts the window cover and a shaft of sunlight streams in, catching her ring, the wave bouncing right into my eye, blinding me with pain. I have to look away, the afterimage etched in my sight.

I close my eyes, the distance between her warm skin and mine widening with each breath, even as we stay in place. She is pressed against me, still snuggled in, yet I'm a football field away within ten minutes.

That day I said I wouldn't let her love me, I lied. I told myself one hell of a whopper, and then I crafted it, an artisanal masterpiece of fakery, in order to get her to leave me with my pain and fear. Having a witness to my weakness was worse than bearing it alone.

It's crazy. I know. Wanting to be married to her is illogical. Impetuous. Silly and immature, a flouting of convention and societal understanding of what marriage is supposed to be and represent. We made a spectacle of ourselves in Vegas, and in the midst of drug-induced spontaneity, we committed an act of utter synchronicity.

For one of us, at least.

By the time we arrive in Boston, we're still sitting next to each other, and she's sleeping, her cheek against my shoulder, but we might as well have the Berlin Wall between us.

And one of us has to defect.

# Chapter Nine

The realities of learning to run a Fortune 500 company come crashing down the second we land in Boston. Gerald's there to greet me with the limo. Amanda and I exchange strangely distant kisses. Lance takes her home at her insistence.

She claims she has a doctor's appointment she forgot about, but it seems contrived.

I invent a meeting with investors from Vilnius. She doesn't question it. Her weekend is "full" with vague events with her mother, and mine is nothing but work catch-up.

We both clearly need some space.

Our parting lingers in my troubled mind as Gerald pulls away from the airport, the other limo disappearing with a finality that makes me sick. We're not on bad terms. Not even a bit.

*Ridiculous.*

That comment, though. Might as well tell me I'm bad in bed. Both are about as true, and both are distinctly impossible.

"Sir?" Gerald asks. "How was Vegas?"

"Don't ask."

"Pretend I didn't, sir." He smirks. The guy has worked for us for years. I don't know much about him, other than the fact that he was a Navy SEAL and he teaches art on the side. Dad likes to hire chauffeurs with military or law enforcement backgrounds.

We haven't had a safety issue since I started working for Anterdec, so this is one of my father's policies I plan to continue.

"What happens in Vegas, stays in Vegas," I add, voice dripping with sarcasm. "Anything new here?"

"No, sir."

"How goes the art project at the community center?" Declan's closer to Gerald, and helped secure a grant from our company's foundation for a proposal initiated by Gerald.

The guy shaves his head and has a face that shows a violent life. Crooked nose, deep scar below his right ear into the jaw, and a hardness in the lines of his face. He's built like a nuclear bunker.

But when he smiles, he becomes a marshmallow.

"The kids love it. The pottery wheels and kiln make a huge difference. Some of the kids are preparing to sell their works at a juried art show. Another one got accepted into a full-tuition summer program for art camp."

"That's great."

"And your brother has offered to model again for my classes. Not for a while, but this fall, after the honeymoon."

I groan. Gerald laughs. "What's my brother trying to prove?"

Gerald wisely shrugs and goes silent for the rest of the trip to my place.

I spend the night alone with my laptop. It doesn't mind being married to me. My laptop is the perfect wife, actually.

It turns on whenever I want it.

It greets me by name.

It remembers everything.

A few strokes of my fingers and it gives me anything I demand.

It doesn't talk back.

I am one floor below the penthouse apartment, overlooking the Seaport District. Lights blink in the distance, different colors from boats sending signals I can't read. Just like women.

I am on top of the world, the city sprawled before me in an endless series of lights in motion, as if its energy exists solely to serve me. Scores of square miles of industry and commerce, tourism and entertainment, financial and educational institutions dotting the cityscape, each representing a system designed to serve.

Serve people. Markets. Government policy.

And I am empty.

She's happy we're not married. Relieved. No equivocation. No questioning. She views it all as one big mess we untangled ourselves from. Whew. Thank God.

We're free.

She's not wrong. My left hand is heavy. It carries the weight of my own expectations, curled into my palm like a fragile fruit, one that bruises easily but tastes like ambrosia. I can stand here in the dark, wine glass in hand, and own the world that stretches before my eyes.

And every bite of victory tastes bitter.

You know what that is?

That's right.

*Ridiculous.*

By Monday morning I'm in the office, buried under paperwork, three hours of conference calls under my belt and a raging hard-on that keeps banging against the shards of my cracked heart. Restlessness does not come naturally to me. As kids, Declan was the one who twitched and fidgeted, his deep calm as an adult a characteristic he acquired as a result of the rush of puberty and growth.

My fingers strum my desktop. My foot won't stop bouncing. My pants are tight. My wedding ring taps out a sickly Morse code that I can't decipher, but if I were a betting man, I'd guess it's saying something about Amanda.

Who hasn't answered my latest text. Twenty minutes without an answer is, well...

Ridiculous.

My executive assistant, Gina, is new. While Declan got Grace a few years ago, I'm stuck with a string of temps.

Why? It's not because I'm an asshole.

I am *particular*.

It occurs to me for the first time that Declan's resignation could result in a big coup for me. Grace. I can finally have Grace all to myself. She's smart and hilarious, motherly and hardened, and she manages details like a drill sergeant.

I smile. Plus, Dec will have a cow if I snipe his longtime admin.

I smile wider.

My phone rings. Gina. "Mr. McCormick? It's Gina?" Every sentence Gina utters sounds like a question. Either she's the most uncertain woman on the planet, or she's from California.

"Yes. I know. You programmed your number into my phone, Gina. I see it on caller display. No need to ID yourself."

"Oh? Oh, right? Well, I'm calling because your father has issued an edict for the removal of—"

"An *edict*?"

"That was his term, sir? Not mine?"

"Tell me about this edict," I say, in a voice that makes it clear I'm not going to like it.

"Mr. McCormick—er, senior—says that Mr. McCormick—uh, Mr. Declan McCormick—is to have all Anterdec privileges revoked, effective immediately, and security needs to escort him out of the building with, um...?"

"What?"

"His exact words were, 'all his personal belongs in a cheap box from a discount warehouse'?"

"I can't do that!"

"Why not?" She sounds like she's about to cry. "Because it would be cruel, right?"

"No!" Actually, it's pretty brilliant. "Because Declan's on his honeymoon right now. He won't be back for a week. Tell Dad we have to wait until then."

Hah. This just gets better. I get Grace, and Dec gets all the luxuries removed. It's like Christmas and Easter rolled into one.

"You want me to tell Mr. McCormick—senior—that you agree with the edict, but just want to delay it?"

"Yes."

"Isn't that kind of mean?" Is she *sniffling*?

Gina's not going to last long.

"And should I let Grace know?"

"God, no!" I reach into my jacket pocket and pull out Declan's resignation letter. Smug. He was so smug, handing over this thin piece of paper that contains words that unravel parts of my professional life. Terry bailed on the family business ages ago, for reasons he and Dad still won't talk about.

Declan can't leave, too. Without him, there's no buffer.

Just Dad and me.

Bearing the brunt of The Full James McCormick isn't fair.

*Fair.*

There's a loaded word.

If Grace knows what's coming for Declan, she'll move heaven and earth to protect him. Besides, I need to get to her before Dad. I know she'd sooner eat live cockroaches than work for my father again (her words, not hyperbole), which means she'll definitely come work for me, if I make sure the price is right.

"Gina, I'll speak with my father. What else do I need to tackle today?"

"Your calendar has all your meetings in it? You're booked solid in person or by phone for forty-six of the next sixty-three hours?"

"Is that a question, Gina?"

"Is what a question, sir?"

Sigh. "Thanks for giving me time to sleep and shower."

"Actually, you're double-booked for an entire hour in there, but I couldn't help it? Someone from a place called Consolidated Evalu-shop insisted on a meeting?"

"Greg?" I fumble for his last name. That's a detail admins should handle, damn it.

"Um, someone named Amanda Warrick? Just got off the phone with her? She said it involves confidential FCC filing information and requires that you clear your schedule for two hours straight?"

"Excuse me?" Gerald got me a coffee for the ride over here

this morning. A double breve. That's Amanda's favorite, but whatever. I'll take all the caffeine I can get. I start drinking as I listen to Gina's explanation and look outside my window, the expansive view of the financial district rolling out to the seaport. I can see my building from here, along with a large tourist ship making its way to the Harbor Islands.

"She did this for today and again for Friday? I know Anterdec is acquiring Consolidated Evalu-shop, so I assume she needs to go over every detail of how to merge?"

And the window gets sprayed with coffee.

"What?"

"Did I explain this the wrong way?" Gina's voice goes up even more when she's worried. If this continues, she'll sound like she's sucking on helium all day.

"No, I got it." And I do. Amanda is grabbing chunks of my schedule in advance.

She's a fixer, all right. Saving the date in my professional calendar for sex?

Damn, she's good.

"Let Ms. Warrick know that the merger talks may go on longer than two hours. Better plan for three."

"That would bump your daily meeting with your dad?"

I smile. "Even better."

"Mr. McCormick—senior—also made a requisition for a change in corporate policy regarding pets at work?"

"A what?" Oh, God. Now I'm doing it. I need a declarative statement to purge this vocal tic. "Please explain."

"He wants Fridays to be Bring Your Pet to Work Day?"

"Fine." No harm in it. "Anything else, Gina?"

"No, sir?"

"Please call me Andrew. All my admins do."

"Yes, Mr. McCormick?"

*Click.*

I finish my lukewarm coffee. Weed through more than a hundred email messages that Gina already triaged. These are the truly urgent ones. I pare them down to eleven that are impossible to solve in my first full day back.

By the time I'm in my spin clothes, my trainer, Vince, has arrived. He's carrying a glass bottle filled with limp, brown seaweed and a foil packet.

"Here's your kombucha," he announces, handing me the seaweed.

"I'm not drinking that crap, Vince."

"It's fermented! It's good for your gut."

"Beer's fermented, too."

He shoves the foil pouch in my hand. Vince has long hair, thick and braided, with a clean-shaven, wide face and a nearly hairless body. In spite of his enormous size, he cycles competitively and does private training for a few CEOs in the area.

He's also merciless.

Which is why I hired him.

"What's this? Kelp botanicals in a druid-tear solution?"

"MCT oil."

"Isn't that illegal everywhere except Colorado and Washington?"

"It's medium-chain fatty acids, not marijuana." Vince begins reciting all the health benefits. It's easier to eat it than to argue. I rip open the top of the packet and suck it down.

"Ugh." It tastes like you think. I just drank a quarter-cup of oil.

"Muscle power."

"If I vomit in the middle of my sprint, it's on you."

"Nope. My reflexes are better than yours. You won't get any on me."

I snort. He shoves me to the twin spin bikes in the workout room attached to my office. "Put up or shut up."

I climb on my bike and wait for the music. The same song opens all of our 60-minute spin sessions for warm-up.

Queen's *Fat-Bottomed Girls*.

Vince doesn't start the music, though. His eyes are narrowed to slits, and he's staring at my midsection.

"The fuck, Andrew?" Unlike everyone else who works for me, Vince doesn't call me Mr. or Sir.

"What?"

"Something you want to share with the class?"

"What class?"

He yanks my left hand off the handlebars. "You got *married*?"

"Oh, that."

"You're wearing a wedding ring for shits and giggles?"

"No."

"You gonna explain this to me?"

"No."

"I have to spin it out of you?"

"Just try."

"Is that a challenge?"

"Burn me to the ground, Vince."

"Done."

The music starts.

Five minutes into it and my legs are screaming.

Ten minutes into it and Vince is screaming.

Twenty minutes into it and *I'm* screaming.

Forty minutes later, the lambs are screaming.

With five minutes to go, Vince's soundtrack shifts to a song I've never heard before.

"You changed the lineup?"

"Sure. Variety is the spice of life."

"Don't do that. Stick to the plan."

"My plan, Andrew. You can't make me do the same damn shit over and over."

When I hired Vince, I told him exactly what I wanted. Technique, pacing, playlist, the whole bit. All he had to do was ride with me and hold me accountable.

"Screw you," he said that day. "I do what I want because I'm the best. Don't like it? Don't hire me."

I hired him on the spot.

"Changing the music makes me lose my pace," I huff.

"Changing the music forces you to adapt. You're too rigid."

"Go to hell, Vince."

"You only say that when I'm right."

I don't have the lung power to answer.

Five minutes later, I'm stretching. Vince is at the blender.

"Smoothie?" I ask, as I feel my pulse in my eyelashes.

"Bulletproof coffee with protein powder."

"Coffee and whey?" I cringe. I uncringe. How did Vince make my face muscles ache like this? Damn. "Do I look like Little Miss Muffet with a latte?"

"Trust me."

"I don't trust someone whose primary diet source is rotten plankton."

He just grunts, then shoves a pint glass filled with beige cream at me.

"Seriously, Vince, what's in this?" It looks like a hot latte met an oil slick.

"Try it."

I do. It tastes like milk blended with coffee and snot. I gag on the first try.

"You're like a chick giving her first blow job, Andrew."

"Now I *really* want to put this in my mouth. You're so inspirational."

"Wimp."

"Asshole."

"You have too much energy left," he declares. "Let's lift."

Verbal abuse is my second language. I'm fluent in it when talking to other guys.

"I'm not lifting. I've got a call with some investors in Turkey."

"Excuses, excuses."

"If you haven't noticed, I run a Fortune 500 company."

"And you're wearing a wedding ring you won't talk about."

"I'm not married."

"Spill it."

Damn. He's not letting me live this down, is he?

I tell him the whole story. The abridged version.

In one sentence.

"Amanda and I drank hallucinogen-spiked wine in Vegas and

93

woke up wearing wedding rings, but it turns out we didn't actually marry each other."

His eyes narrow.

"Why are you still wearing the ring?"

I shrug. "Haven't had time to take it off."

His eyebrows go up. "You haven't had two spare seconds?"

Damn.

"Fine." I reach down and slide the ring off my finger, holding it in my palm. "See?" I curl my fingers around it, protective.

"Don't take it off for my benefit. I'm not the one who gets fake married and then comes home in real denial."

"Denial?"

"All I'm saying is that the chick you almost-married must be one hell of a woman if you're still wearing a wedding ring you don't need to wear. Most guys would have ripped that off their finger the second they could."

"I'm not most guys."

"No, you're not. And speaking of that special woman, how are you doing on your wasp lessons?"

Back up. *Wasp lessons?* I know what you're thinking. It's not —well—

"I'm doing fine," I grind out, covering my mouth with the lip of the glass filled with caffeinated snot.

"You're practicing?"

"I don't need to practice."

You ever hear metal grind against an orc's bowels? That's the sound Vince makes.

"Andrew." He grabs the rest of my bulletproof coffee and drinks it, then slams the glass on the counter like he's Thor, demanding another tankard of ale. "You came to me a few months ago to ask for help dealing with your fear."

"Don't use that word," I snap. "It wasn't—"

"*Feeeeaaaaarrrrrr.*" He draws out the word slowly, eyes glowing, boring into me like a laser. "And I came up with a plan. When I work with clients, my training programs are all-encompassing, and designed for success. Your wasp lessons were maximized for optimal outcome. Eradicating fear was the goal."

"Quit calling it—"

"*Feeeeeeaarrrrrr.*"

My hands curl into fists, the wedding band digging into my palm. He looks just like Declan when he says that damn word.

"Look." I grab my hand towel off the bike and start to walk away. "I've got a call with some officials in Bhutan in ten minutes, and then I—"

"You said Turkey a few minutes ago."

Shit.

"Turkey, Bhutan," I say, dismissive like my dad.

"Even *I* know those are very, very distinct countries and cultures, Andrew." He gives me a sour look.

"Investors blur together. They're all the same." That's a huge lie. "I don't have time for this."

Not a lie.

"You taken your fake wife out on a real date in daylight, Andrew? Outside?"

I freeze. It's a split second pause, but he catches it.

The huff of dismissive reaction makes my blood boil.

"Look, Vince, shut the hell up."

"I'll shut up when you man up."

"I'm plenty man."

"Not if you expect your woman to live like a vampire. You bite her already and turn her into one of you? Humans need sunlight. Air. A man who doesn't live in fear of an insect's shadow."

I've never told Vince why I live a carefully-constructed life. A life designed to mitigate risk. A life that reduces down to near-zero the chance that I'll be stung.

A life that makes sense.

"She's agreed to your weird-ass lifestyle crap?"

My head feels like a balloon within a balloon within a balloon filled with glitter and jelly beans. I can't have this conversation.

"She's off limits as a topic." I take the ring from my palm, slide it back on, and give him the bird.

His eyes narrow, hands on hips, breath steady. "You're hardcore, Andrew. Seriously. I don't say that lightly. I work with guys like you. Most of you are a dime a dozen. That's why I don't work with most of you. But you're not the strongest client I have."

"Vince, you train Olympic weightlifters. Of course I'm not." He's playing head games. Won't work on me.

"Not that kind of strength, man. I'm talking about inner strength."

He might as well have sucker-punched me, gloveless, while wearing brass knuckles.

"Fuck.You."

Vince shrugs, shaking his head slightly, never breaking eye contact. "There you go. Baring your fangs when you should be showing me your belly."

"What does that even mean?"

"Real strength comes from being vulnerable without flinching. Real strength comes from admitting when you feel weak— and asking for help to become strong again. You did that when you came to me and asked for help with the wasp thing."

I snort. "Okay, Dr. Phil."

"And now you're backpedaling."

I roll my tongue in my cheek and say nothing, pivoting away. My hand shakes as I reach for a folder.

"It's Monday. We used to meet on Fridays at two out at that park in Waltham. You gonna be there?"

"Do I pay you to bully me?" I'm not answering his question. I'm not answering because I don't know the answer.

"No. You pay me to train you."

I shoot him a dirty look.

"The bullying is a bonus."

As he walks out, I hear him say to Gina, "Two o'clock Friday in Waltham. Add it to his calendar."

Balls.

But I don't object. I'm man enough to admit he's right.

Just not to his face.

As I'm bending down to sit in my office chair, eyeballs deep in some contract made up of more legalese than a pre-nup for Rupert Murdoch, in breezes a bundle of creamy flesh, lush hair, big, round eyes and red lips that don't even get a chance to talk before I'm across the room, kissing them. She's soft and sweet, tasting like honey and tea, and her curves melt under my hot hands.

My hot hands that wear our wedding ring.

For a marriage that didn't happen.

*But it will*, I think as the kiss deepens. The shift from talking smack with Vince to having her skin pulsing into my palms is dizzying.

Or maybe that's just the effect of having Vince beat the shit out of every electrolyte in my body.

As she makes a small sound of pleasure in the back of her throat, my thumb migrates, the pad resting lightly on the pulse at her collarbone, seeking to feel the sound. Our hips press into each other, my erection painful in these cramped, tight shorts, and all I want to do is free myself, then be caged within her warm, wet madness.

Losing myself in her is the best form of escape.

Her hands slide up and down, one north to the nape of my neck, one south to the curve of my ass, which tightens at the initiation of her touch. Her hand is insistent, demanding, righteous and full of assumptions.

She acts like she has the right to touch me like this.

I like that.

I break the kiss and bend, thighs screaming, hamstrings ready to defect, put one arm under her knees and the other around her back, palm cupping her breast, and she's in my arms, then on my desk.

And I'm on my knees.

Ignoring the shaking muscles in my legs, which tremble from strain and desire, I part her legs, finding black silk, lace, and nothing but barrier. It's beautiful, but this will not do.

"Not here!" she gasps, but her voice isn't firm, the protest half-hearted, as if she needs to check a box on a list of How To Be Professional qualities she should have in the workplace. She's turned on and ready, the illicit desk sex and my mouth too much to let her mount another argument, her head lolling back as I dive in, pushing aside the piece of cloth and finding my way to give.

Sunlight glints off the wedding ring on my hand as I reach back, my hand resting on her knee.

It's the last thing I see until she chokes back a cry from her orgasm, her fingers pulling tightly on my hair, and begs me, "Please. In me. Now." Normally talkative, Amanda loses access to part of the speech center of her brain as we spiral deeper into lust and passion. It's a tell.

I love this tell.

Within seconds, the bike shorts are across the room, and we're on the floor, her skirt around my hips, Amanda riding me. Not only is this one of my favorite positions, but she doesn't know that my legs are so blown from Vince's workout that I'm not sure I could remain standing for any testosterone-injected positions that require balance or strength.

Not going to admit that, so instead, I let her take the lead, which kills two orgasms with one stone. Or something like that. My own speech center is devolving as she moves up, the friction turning me into an animal, atavistic and primal.

Besides, this leaves both hands free, which means I can unbutton her shirt, unleash her breasts, and watch her beautiful face as she rides me, coming with a tight clench and a full-throated cry, her face flushed and lips parted, one look at her pushing me over.

As we come together, I stare at the sight of my left hand on her breast, the ring stroking her sweet nipple, my mind processing only this as my body roars with a pulse and thrusts that move us up to a new layer of abandon.

She leans down for an open kiss, her mouth pausing as a small pulse ripples between us, a little more that usually comes from her after the main event, as if her body isn't quite done with her yet, like a stinger at the end of a Marvel Comics movie.

Hair. Suddenly, I'm surrounded by long, lush hair, covering my cheeks and neck, tickling me. Her uncovered torso presses into mine, her body loose and liquid, hands curled on my sweaty shoulders, her nose in my ear.

"God, I needed that," she mutters.

"You needed that? *You?*"

"It's been two days."

"I know it's been two days." I tighten, making myself twitch inside her, which unleashes a torrent of giggles from her. "But you turned me down last night." My booty text went unanswered. Same thing as rejection.

"Did not!"

"Did too."

"Are we seriously going to fight about sex while I am still pulsing around you? Not the best management technique, Mr. McCormick!"

"You're not my employee. It's not as if we're acting out a scene from 'Who Moved My Cheese,' Amanda."

She laughs. The movement pushes me out of her.

*Bzzzzz.*

"Mr. McCormick?" It's Gina, on the damn intercom Dad insists we use.

*Insisted.* Past tense. He's no longer CEO. Note to self: abolish the intercoms and just use texting.

"You answering that?" Amanda rolls off me and onto her back, staring up at the ceiling, her eyes darting to catch mine as I stand, slowly, and look down on her.

What a vision. Skirt around her hips, thigh-highs slipped to her knees, her panties hanging off the edge of my trash can in my peripheral vision, she's all creamy skin covered at the edges by lightweight gray wool and white business cloth. Her hair slips over the carpet like an oil slick, lips red and raw from kissing, her expression telling me everything her body just said.

"Thank you," she whispers, eyes digging into my soul, slowly standing and beginning to re-cover that which belongs fully exposed for my eyes to feast on.

"Thank you."

"We're a grateful pair." Her left hand comes up and strokes my cheek.

Her hand is bare.

My solar plexus curls up into a shriveled ball, like a tiny leaf after the first fall frost. I shouldn't be bothered by her lack of a ring, but I am.

I am, deeply.

All the pain Vince injected into my muscles comes roaring into my center, aimed straight for the safe confines of a compartment inside my heart. The unbearable ache of the journey is nothing compared to the agony of closing the door on that shattered piece of me.

This should not bother me.

It does.

I should not let it hurt so much.

But I do.

*I do.*

Post-sex bliss drains out of me like I've been slashed, mugged for the bounty of some richness inside me and left to bleed to death. Amanda's chin is pointed down as she looks at her buttons, and my chest spasms, threatening to rip a sound from my throat that I can't let myself make.

I'm ice cold, then burning hot. My legs tremble and tense, my arms itching to touch her, to smack her, to make her want what I want.

To make her want me.

"What's wrong?"

I don't pretend. "You're not wearing your ring."

"We're not married, silly!" she says with a laugh that dies as she looks at me.

"No," I say softly, mournfully. "We're not."

She reaches for my left hand and strokes the ring. The movement of her steps, the new proximity to her, brings a whiff of our mingled scents, hers rosy and sex-laden, mine sweaty and metallic. Minutes ago, I was buried so deep inside her that I could push up and skim heaven.

And now I feel like I've descended into hell.

Her brows twitch, pulling down and in, and her wide eyes search mine. "Why are you so upset? You were really weird on the plane ride. And," she asks, faltering, her fingers seeking my ring, "why are you still wearing yours?"

"Maybe I don't want to take it off."

She pales.

"Why not?" Amanda's breath quickens.

"Maybe I've gotten used to wearing it."

"Maybe? Andrew, you don't use the word *maybe*."

Maybe she's right.

# Chapter Ten

"You said the idea of being married was 'ridiculous.'" I resort to finger quotes.

Yes, I'm desperate.

"I did."

"What if there is no conflict?" I ask.

Her eyes narrow. "What do you mean?"

"Why do we need to have some big dramatic moment about this? You confessed that the idea of already being married is terrifying, yet I think you also find it appealing. I didn't take my wedding ring off until my trainer hassled me out of it—and then I put it right back on. Maybe we both want this."

"Want to be married after kissing in closets for two years, only dating for a few months, breaking up horribly, and reuniting when I took a dog and kitty bath and nearly drowned?"

She's got me there.

Truth always wins, though.

"Yes." I shrug. I reach for her, my finger tracing the strong line of her jaw.

She manages to frown and widen her eyes at the same time. "That is crazy, Andrew! People don't magically just go and get married like this, and have it last."

"Says who?"

"Says everyone."

"I don't care about everyone. I care about you."

"But we can't just—"

"Says who?"

"You truly want to just run off and *marry* me? After rejecting me less than two weeks ago during Shannon and Declan's wedding rehearsal fitting? What happened to the man with the cold eyes and the closed heart who told me he wouldn't let me love him?" Her throat makes a strangled, hitching sound that feels like a line to my heart, which twitches in response. Amanda's palm begins to sweat.

I hold on.

"I'm sorry. I'm so sorry." I strain to find the right tone, the right words, that match the utter fury I hold inside toward myself. That day of the wedding party fitting, when I stormed out half dressed, needing an excuse to be angry and finding it in the paper-thin argument that no one had told me the wedding was outdoors, in daylight, in July, the beast inside me was looking for a fight, and invented one.

"When I told you I wouldn't let you love me, it didn't mean I didn't love *you*," I confess, trying to find a lifeline here, a rope attached to a buoy as I drown in memories of my own stupidity. "I knew that so long ago."

"Knew what?"

"That I loved you."

"How long ago?"

This tell-the-deep-truth part is hard, isn't it? Few aspects of my life are truly new these days. Information, sure. Details and experiences, travel and people are new.

Emotional realities, though—going into new territory is rare.

With Amanda, it's become the rule. I don't know how to be in a relationship with her and not explore new layers of love with her. Holding back from that journey feels unfair. False. Fake.

If I wanted fake, I'd date Jessica Coffin again.

I want real.

I close my eyes, remembering the moment she walked into the boardroom as Dad, Declan and I conferred before Greg and his staff appeared for the mystery shopping account meeting. More than two years ago. A lifetime. An eternity.

A blip.

"The day we met, you were wearing a long, gray pencil skirt that hugged your hips like a treasure map for my palms. The slit up the back was a portal into another world. Red silk shirt under a black blazer, and your lips matched the silk. I wondered if you were wearing a red lace bra underneath."

She's spellbound, eyes watching me as if my words hypnotize her. "I was," she rasps.

I knew it. "You were the epitome of 'fuckable secretary' from every fevered fantasy I've ever had."

"You really are a pervert."

I shrug.

"Hey, if we're telling the truth..." I pause. "But I don't have those fantasies about *my* secretaries."

"Right." She's skeptical.

"I haven't. Not since the day we met."

"Really?"

"Yes. You've ruined masturbation for me. I can't even cheat in my mind."

"You're such a romantic."

"I quoted Dickinson to you on our first date!"

She makes a gesture of concession. "Go on."

"Red silk shell and black blazer. With the black hair and red lips, you had the look down. That day I looked up, expecting to just glance at the client's staff, shake hands, and sit down for the boring but necessary details before signing the deal. That's not what happened, though. I did a double take."

"My *breasts* made you do that," she says with a soft laugh.

"No." I reach for her chin and lift it up until she can't look away from me. "You did that. *You*."

She sighs and smiles, nice and wide.

"Your breasts were just the closer," I add, flinching, ready for the punch that I know follows.

The kiss surprises me, a welcome substitute for the punch I deserve.

"Why?" she asks, talking against my mouth. "Why did you wait so long? Why did you steal kisses and make me live with ambiguity?" I can tell she needs to know, and my own murkiness makes me feel inadequate. I owe her the truth, but what do you do when you don't even know your own truth?

"Because I didn't know how *not* to live with ambiguity. It's all I knew."

"What changed?"

*What changed?*

"I tortured myself for those few days before Dec and Shannon's wedding. Got Vince to take me out for some more desensitizing sessions."

"De-what?"

"Never mind. I'll explain later. It's not important."

"Every part of this is important."

"*You* are important."

"*We* are important."

And our future, too.

You aren't supposed to know, with great certainty, that an idea is true. High school and college philosophy teach that absolute truth is impossible, a sign of weakness, a warning bell that someone is rigging the system in an effort to meet some non-truth goal. Certainty is an illusion, ever-morphing, and in the absence of absolute truth, all you can do is work to be as antifragile as possible. Flexibility and pivoting are hallmarks of a resilient mind.

But the heart is different.

Absolute love is real.

Ask me how I know.

"What if I told you I don't have words to explain it?"

"Andrew James McCormick, if you tell me I have to live with ambiguity, I am going to rip your nipples off and turn them into human jerky."

I stare at her. "Are you related to a guy named Vince Retigliano, by any chance?"

"What?"

"Nothing." I blow out a puff of air, buying time. Willing my shoulders to relax, I try to go blank, so I can find some space for my emotions to line up and make sense.

Fat chance.

Instead, they all dance and hoot and holler like they're at a Mardi Gras parade, flashing boobies and beads and everything.

Emotions Gone Wild.

"I am a walking paradox. My life is about reducing uncertainty. Carefully crafted procedures weed out as much fragility and exposure to risk as possible. In business, I can go on gut instinct. In life? No."

She just watches me, carefully silent. Some part of her knows I need space. Lots of space. If she talks, the space fills, and then there's no room for my heart to roam and find its way to the end game.

In space, no one can hear you scream.

But they sure can watch you fumble for homeostasis.

*Bzzzzz.*

"Damn," I hiss, all the bravado leaking out of me.

The spell is broken. Amanda stands, straightening herself, and gives me a hard-to-read look.

"I have to get back to my office. Greg's going nuts with all the procedures involved in selling the company to you. By the way, what's going to happen to the cars?"

"Cars?" The topic change has me reeling, but I harden. Go with it. Don't show any weakness. She's probably weirded out by me already. I don't understand how I can manage a nine-figure deal but can't get a single conversation about love to make sense.

"The promotional cars?"

My mind goes blank.

"Turdmobile?"

"Ugh. What about it?"

"The contract for the cars lasts for nine more months. Greg has a marketing contract for—"

"Anterdec sure as hell doesn't want them!" I say dismissively. If I don't look at her, I can pretend she's just another worker.

One eyebrow twitches. "That's a hard no?"

Our eyes meet. I can't help it. "A hard no?" I repeat, my voice turning up in a question, but my jaw's clenched tighter than my dad's tennis grip. Great. I'm turning into an angry Gina.

Her gaze locks with mine for seconds, then minutes, an eternity passing between us in the blink of an eye. I keep my eyes hooded and impartial, steely and protected.

"A hard no. I'll act accordingly." She repeats my words in the declarative, turning away, leaving the faintest scent in her wake, and the firm *no* that feels like a stone slab across my chest.

No.

*Ridiculous.*

# Chapter Eleven

Six days after returning from Vegas, I'm no longer wearing a wedding ring, the Sultan has agreed to an in-person meeting with me in Dubai, and I am surrounded by Subaru Outbacks with roof racks and COEXIST bumper stickers.

Still better than Amanda's Turdmobile.

My brother Terry lives in Jamaica Plain now, where Dad claims young hippies go to turn into parodies. He owns a duplex I've been to exactly once before, and that was a few years ago, when he insisted I come up and see some painting he did in Mom's honor. He travels a lot, a guy in his mid-thirties who looks like he was the first hipster ever. For years, he rented out both apartments in his building, but he's returned to the city recently. Dad doesn't do big family holidays, and as we've gotten older, we've just drifted.

We're not exactly close.

He was in college when Mom died, and never came back.

With Declan gone, and Vince out of town on some fitness boot camp retreat thing, I have two choices for hanging out with friends.

My chauffeur, and my biggest brother.

If I were dating again, I'd just have Gina arrange a business meeting with some local female executive I could charm into bed.

But I'm not dating.

SHOPPING FOR A CEO'S FIANCEE

At least, I don't think I'm dating. I'm with Amanda, but the definition of *with* is as slippery as Bill Clinton's *is*.

Damn it. I need to talk to Declan.

And the fact that I need to talk to him makes me seethe.

Seeing Terry in Vegas was a reminder, a nagging pull. Amanda set up that crazy hotel scenario two years ago to get Declan and Shannon back together. She barged into my office to demand compliance and walked out of it with my heart. I just didn't know it.

Terry was part of the scheme, and thinking back, I didn't question his presence. Amanda may damn well have been the first person other than Grace to get me, Dad, Declan and Terry to do something together.

Another reason she's amazing.

Terry never answers his cell phone. I know he has one—has had the same phone number since the late 1990s. He's called me a handful of times over the years, but he never answers when I call. Same for Dad and Dec. It dumps to voicemail. I don't understand my biggest brother, but I'm about to turn to him.

I knock on his front door. All of my limos are SUVs now, to be less conspicuous, and Gerald's waiting in the road. The duplex is pretty shabby, but my sense of "nice" in a neighborhood like this is skewed. Who chooses to live in a condo without a doorman and an indoor pool?

I knock again. I know Terry.

I call again, and this time, a deep bass answers the phone, like someone plucked a string on an electric instrument. "Hello?"

"Terry. It's Andrew."

"I'll be right down."

The phone disconnects and I hear *thump thump thump*. I don't even know if he lives upstairs or downstairs, or how this building works.

I know so little about him.

The door flies open and I'm face-to-face with him, looking down slightly. He's covered in little smears of colored paint, his hair streaked with occasional long strands of grey, and he hasn't shaved in forever.

Wild brown eyes meet mine.

"What's wrong? Is it Dad or Dec?"

"What?" I slide a hand into the front pocket of my suit trousers and hold my clenched fist in there. "What are you talking about?" My other hand holds a bottle of Terry's favorite wine. At least, Grace told me it's his favorite.

Terry's breathing hard, looking like someone who just sprinted across a basketball court. "Did something go wrong with Dad? Is Declan hurt?" He's always had this crazy-deep voice, something I envied when I was an awkward teen who hadn't gone through puberty yet, when I was all paws and gangly limbs but could still qualify for the Vienna Boys' Choir.

"Why would you think that?" I ask slowly.

"Andrew," he says, the single word ringing out like a low gong. "You've never been to my place. Ever."

"I was here," I protest. "To see that tribute painting to Mom."

He frowns. "That was eleven years ago. You couldn't grow a mustache back then."

I resist the urge to touch my chin in protest. "Right. But I was here."

His eye roll is epic. Ah. There it is.

The resemblance to Declan.

"No one's hurt?"

"No. I tried to call. It went to voicemail." *Like it always does.*

He grimaces. "You're here because....?"

I hold out the bottle of wine, wrapped in a handmade fabric sleeve with a handle. "To get to know my brother better."

His eyes narrow and he chuckles. It feels like boulders rolling down a mountain.

"I'll take the wine, and come on in, but you're setting off all my Stranger Danger alarms."

The scent of old wood and fresh paint fills the air as I follow Terry up a set of gleaming, varnished stairs. The window at the top of the landing is stained glass, a modern abstract combination of colors I didn't know glass could hold, vibrant reds and near-neon greens. Another short set of stairs and we're in an open, loft-like room with a kitchen set-up against one wall, the ceiling soaring to a tall inverted V, support beams crossing the entire room. Dried herbs and various stained glass ornaments hang from all the beams, many of them containing lights.

And the furniture is, well...what the hell is this?

Terry goes to the kitchen—if you can call it that, with speckled granite counters atop wide barn-wood cabinets, the length of the fridge, oven, sink and dishwasher about the size of one of Dad's limos—and searches through the drawers for a corkscrew.

"Have a seat," he says.

I look at the furniture.

"Where?"

His laugh rumbles again, like stones in a clothes dryer.

His living room is one wide-open space, with an easel and a workbench by an enormous window at the peak of the front of the house. Three huge area rugs cover the floor in primary colors, thick shag. Red, blue, and yellow.

And surrounding those carpets are beanbags.

That's right.

Beanbags.

"You run an unlicensed day care center from your home, Terry? Is that how you supplement your income? I know you can't live off the money from Mom's family trust alone."

He snorts. "Of course I can. It's more than triple the average income in the United States, Andrew."

I know damn well how much it is, and I also know you can't live on that amount. It wouldn't even cover the mortgage on my condo in the Seaport District.

If I had a mortgage.

"What's with the beanbags?"

"Sit before you judge."

"I'm not judging."

"Right. Of course you're not. You're just looking at my apartment with a discerning eye. Not judging at all."

"Exactly."

"You are Dad's little mini-me, aren't you?" he says with a laugh.

I stiffen.

Then drop.

"What the hell is this?" It's an enormous beanbag chair the size of me, about seven feet long and three feet wide. Bright red. It molds to my body as I sit on it. Terry moves behind me and pushes on it, turning it into a big pile of something that gives me back support and is comfortable.

He names a brand.

"The place with the store at the mall? That's what all of your furniture is?"

He grins, handing me wine in a glass that has been hand painted to look like stained glass. "Yeah. It's comfortable as hell."

"It is," I grudgingly admit, yanking on my trousers at the thigh to give the boys some room. I didn't dress for sitting like this.

"Let's toast," he says, dropping into a blue beanbag with a lithe grace that belies his larger frame. "To not being married to a cat!"

I groan. "You heard?"

"I was there for part of it, Andrew."

"You were?"

"You don't remember?"

"My memory has decided to be selective." I sip the wine. "And I assure you, this wine is not entheogenic."

"Nor homeopathic?" he jokes.

"Just grapes."

He crosses his legs and laughs.

Something behind me makes a jingling sound, and then a pile of ribbon and hair plunks itself in my lap, wriggling. Two serene brown eyes meet mine and a pink tongue starts licking my chin.

I nearly tip backwards.

"Mr. Wiffles!" Terry booms. She completely ignores my brother. Yeah, *she*. Terry has a long, ridiculous story involving a modest Amish teen girl breeder who picked the dog's name without ascertaining the true sex, but I blame Terry for being *that* weird.

"How's your transgendered dog?"

"She's fine," he grunts.

I pet her with my free hand and make a note to have Gina prepare a fresh suit for me. "She misses me."

"Then it's Stockholm Syndrome, Andrew. You stole her from me last spring."

"Borrowed."

"Semantics."

"Truth."

"Speaking of dogs, how is Amanda?" He raises his eyebrows and takes a sip.

I choke on my wine.

He pauses, frowns, and bursts out laughing. "Oh, man, that sounded awful, didn't it? I don't mean she's a dog. In fact, she's gorgeous. You picked a hot woman." He holds his hands up where his breasts would be if he had them, and wolf whistles.

"You're not doing a good job of digging yourself out of that hole, Terry." I simmer, tongue rolling in my cheek, wine gone to vinegar in my mouth.

Terry sighs. "You invented that hole. I'm just trying to have a nice conversation with my brother, who never visits, while we dance around the real reason you're here."

"Insulting my girlfriend isn't a great start."

"When I said speaking of dogs, I meant that Amanda reminds me of dogs—" He holds up one palm to stem my protest "—because of her rescue of so many, and her mom's little teacup Chihuahua."

I give him a gimlet eye. "Right."

"Convinced?"

"No."

"You're so uptight. Always have been. Even as a little kid."

Great. Here it comes. The big brother who knows all because of age.

Mr. Wiffles moves out of my lap and trots to a water dish

under the counter. The sound of lapping fills the silence between Terry and me.

"I'm here because I need advice."

A man with a voice like Terry's shouldn't be capable of hooting.

"You what?"

"Declan is on his honeymoon, and my trainer isn't exactly the guy to talk to. Dad would be impossible on this one, and the chauffeurs, well…"

"You're flattering me. At what point in your lineup do I fall? Before or after the woman you hire to water your plants?"

"She was at the dentist today."

Terry drains his glass, reaches behind him for the wine bottle, and pours himself another. He motions toward mine. I cover it with my palm.

"So?"

"Why did you leave Anterdec? Dad won't talk about it. Just says you decided to become a hippie."

"I thought we were talking about you?"

"We are. In a roundabout way. But I can't get to my shit until I understand this."

He looks at the wine bottle. "We're going to need another bottle for this conversation. And some food."

"And better seating," I mutter.

"There's a great Turkish restaurant nearby. We can walk." He names a place.

"Gerald's out there. We can drive."

"But it's only five blocks away." He's shifty-eyed. I know what he's doing.

"I'm in a suit. I don't want to get sweaty."

He looks at my lap. I look down.

Mr. Wiffles sheds a lot, huh?

"If you're worried about appearances, too late. Might as well get sweaty. Besides, you know I hate limos."

"It's not a limo. SUV. Satellite internet connection. We can track the markets and watch for—"

"My legs could use a stretch."

Side-eye.

Damn it.

"Fine. Meet you there. I need to check email and some oil stats."

Before he can argue, I'm out the door, into blinding sunlight, then back inside the cocoon of the SUV.

I bark out the address and turn on my laptop.

Funny how the markets haven't changed much in ten minutes.

I blink a few times, and Gerald says, "We're here, sir."

"Short blocks," I mutter.

By the time I turn off my laptop, find my phone, check texts and answer a few, Terry's next to the SUV, shaking his head, a half smile on his mouth.

I get out of the car and ignore him.

"Busy markets?"

"If I hadn't checked, I'd have missed a critical message." He doesn't need to know it was from Gina about my massage appointment tomorrow.

"You're an important man." He always had that shock-jock voice. Terry could have made a killing in radio.

That makes me halt. "Is that what this is about? You're jealous Dad picked me for CEO?"

"My God, Andrew, you figured it out. Exactly. I'm jealous. Now get in here and order for me. Take charge. Be the controlling sonofabitch Dad wants you to be. Order the hell out of the hummus. Dominate that kebab." He says this with a mock intensity that would come across as scathing sarcasm from Declan, but seems jovial in Terry. Like having Santa Claus sing CeeLo's song "F*** You."

It's unnerving, but I'm too pissed to let it rattle me.

We're seated at a low table with soft cushions on benches. The place smells like incense and an earthy spice I can't name. Terry looks at me with a smirk, but it's a friendly, playful expression. I'm good at reading people, but hell if I can understand my own brother's nonverbal cues. He looks like a blend of Mom and Dad and acts like no one in the family.

Scratch that.

He's more like Mom than anyone else.

"What's good here?" I ask.

"You're the one in charge."

The server approaches and before she can say a word, I order. "We'll take your best two-person platter."

"Meat or vegetarian?"

"Meat. And wine. Whatever your best bottle of red wine is."

She nods and retreats. A man approaches, fills our water glasses, and disappears.

"So?" I ask.

"So what?"

"Why'd you leave Anterdec? I didn't pay much attention back then, but you were in your junior year of college. Dad's protégé. Eldest son and primogeniture and all that. Inherit the family business. Titan and son."

His eyes drain of emotion. A wave of regret pours over me, but I hold fast. For some reason I can't quite understand, I need to know this.

Need to know it *now*. On the surface, it has nothing to do with my feelings for Amanda.

Deep below, though, it is everything.

If I were having this conversation with Dec or Dad, I'd get exchange after exchange of deflection. We'd spar and tussle, verbally jabbing each other, and the only information I'd get would need to be gleaned afterwards, reading between the lines.

Terry meets my eyes and says, "It was all about Declan."

Didn't see that coming. On multiple levels. I wait for him to explain, and as he opens his mouth—

"Andrew!" a female squeals. "My goodness, what a coincidence running into you here!"

I turn to find my face in a woman's cleavage, her scent a fine perfume that takes me back to high school.

She pulls away and I fumble, looking up, standing quickly.

"Jessica?"

Definitely didn't see *that* coming, either.

Terry's eyebrows are the opposite of his voice: nice and high. The server delivers our wine, setting the bottle on the table.

Jessica's hip bounces against mine with a misplaced intimate nudge. She's animated and alive, eyes sparkling as they cut over to Terry.

"Terry! The reclusive brother! I haven't seen you in years," she gushes, offering her hand for a handshake. He takes it, her slim-fingered appendage swallowed by Terry's. He gives her a man's-man handshake and I see the muscle in her jaw twitch with the unexpected force.

"Jessica! Fancy meeting you here," he says. "Given my hermit-like state, this must be divine intervention."

She quirks one eyebrow, extracting her hand, and using it to shove a wall of straight, blonde hair behind one ear. "You always did have a voice that could melt frozen butter," she teases him.

"Join us," Terry offers.

"And panties," she says under her breath, out of Terry's earshot.

I groan internally, but move aside as Jessica plops her ass on the cushioned bench next to me. The server instantly appears with another table setting and a wine glass.

"What are you drinking?" she asks, her face going shrewd.

"Merlot," Terry answers.

She gives him a hard look, then openly crawls over him with her eyes. "My goodness, Terry, you're covered in paint!" Her giggles pierce the calm environment, bridging the line between mocking and mirthful. The fact that I can't tell the difference sets my teeth on edge. "I'd imagine being out of the limelight means letting yourself go. Must be nice."

She waits patiently. Too patiently, hands in her lap, making eye contact with Terry, then me.

I reach for the wine bottle and pour obediently.

Her smile is my reward. I guess.

What is she up to?

"That wedding was something else, wasn't it?" she says with a throaty, condescending laugh. "As if poor Declan weren't dragged through enough with the gaudiness of all that Scottish crap,

Shannon made him escape in the helicopter. Hello—decorum! I give the marriage two years. I hope James insisted on a pre-nup."

Terry and I share a look. He guzzles his entire glass of wine in one long gulp.

The fastest way to make two people bond is to give them a common enemy.

He reaches for his phone and starts tapping, then puts it away, watching us intently. The man doesn't actually use his phone. Why now?

"And then the bridesmaid fell in the water and you saved her!" she adds with glee, clapping her perfectly-manicured hands. She is golden tan, a color never found in nature. Her skin is impossibly smooth. Something seems slightly computer-generated about her. Jessica triggers the Uncanny Valley reaction in me.

"What a ridiculous spectacle," she continues.

I bristle at the word *ridiculous* and tune her out as I drink my glass and Terry refills it.

"The only good to come from that wedding is the confirmation that you're not a vampire, Andrew."

I am in mid-swallow, and as I finish, the wine feels like an endoscopy tube doing down.

"Between the cat as a flower girl, the half-naked bridesmaid who was clearly doing it for attention, the crazy mother of the bride thinking the President of the United States had come to her pathetic daughter's wedding, and what you had to do to rescue that frumpy oaf."

Did she just call Amanda a *frumpy oaf*?

"I am so sorry your brother has dragged down the family name by marrying into that mess." A blindly charming smile aimed directly at Terry gives her nothing but my brother doing his best imitation of an Easter Island statue. She tries to use it on me.

"Oh, no," I answer, turning in the booth, putting space between us as I stretch one arm across the back, behind me, the other holding my very full glass of red wine. "If anyone dragged down the family name, it was me. Going back to high school."

Terry and I exchange a look. He smiles.

Turkish food always makes McCormick men so clumsy.

As the entire contents of my glass pour into her lap like the Hoover Dam in a disaster movie, I try to savor every second. I didn't tell Amanda the entire story about my dating Jessica Coffin when we were flying home from Vegas. Truth is important in relationships, yes.

And as Jessica leaps up, Terry tries—oh, how he tries—to grab the half-full wine bottle before it tips toward her and pours even more wine all over her lap.

But he fails.

We're a bucketful of family fail right now, aren't we?

"I am so sorry!" he says, jumping up, grabbing the bottle and fumbling, tipping the neck up so the wine burbles up in a parabolic stream, hitting between her breasts.

"OH MY GOD!" she screams, batting at the stains, Terry's hands, making the mess turn into a wine Vesuvius.

The server rushes over with a towel and a look of horror. "Miss! Miss! Can I help?"

"Of course you can help, you stupid idiot! Get the manager!"

A flash from a far corner of the restaurant registers and I turn toward it.

Twenty-somethings taking pic after pic after pic.

Like Jessica at Dec and Shannon's Boston wedding.

Terry's eyes cut over to the flash, too, and he gives me a look, winking.

"You are having some sort of breakdown, Andrew! I've never known you to be clumsy!" Jessica rants.

"People change. I am so sorry." My tone makes it clear I'm not.

"My dress is ruined!"

I look at her, softening my eyes, working on a convincingly sexy body crawl that she picks up on instantly, minus the fakery.

"It was a year out of style anyhow," I say, her reaction a hiss. "I probably did you a favor." *Wink*.

The server is mopping up the destroyed tabletop. A pool of wine on the cushion means I can't sit. Jessica's gawking at me, gape-mouthed, her hand curling and uncurling in the universal gesture of outraged women.

I'm about to get slapped.

I give her a one-shouldered shrug and turn away, making a call.

"Gina? Jessica Coffin will call you shortly. Take care of her dry cleaning bill and replace the dress I ruined just now."

"You asshole," Jessica mutters.

"Yes, sir?" Gina peeps. "Wait. *The* Jessica Coffin? I follow her Twitter stream? She's the best? You ever read about #poopwatch and #hotsanta?"

"She's the best, all right," I say, giving her a glance. "And yes, I'm intimately familiar with those." I tense.

"You'll pay for this!" Jessica screeches, the worst of the wine mopped up. The manager appears, urging us to a different table, while Jessica heaps abuse after abuse on the server.

Terry meanwhile, is just trying not to laugh. He grabs the wet bottle, dries it off, and pours the rest into his glass.

He gets a half inch.

"Why would you do this?" Jessica screams.

"These things happen."

Her eyes go wide. She looks like a Rorschach test with eyes.

Those words? *These things happen.*

That's the exact phrase she used when I caught her in Declan's lap.

I watch her watching me, and my conversation with Amanda from the other day comes back to me. She thinks Jessica has power. Influence. That she *matters*.

More flashes from the peanut gallery in the corner. Then a pause. Probably uploading.

A bitter, airy laugh greets me as Jessica shoulders her purse. "You've waited all these years to get back at me for choosing your brother over you and this is all you've got, Andrew?"

"The wine was an accident."

"Like hell it was."

I get in her face, my hand on the small of her back, pulling her in like a confidante. Her perfume is the same, made for her mother in a French perfumery, and it tickles the senses, delightful and sinister at once.

Her blond hair is like corn silk spread over cadaver flesh as I whisper in her ear. "Back off. Back off Shannon, back off Amanda, back off my family. You tweet about, or to, any of us again—and that includes any Anterdec properties—and I'll unleash the video."

"What vid—oh, please!" she says nervously. "That video? Doesn't exist. I got all the copies long ago."

I let go of her.

"Fine. If that's what you need to believe to sleep at night." I flash her a grin that is usually charming, but I up the malevolent factor enough to make sure I look a little evil.

It works.

Pale on pale makes her turn into a bedsheet.

"You realize that could ruin me."

"Really?"

"My entire reputation in public health would be destroyed."

"How awful." The words come out through gritted teeth and steel. "Can you imagine what it must be like to have a social media shitstorm sent your way? Oh. That's right. I'm sure you can."

Her nostrils flare.

"But normally you're the one aiming the fire hose."

"I have enough dirt on you and your family to—"

"To what? Dirt?" I laugh. She's annoying. Shannon and Amanda have built her up to be this unstoppable force but she's a toddler. A toddler with no one telling her *no*.

Time for me to be her *no*.

"I could destroy you," she says, seething.

"With a tweet? A picture? A rumor? That's your currency, babe." She hated that term of endearment in high school, and from the look on her face, I hit my target. "And it's overvalued. Like you."

"You think being CEO of Anterdec means I'm supposed to bow before you?"

"I wouldn't accept even if you did, Jessica. I have standards."

Her head darts to the left, looking out the plate-glass window.

"Standards like *that*?" She points and smirks.

I follow her arm to find her pointing at the Turdmobile. Amanda's in profile, bouncing to whatever song is on her radio, and she's at a stoplight. Consolidated Evalu-shop is one town over, and this restaurant is right on the main drag of town, on a numbered state route.

"If that's your baseline, you're a fool, Andrew."

"What does it say about you that I'd pick a woman driving a car that literally looks like a piece of shit over you? Bring it on, Jessica." I spread my arms wide, back to the road. "Do your worst."

She is steaming, red with anger, her eyes hopping between me and the road. Then her mouth curls into a vicious smile and she does the one thing I never expected.

Throws herself into my arms and kisses me.

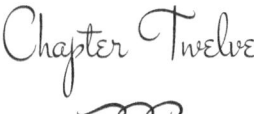

Chapter Twelve

Shoving a woman who is not much more than a warm toothpick wearing five-inch heels and a ruined designer dress is harder than you'd think. But I do, and do it with mastery and grace, so she plunks down on the chair in front of me, but not before she pirouettes me into a full three-sixty.

I'm left with the lingering taste of bitterness and anti-aging face cream.

Horns. Lots of beeps, suddenly, from the road.

I whip around to find the source of the cacophony.

Amanda's stuck in front of the green light, mouth open, staring through the window. It's that time of day and just cloudy enough that the clean, clear glass shows everything.

"Hmph," Jessica says with triumph. "Good luck fixing *that*."

Amanda gets out of the car. I repeat: she gets out of the car, abandoning it in the middle of a New England town center, with three lanes and five different directions.

Her march is steady, straight, defiant, and dead on.

And she's *not* looking at me as she bursts through the restaurant's main door and goes straight for the jugular.

"Touch him again, and I'll rip every weave out of that hair of yours," she says pleasantly to Jessica, a smile on her face and the biggest case of the creeps shining through her eyes.

"Oh, I like her," Terry mutters, crossing his arms without letting go of his wine glass.

I have never seen Amanda fiery. Pissed. Livid.

Out of control.

"Excuse me? Did you just *threaten* me?" Jessica squeals, looking around the room as if collecting witnesses.

"Yes. You like those eyelash extensions? Because all I need are some manicure scissors and two friends to hold you down." She scrunches up her face. "Or a really small blowtorch."

Amanda's voice sounds like a serrated butcher's knife that's just about to go through Jessica's trachea.

And...I'm hard.

"You can't do that! How dare you threaten me?" Jessica protests.

"Just did," Amanda declares. She still hasn't looked at me, but her eyes rake over Jessica's dress. "You're such an alcoholic, you can't keep the wine in your glass?" she says in a loud, over-enunciated voice.

*Flash.*

The people in the corner start taking rapid-fire pictures, and I see someone holding up a smartphone. Videotaping.

"I—what are you talking about?" Jessica protests. "He poured it on me!"

I twist a finger around my ear and say, "We tried to do an intervention." I shrug. "She wouldn't listen to reason."

"Liar! He spilled it on me to get back at me for cheating on him with his brother when we were in high school!"

Titters begin from the other patrons.

"So you admit it," I say slowly. I want to add, *smile for the camera*, but I'm not ready to tip my hat just yet.

"You're an alcoholic," Amanda says, her voice dripping with contemptuous pity. "Explains so much, doesn't it?" she says loudly to Terry.

He makes a fake compassionate face. "She's really lost her touch."

"And quit trying to steal my man!" Amanda shouts.

I do a double take.

Wait a minute.

This does not add up.

Without touching me, Amanda passes by, glaring the entire time, and walks to the other side of the table, across from me.

Where she grabs Jessica and kisses her.

That's right.

*She.Kisses.Jessica.*

Terry's mouth drops.

I stare, uncertain whether to be angry or aroused. My body decides both.

Angry boners suck.

A camera flashes.

Pandemonium ensues.

First, Jessica flees.

Second, the people in the corner clap. And snap. And flash.

Third, Amanda wipes her mouth and drinks the rest of Terry's wine.

Fourth, Terry and Amanda fist-bump each other.

Fifth, a police car appears.

Sixth, Amanda sprints out to retrieve her abandoned car.

"What the hell, Terry?" My fingers are two seconds away from grabbing his shirt and giving my big brother a right hook.

He holds up his phone and shakes it. "Not just an expensive clock. I know how to use it."

I pause. "You texted Amanda?"

"I knew there was a reason Dad picked you for CEO. You're quick."

"Screw you. My wife just kissed Jessica!"

"Your *what*?"

"My, uh, girlfriend."

"It was entirely for show. She wasn't sure who to kiss."

"*Who* to kiss? You texted my girlfriend back and forth and considered kissing her?"

He shrugs. "It was for show."

"You ever 'show' my girlfriend, I punch you."

Terry holds up his palms. "Fine. I'll stick to kissing Mr. Wiffles."

He just told me too much about his love life.

Horns blare outside. Cop lights flash in the window. Amanda's screaming my name and—is that cop putting *handcuffs* on her?

I'm the only one who's supposed to do that.

I run, dodging moms with babies in carriages and gawkers watching the scene, coming up on the cop's left while another cop stands across from me, glaring.

"Officer, I can explain," I say, mind scrambling to figure out what exactly to say. "This is all a big misunderstanding."

"Always is, bud." I get a good look at the cop. Balding. Paunch. Mustache. His specialty is glaring.

Great. This will be easy. As James McCormick's son, I'm not just fluent in glare. I could teach a class on it.

"This is my girlfriend." I measure my breathing, pull up to full height. Time to show the cop who's in charge here. "She saw me in the restaurant in a moment of distress. Came to help."

"Help? You needed help so bad from her she had to abandon her car in a busy intersection?"

Amanda's biting her lips and looking down. My heart starts racing, but my face tightens. The only way out of this is through sheer dominance.

"I'm sure you can find a way to let her go. We're making a bigger mess right now than—"

"SHE ASSAULTED ME!" Jessica screams, coming around the corner in all her wine tie-dye glory.

"I'm gonna need backup," the cop mutters to his partner.

"Sir," I say, changing tactics. I shrug and give him a look that I hope engenders some sympathy. "I've got two women fighting over me."

"Lucky you."

"She just kissed me without my permission!" Jessica wails, pointing to Amanda, who slips her free hand into the crook of my elbow and gives the police officer a smile so sweet you'd think she'd just been crowned Miss Cornhole in a tournament in Lima, Ohio.

"This is my boyfriend's ex-girlfriend. She's stalking him all over town. Her name is Jessica Coffin and—"

"*The* Jessica Coffin? From Twitter?" the cop asks, eyebrows up as if impressed.

Great.

"Yes," Jessica crows, flashing mad eyes at me.

"The one who made fun of the Arlington cops when we held our Brony dance for local kids?"

"Uh..." Jessica's face freezes in a mask of uncertainty. Or a bubble in her Botox treatment hit a vein.

He gives her an up-and-down look only a cop can give, eyes turning from careful guardedness to a knowing cynicism I've only seen one other place.

Dad.

"Have a little too much to drink?"

"He poured wine on me!" she says, pointing at me.

Amanda shakes her head slowly and says, "She keeps stalking him. Ask the people inside the Turkish restaurant. They have pictures and film and everything. She's obsessed with Andrew's sister-in-law."

"Hold on. Andrew. You're Andrew McCormick?" The cop looks impressed. He should be.

"Yes."

"And your sister-in-law is #poopwatch, which makes your brother #hotsanta."

"Something like that," I mumble.

"You're the one who kissed me!" Jessica screeches. "Wait— someone was *filming* in there?" She starts to turn, as if to go back into the restaurant, when the cop's partner clears his throat.

"I'll need to take you in for questioning, ma'am," he says.

"As well you should!" Jessica huffs, giving Amanda a victorious grin.

"I meant you."

"Me!" Jessica cries out. "Why?"

"You're clearly drunk."

"I'm not!" She fumbles with her purse, pulling out her phone.

Which drips with wine.

Amanda lets out a low whistle.

"Who poured wine in my purse?"

I look back covertly toward the window of the restaurant, where Terry turns away, his shoulders shaking.

Amanda squeezes my arm. I can't get the looping image of her and Jessica kissing out of my head. I'm trying.

Really. I am.

Not too hard, but...

Five minutes later, Jessica has stormed off, released by the cop, and Amanda's moved her car to an open metered spot in front of the restaurant. I'm avoiding being anywhere near the Turdmobile. It's one thing to make a scene.

Quite another to be publicly humiliated.

Add the Turdmobile, and you might as well give up.

"What the hell was that? You kissed Jessica?"

"It was her or Terry, and I figured you'd punch Terry. Kissing Jessica was strategic. Now you have a fantasy come to life." She winks.

"That's not my fantasy."

"Every guy fantasizes about being with two hot women who are all over each other."

"But not you and Jessica."

Her eyebrows go up. Damn.

The cop reappears and Amanda goes up to him, arms open, and embraces him with a huge hug.

I didn't think I could be shocked more today, but she surprises me.

"Hey Al, thanks."

Al. Why does that name ring a bell?

"Let me introduce you two," Amanda starts.

"You know each other?"

The cop laughs, his face lighting up. He looks ten years younger when he smiles. "You could say that. Me and Amanda go way back. She called me when she realized your ex-girlfriend had gone nutso on you. Didn't mention it was Jessica Coffin! That was a nice twist. She skewered us when we did the Brony dance for local kids with special needs. Could have really given that event a boost, but instead she poisoned it." He makes a face.

Al.

Al—

"Al Barkin?" My voice goes up and down like a puberty rollercoaster.

Amanda turns bright red.

The guy standing in front of me, balding and in uniform, an actual gun on his hip, is the man who took Amanda's virginity on prom night.

"Yeah." He looks at Amanda with a questioning look. "How'd you know?"

"Amanda and I have been together a long time," I say, trying to recover, wrapping my arm around her. "The name rang a bell."

A twelve-foot gong.

"We had some good times back in high school, didn't we, Mandy?" He reaches for her hand and uncuffs the metal handcuff on there, sliding it back on his belt.

Her smile to him is so genuine, I see the seventeen year old in her.

His smile back makes me want to rip off his balls and stuff them down the nearest Brony's throat.

My phone buzzes. I reach into my pocket and read a text from Terry.

*Gotta go walk Mr. Wiffles. Have fun!*

Al's walkie-talkie crackles with some numbers.

"See ya," he says curtly, jogging off to his squad car.

Leaving me alone with—

"Mandy." I look down at her, wondering what the hell she just orchestrated to make that sequence of events unfold without anyone ending up in handcuffs or jail.

"Andy."

I bristle.

Her laughter blends with the sound of a church's clock, the peals mingling with music, until I have to join in, too.

"As lovely as this accidental meeting is," she says, "I'm late for a meeting with Greg."

A kiss. A deeper kiss. A promise to explain later.

She's gone.

And then I realize that I still don't know why Terry left Anterdec.

Damn it.

Chapter Thirteen

Unlike the morning after Shannon and Declan's wedding, this time I'm waking up with my face between Amanda's thighs and the only person shouting at me is *her*.

It's a good kind of shout. The best kind.

The kind only I can elicit.

She arrived late last night, and before we could talk about the craziness at the Turkish restaurant that afternoon, we were in each other's arms, then bed, then out cold, tired and spooned, curled against each other in sleep as if we made each other into a fortress.

And now we have our morning spread out for us.

At least, *she's* spread out.

She has this sound she makes when she's about to come. We all do. Everyone has a sex tell. If you think you don't, you're wrong. Amanda's tell transmits a signal to my brain that says *Congratulations*.

Achievement unlocked.

Except it's not the achievement you think. Not a sex goal. Those are easy. Anyone can do that with the right skill and enough alcohol.

This is love. Complete release and abandon with someone you trust so deeply, you take the leap of faith that they'll catch you.

You can only catch the tell if you have that kind of love.

"Andrew," she says in a voice reserved for when we're between the sheets. "Andrew." Her hand is threaded in my hair and as I rise up, I taste the silky smoothness of her skin, which unfolds before me like a perfect, lush valley, hills and curves, rolling sweetness and a place of discovery. No woman captivates me like Amanda, and when our eyes meet and I slip into her, the way her head tips back and her throat begs for a kiss makes me offer up *my* tell.

It's the sound of gratitude. I'm not grateful for sex. I'm grateful for having *her*.

The balcony doors are open and a massive breeze pushes the curtains in, the sound of billowing fabric catching my ears as the rush of ocean air chills my back. The sunlight in the room dims suddenly, making the room surreal, as if we're in the eye of a storm and chaos is about to be unleashed.

Which is apt.

She's so damn beautiful under me, her hands on my back, my shoulders, my ribs, just touching me with a possession that fires my soul. Her hair tickles her shoulders and it's thick and tousled, makeup long gone, her lips bright red from long kisses all night. Those impossibly-big eyes peer up at me and make me stop breathing, though I keep moving, making love to her with long strokes like a clock tower bell calling out the hour, the slow, sonorous beat designed to mark time.

Now.

Now.

Now.

Now.

I dip my head down to take one nipple and it tastes like salt and velvet, like my fingerprints and her secrets. She arches up, a simple gesture that asks for more, and I'm grateful again. Fire courses through me, sweat making the slick friction between our skin even easier, the glide of body against body allowing for the insatiable build-up between us sparked by each stroke.

Amanda reaches up, one hand on my ass, her fingertips digging into me, her mouth on mine, tongue searching for more connection. We're as close as two bodies can get, her hands clinging to me, her breasts smashed against my chest, and I know this tell, too. When she tightens her hold and her touch becomes damn near frantic, she's about to come, and I pause. Just for a second, just long enough to honor what's inside me without interrupting what she needs.

Because in that pause, I feel all the emotions at once, thousands of feelings connected to her sighs, our kisses, the strokes and caresses, the push of being in her, the warm softness of being enveloped, the wet moans and worshipful sighs and eager urgency that all rolls into a whirlwind of energy and emotion that is the tornado within.

And then we roar together.

A crack of lightning makes us both startle and jump, the rhythm interrupted, the cacophony of a sudden, explosive rainstorm outside changing the air, ozone and salt on the tip of my tongue, replacing the taste of her from moments ago.

"You timed that, didn't you?" she says, laughing under me, the push of muscle nearly evacuating me from her body, but we shift, holding closer, and I stay inside her.

The pounding rain makes it hard to hear. She reaches up and pushes the hair from my forehead using the same hand that was in those strands moments ago, urging me.

"Even I can't orchestrate that," I say with a laugh, picking up the rhythm, her eyes closing, breath quickening. We've lost what we had but we'll find it again.

That's the beauty of knowing.

You'll always find each other again.

My throat tightens as we crest together, caught up in the crazy storm of arousal and climax, of pleasure and desire, of the mix of the squall outside and the tornado within, whirling and whirling until there is no more Amanda, no more Andrew, just a tight clinging to each other that comes from certainty. From trust.

From some feeling deeper than love, threaded together by those thousands of emotions I felt in that single pause.

The storm outside becomes louder, and suddenly I feel wetness on my back.

"Is it raining on the bed?" Amanda squeals.

I jump up, almost mournful as our bodies separate and I pull out of her, the feeling of separation like a prison sentence, and I remove myself from the unnamed half of the wholeness I feel when I'm in her. I turn into just Andrew, a naked guy in his waterfront loft who faces a stinging wall of ocean rain and wind.

I shut the balcony door and turn around to find Amanda giggling, then snickering, and finally snorting with laughter.

I am *soaked*.

"You look like a wet squirrel."

"That's not the spirit animal I would pick for myself. How about a bear? A wolf? Give me some credit here, Amanda. I would be a big, alpha animal."

She scrunches up her face in contemplation, her eyes relaxed and happy, her body loose and half-exposed between the twisted sheets. "Ferret?"

"Hmph. How about a nice, big hug?" I say, not giving her the chance to reply in the negative, jumping on the bed and covering her with wet kisses.

She screams, wriggling under me, and damn if I'm not getting hard again.

"You're salty!" she says with a laugh. "My lips are stinging." I'm kissing her, face coated in rain, and she slowly stops her giggles and lets them dissolve into little sighs.

There we go.

The storm outside can rage on, but the one in here has its own tempo, too.

"I love you," I whisper, kissing her neck.

"Love you, too," she says with a little sound of contentment. "But I need coffee."

"You need coffee more than me?"

"Only sometimes. Especially at 6:17 a.m. on a Friday."

I squint at the clock. Oh, hell. "You're as bad as Shannon." But I let her go, enjoying the view as she stands and walks to the door, grabbing my robe. Watching her put it on gives me a sense of pride. Possession. The robe swallows her. The gesture is domestic. Casual. Understated and assumed.

Wifely.

"If I'm as bad as Shannon, will you buy me my own coffee chain?"

"You have to marry me to get that. Dec bought it for her as a wedding gift."

"I'll keep that in mind."

Every part of the room tilts. My blood stops pumping. My mind stops racing. The crazy rain outside sounds like white noise. A ringing forms in my ears, and it's like I'm watching her through clear, transparent molasses.

Wife. Marry. Wedding.

Those words make an appearance again.

*Bzzz.*

She groans. "Your phone? Again? Can't you just turn it off?"

"Between Dad's inability to turn over the CEO role to me in full, and now Declan's resignation, work is crazier than ever. I only have so many hours in a day."

"Some of them should be for me!"

"What do you call what we just did?"

"Seventeen minutes."

"You *timed* it?"

"I happened to look at the clock right as you woke me up, and then, uh, after."

Seventeen minutes, huh?

I can do better.

I *will* do better. I reach for her, cupping her sweet, creamy breast, the curve of it so—

*Bzzz.*

But not now, apparently.

I grab the phone and check texts, fingers flying as Amanda sighs, gets up, and walks out of my bedroom, removing the robe and walking into my bathroom. I hear the shower turn on.

What a difference a few weeks makes. The first time she spent the night, she was more shy, more inhibited, and clearly working to figure out the lay of the land—physically and emotionally.

We're more comfortable with each other now.

Which is why I can ignore her and work.

The glow of my phone screen is all I need as the storm rages outside. Sitting upright, under the covers, I crawl into the phone, tapping and answering texts from Dad, Gina, Grace, my IT guy, and a host of other people. I try to keep it simple, but within ten minutes my laptop's on a pillow in front of me, email open and my phone cradled between my shoulder and jaw just as Amanda walks into the room, now hair wet and freshly combed, framing her face in a dark wall, carrying two cups of coffee.

I get an epic eye roll from her.

"Get off that damn phone!" she hisses. "It's like Shannon's vibrator!"

"What?" I drop the phone onto the bed, horrified by the comparison.

"Declan calls Edward Cullen her secret lover." I now know way too much about my sister-in law.

"You're comparing my working on my phone to my sister-in-law's electronic substitute for my brother?" Flashing her a smile that I hope makes up for this work episode, I take the coffee, grateful.

Truly.

"Yes. Both are things you turn to when you're frustrated and need to feel a sense of accomplishment."

I open my mouth to respond. Women must view orgasms very, very differently than men.

Accomplishment? No.

Therapeutic? Yes.

Amanda grabs my phone from my neck and shoves it down the front of the robe.

"What are you doing?"

"Hiding your phone."

"And you think I'm *not* going to find it there?"

"If it's out of reach, you can't be on it constantly."

I grin. "I have no problem playing hide and seek." Her breasts rise and fall as her anger intensifies.

"And then what? Will you text over my shoulder in the

middle of sex? What's next, Andrew—an emoji instead of a groan?"

"Would that turn you on?"

She takes an angry sip of coffee. Where's the ire coming from? I always squeeze in work between every other part of life. Amanda should be used to it.

"Is this how it's going to be?" she asks, faltering, the anger draining out of her. "Dating you means accepting that you live your job." A crack of lightning punctuates her words as she bends down for a sip, suddenly contemplative.

"I—"

"Shannon told me it's like this with Declan. Said she comes second most of the time." Amanda blinks rapidly, her face a series of tiny muscles under the surface that seem to rotate through scores of emotions, trying one on for size and discarding it over and over. "I've been sympathetic for the past few years, but now I see I never really understood."

My hands stop over the keys, mid-stroke, eyes stuck on the screen. Our chief financial officer has a report on a huge lawsuit we're currently losing, and the financial fallout could hurt our quarterly projections.

But not paying full attention to Amanda right now would hurt even more.

I close the laptop and set it aside. My mind's in work mode, so this is harder than you'd think.

Much harder.

Compartmentalizing means that Sex Brain Andrew, once satisfied, is ready to move into the CEO Andrew box, and once I'm in that compartment, going into Relationship Andrew is harder than you'd think.

Like learning to play piano while unicycling.

"Talk to me," I say, unable to find the right words to even start. I drink my cup of coffee and the image of all those unread emails taunts me, each line etched into my mind. The curse of having a photographic memory.

"I am." She gives me a bitter smile and slowly opens the robe, revealing my smartphone tucked neatly under one breast.

She must have magician's genes in her. How does it stay in place?

I reach for it, the metal warm, the glass slightly wet with her perspiration.

"Tell me what's going on behind those beautiful eyes."

She looks up, coquettish yet guarded. "Shannon says they fight all the time about Declan being a workaholic."

"Doesn't surprise me."

"And that you're worse."

"Worse?"

"You work even more hours than he does."

"I do. That's how this works. I'm CEO now. It's not a job—"

"It's a life," she says, echoing me.

"Dec says that to Shannon, too?"

She nods.

I tip her chin up. "I work so hard and so many hours because I'm taking over Dad's legacy. But truly? I've always worked so much because I didn't have anything else in my life. Anterdec was it. Until now. Until you."

She melts.

I knew she would.

All I want is to spend the day in bed with her, our only interruptions the delivery people bringing food. How many orgasms can we generate in a twenty-four-hour period? My competitive nature rises up.

Among other things.

"I know your idea of work and my idea of work are in different columns," she says seriously. "Work is what you do to get ahead. To pay the bills. To find meaning."

"Work isn't some separate category," I add. "It's integrated into who I am. I am Anterdec now. I am not just the face of the company, Amanda. Being a CEO is different than having any other job on the planet."

"I know."

"I'm not saying that to be arrogant, or brag."

"You don't have to explain it to me, Andrew. I understand."

"Do you? Really?"

"I'm trying to. Your reality is different from most people's. Your family lives a life very removed from most of us."

"You make me feel like I'm exiled," I say, half joking.

Half.

"In a way, you are. Sometimes I feel sorry for you."

"Excuse me?"

"Not in a poor-little-rich-boy kind of way. But fame and fortune have costs I never realized before."

"Like what?" I settle in, setting aside my work mind. I'm intrigued.

"It's not just the busyness. Not just the demands on your time, or the fact that, like you said—you are Anterdec. All of you except Terry. I'm seeing that better now. Your company isn't some institution your father created to make money. It's like giving birth to a child and raising it. And you're being handed your father's baby."

"Is this part of the whole 'you're bad at analogies' problem? Because *I* am my father's baby." Sounds weird to say it that way, but truth is truth.

She laughs. "So is the company. And you're struggling with the transfer of power. You're in massive transition right now."

"In more ways than one." I take her hand and watch as she reacts, changing before my eyes. "We're in transition, too."

"Yes."

"Each of us, separately, and both of us, together."

"Mmm hmmm." Her mouth is full of coffee.

"What about you?" I ask. "Did you always want to be a mystery shopper manager? Work in marketing?"

As the words come out of my mouth, her eyes change from purely curious to suspiciously confused. "What?"

"Was this your career goal?"

"You're joking, right?"

"No. Why would I joke?"

She sighs. "Exhibit #1, Your Honor."

"I'm on trial? For what crime?"

"Being exiled." She frowns. "I went into marketing because it was a job. With a paycheck, and the holy grail of full benefits. I didn't set out to be in this field, Andrew. I found it out of necessity."

"What did you want to do? When you were younger?"

"You mean, what's my heart's work? Follow your bliss and all that?"

I groan. "God, no. I hate that phrase."

"You do? Why?"

"Because no one actually finds meaning and money in their bliss. You can't. It's like..." I fumble for the right words.

"Trying to orgasm and pee at the same time?" she offers.

"Exactly like that."

"Maybe I don't suck at analogies after all."

I kiss the top of her mussed head. "No. You do."

We chuckle as the wind whips the rain against my closed balcony slider. It sounds like a phalanx of kids with BB guns shooting at us.

Amanda looks at the rainstorm. "Glad I don't have to go anywhere immediately."

"I can just have Gerald or Lance take you wherever, anyhow. You never need to set foot outside."

She gives me a funny look.

I drink my coffee and shut up.

"I assumed you'd have your pick of careers. You were raised with wealth. Access. The finest educations and all that. I'd assume kids raised the way you were raised could major in basket weaving and not worry about money."

"That's not how it works."

"Illuminate me."

"Maybe it works that way for some of the kids I went to Milton with. But if it did, I didn't know any of them. The rest of us had the pressure put on us in preschool. Like a fire hose aimed at your permanent record nonstop."

"Why?"

"Why? Why did our parents hold us to high standards?"

"Yeah."

"For Dad, it was about making sure we could take over the

company. Keep the McCormick name in stellar shape. Grow Anterdec and turn it into an international giant."

"So far, so good."

I shake my head. "It's been Dad, mostly. Dec's done some good deals for the hospitality branch, but it's all on me as we move forward." A rush of responsibility fills me, like the crush of a crowd trying to make it to the front of a stage at a huge rock concert. Thousands of work details, big and small, shove at me.

"You'll do well. James wouldn't have picked you if he didn't believe in you."

"You really think that?"

"Sure. Why not?"

"I think Dad picked me to punish Declan." There. I said it. Amanda's the first person I've ever confided in.

"Really? He's still mad? After all these years?"

"It's never going away. Never."

"I don't understand that kind of anger. Why keep it inside? Why let it eat away at you?"

"I don't know."

"Maybe he doesn't know any different." Amanda finishes her cup and plucks my empty one from my hands, turning away, walking through the door.

Leaving me dumbstruck.

I grab my phone. Text from Vince.

*Outdoor session canceled. Meet me at your office. Will turn you into a puddle indoors.*

I snort.

Or whimper.

It's hard to tell the difference.

I am still texting just as she returns, steam spooling up from the two fresh coffees in her hand.

"Work?"

*Need to talk. Want to know the rest of the story*, I text Terry.

"Yes," I say, smiling as she hands me the coffee, dipping down for a kiss.

By the time Terry replies, I'm buried.

In her.

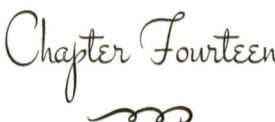

# Chapter Fourteen

"I can't believe we have to suffer through this," I grumble as we climb out of the SUV, Gerald dropping us off at Declan's building. We've been home for two weeks, barely enough time to catch up, and now we have to spent a rare Saturday night being tortured by my brother's mother-in-law.

I am not legally related to her.

But crazy has its own gravity, flowing from older brother to younger.

"You're the best man. I'm the maid of honor. We have to go to the wedding-gift-opening party."

"Terry *was* the best man, technically."

Amanda gives me a look that says I'd better shut up or I'm on the fast track to a no-sex night.

I shut up.

"Dec and Shannon have nearly seven hundred wedding gifts to open, and we're all going to help them."

"Great. Just what I want to do with a Saturday night. Spend it at my brother's house with his crazy mother-in-law, opening china and tablecloths, *oohing* and *aahing* over crap no one really uses. Let's take wagers on how many fondue sets they get."

As we enter the elevator, she gives me a funny look. "That's what you really think about weddings and registering and gifts?"

"Yes."

She laughs, giving a sigh of relief. "Me, too."

My thumb worries the spot where my wedding ring used to rest.

I miss it.

We're the last to arrive, the room filled with the same people who were at the rehearsal dinner. Has it really only been a month since that night? I count back.

About six weeks.

Not long enough between parties involving Marie.

Even my cousin Hamish is here, which is strange. Why would he be here?

Oh. Right.

A party involving Marie. That's why.

"Andrew! Amanda!" Marie squeals. She's wearing a purple get-up that sets her now-platinum hair apart, like corn silk on top of a lavender field. For the wedding, she dyed it auburn for some reason, but now she's back to normal, whatever *that* means for Marie.

Her eyes are bright and cheeks pink. Her hug comes with alcohol-soaked breath. "I'm so glad you're here. Now we have two best men!"

I look over her shoulder at Terry, who gives me a fake smile, a thumbs-up, and points to a beer in his hand.

*Hell, yes*, I mouth.

I'm going to need plenty of alcohol to get through tonight.

"Six hundred and fifty-seven presents Shannon and Declan got for their wedding!" Marie calls out as she lets me go and Terry mercifully appears with a beer for me.

"I'd rather listen to you tell me what happened with Dad after Mom died than sit through the next two hours," I say before swigging half my beer like it's an antidote to being wedding-poisoned.

"Come on. Marie's not that bad," Terry replies with a wink.

"Dad dropped you on your head, didn't he? That's the true explanation."

He gives me an even, neutral look before whispering, "Some

other time. Not now. You clearly have enough tragedy to work through." The corner of his mouth twitches.

Amanda gravitates to Shannon, who is tanned and smiling, Dec's arm around her as he pours red wine into a series of glasses.

He looks pretty damn relaxed, too. Honeymoons will do that, I guess.

Can't wait to find out for myself.

"Look at all those gifts!" Marie says, pointing. Tables have been set up in the living room, and about twelve file boxes are stacked neatly, labeled McCormick Wedding Gifts. About a hundred wrapped presents of varying sizes are piled around them on the floor and tables.

Looks about right for a thousand-guest wedding.

That Dec and Shannon abandoned.

"It's going to be a long night," Dad says, appearing behind me, his voice tortured. "Six hundred gifts and Marie in her glory."

"Can't an admin at Anterdec handle this?" I mutter.

"That's what Declan and I said, but this is all Shannon and Marie's idea."

"You mean this is *Marie's* idea."

He laughs. "Your brother's the one who chose to marry into the crazy family."

I look at Amanda, who is chatting with her mother, who has her teacup Chihuahua in her purse, feeding it nibbles of cheese from a platter. Terry walks over and gives Spritzy a kiss on the forehead, making baby talk to the little drowned rat.

Right.

Crazy family.

Dec peels himself off his new wife and approaches me with a smirk. "Figured out you're not married to anyone, huh?"

"Confirmed bachelor." A hollow gong rings in me as I say it.

"How's business?"

I give him an evil grin. "Good. How about you?"

"Funny thing, little bro. I came home from my honeymoon and went to work. All my passwords were invalid. Gerald informed me I have a week left of limo services from Anterdec.

Grace told me I have a week, too, of her services. Any secured systems I need to access have to be done through her accounts."

I go cold. "Dad didn't talk to you first?"

"So you knew about this?" His eyes narrow and his jaw tightens.

"I knew. You resigned. I offered to talk to you first about the transition, but Dad said he wanted to do it."

"Well, he didn't. The New Zealand account's going to blow up if I can't get back on track. And then there's Grace."

I chug my beer. I can tell he's upset, but he's not pissed. I expected fiery fury. Instead, I'm getting a cold, reserved kind of anger, as if he's suddenly turned British.

"We can manage New Zealand. And Grace, well...she's an Anterdec employee. If you want her, you have to try to make her join your new company."

"I tried. She refused."

SCORE! I try to contain my glee. I finally get Grace as my admin. Buh-bye, Gina.

Or, I should say, *Buh-bye, Gina?*

I shrug and reach across the counter for another beer. Halfway through it, I pause and say, "Transitions. Changes. They all have their ups and downs."

"Being stripped of all Anterdec privileges is one hell of a change."

"What did you expect?" I drain the second beer, welcoming the warm buzz that begins in my hands and feet.

He pauses mid-sip with his wine glass, brows turning down. "Not sure. But not this."

"You have your own company now. Anterdec has security issues with a VP as high as you up the food chain having access to sensitive systems."

"I'm the owner's son."

"And it's the owner who did this to you." I swallow an *I'm sorry* because I'm not the one who's responsible. That's Dad, and Declan'll have to hash it out with him.

"If we're talking business—"

"Do we have to?"

He gives me a look that says, *tough shit.* "I want to buy the Turdmobile."

"You *what*?"

"Well, Shannon does. Anterdec is acquiring Consolidated Evalu-shop. They have a contract with the advertising company that manages the crazy promotional cars. Shannon's shown me the stats on that damn piece of shit car—"

"Literally."

"—and it generates a ton of business for the coffee shop it's intended to advertise. We just acquired a chain of coffee shops, so...I want to buy out the contract from you."

"You can have the damn car."

He laughs. "I thought the same thing, but once I saw the metrics, I was convinced. Besides, Shannon will need a car. No more limos."

"Poor baby."

He glares. "I'll have my people talk to yours about the Turdmobile?"

"You have *people* already? When did your new company get people? You were on your honeymoon last week, for God's sake! You haven't had time to acquire people."

He shuts down. "Just be aware we want to move fast on this."

"Like I said, you can *have* the damn contract. Consider it a wedding gift."

He pulls out his phone and texts. "Okay. Done. Expect a call tomorrow to make it happen."

Great. So far, I've managed to avoid ever riding in that piece-of-shit car. Amanda's offered to drive and I've skillfully avoided it.

Done. Forever.

That car is out of my business and out of my life.

Amanda's eye catches mine and suddenly, Dec doesn't exist. She's giving me one of those closed-mouth smiles that says she's thinking about me, naked. Her nose twitches as she moves her lips, the sexy curve of her mouth one I can imagine in intimate places. The beer is getting a nice grip on me, and if I can get my girlfriend alone, I'll bet she could get a nice grip on me, too.

Dec looks at me, his eyes cutting over to Amanda, and he

does an epic eye roll. "You think with your pants."

I snort. "Like you're any different?"

He frowns. "No."

We might not talk about feelings in our family, but sex is open territory.

"Speaking of which, how was the honeymoon?"

His face goes blank. "Don't want to talk about it."

"That bad or that good?"

"Not talking about it."

Before I can press for details, Hamish approaches, hand outstretched, a shit-eating grin on his face. He's taller than me, and a wall of broad muscle. If he weren't a kickass soccer player, he'd be a rugby man, for sure.

"Andrew!" The Scottish lilt in his voice makes me smile. "So good to see you." He claps his hand on Dec's shoulder. "Already said my congratulations to this one, but he couldn't really talk with the dog collar attached to his leash."

Dec's expression tells me this joke has been made before, many times.

"We can't all sleep our way through Europe on a football tour," I tell him with a wink.

"Ah, but it's fun to try," Hamish says with a deep, dirty laugh.

Behind him, I see Amy and Carol in a huddle around a tray of chocolates. At his words, Amy opens her mouth and sticks her finger down her throat. Carol bursts into giggles.

I see Amy's well acquainted with Hamish.

"At the rehearsal dinner, you were talking about endorsements. How's that going?" I ask.

It's hard to believe we're related. Dad's older half brother from his father's first marriage is Hamish's father. Dad doesn't talk about the family history, so I don't know the details, just that my grandfather had a "first family" in Scotland before emigrating to the U.S. and marrying my dad's mom. Hamish is a fiery ginger with bright green eyes and a broad face covered in freckles. He's the size of a Viking and thickly muscled, the kind of man who looks like he shouldn't be good at soccer but is light as hell on his feet.

He's the biggest European football star to emerge since David Beckham, and a McCormick, to boot.

"That's why I'm here, actually," Hamish says, chugging a dark lager. "New product roll-out for a company based here in Boston, so I have meetings in the morning with my agent. Might be a seven-figure deal."

"Pounds, or dollars?"

"Oh, dollars, aye? If it were pounds, I'd offer up my right stone."

"Stone?"

He cocks an eyebrow. "You know. Balls."

Ah. I get it. "Don't give up the nuts too early in the process," I say. "Hold out for eight figures."

He grins, face splitting with a conspirator's grin. His top teeth are impossibly straight and white, bottom teeth a bit crooked, his nose wandering off at an angle that says it's been broken a few times. His hair is super short on the sides, a little longer on top, and he has the look of a freshly-manscaped guy unaccustomed to that kind of detailing.

"*Nuts*? Only Americans would pick such a wee thing to compare them to." He laughs. "But I like your thinking. You're a shark, aren't ye, cousin? Maybe I should fire my manager and have you negotiate for me."

"Not looking for a new job, Hamish." Not to mention the pay cut would be enormous.

His laugh is bold and open, booming and unpretentious. "I'd imagine you have your hands full." With that comment, he eyes Amanda. "Very nicely full."

And he winks at me.

"Andrew!" Shannon says, coming in for a hug before I can decide how to answer Hamish. "How are you?" She smells exotic, a new perfume tickling my nose. Our embrace feels like hugging a sibling. None of the typical feelings stirred up when hugging a woman appear.

Good.

"I'm great. How was the honeymoon?"

Her face goes slack, just like Declan's. "Fine."

"Just fine? Shouldn't a honeymoon be more than fine?" Hamish asserts with a leer.

"Would you like a rum-soaked truffle?" she asks, shoving a heavy silver tray right into Hamish's navel, so hard he emits a grunt of surprise.

And then she walks away to chat with...my father?

What the hell happened on that honeymoon? Must be bad if Shannon's avoiding the topic by choosing conversation with *Dad*.

"Was the sex that bad?" Hamish grumbles, looking at the tray of truffles that are now in disarray, perfect tops pointed down, scattered like drunken sorority pledges at an outdoor frat lawn party.

"Don't say that anywhere near Declan if you like your teeth, Hamish."

We share a grin and each try a truffle.

Rum. They're rum truffles.

A hand strokes my ass, making me choke. Hamish's hands are in view, so—

"Hey," Amanda whispers in my ear. Her breath smells like cherry liqueur. "The candies are all filled with alcohol," she says, blowing in my ear.

"You don't say?" I snake my arm around her waist and start to think that maybe coming to this present-opening party wasn't such a bad idea after all.

I'm glad I pushed her into coming.

"Is Gerald picking us up?" she asks.

"Of course. Why?"

"Then I don't have to drive home? I can drink?" Her fingers roam a little more.

"You can do whatever you want, baby."

She does a double take, dimples blooming on her cheeks like daffodils in late April. "You've never, ever called me *baby* before."

"You've never, ever grabbed my ass in public before."

"Last time we were here, it wasn't exactly a pleasant situation between the two of us."

"Tonight is definitely better," I agree. Last time we were

together here at Declan and Shannon's place, it was the rehearsal dinner from hell. I was being stupid (I admit it), Dad had just been diagnosed with cancer, Amanda was being weird, and the night unraveled layer by layer, a train wreck no one could stop.

And, I'm reminded, we never did have sex in the walk-in closet where we fought and half made-up.

"Definitely," she purrs, eating a decorated truffle from the plate Hamish has abandoned. He's now chatting away with Shannon and Dad. I overhear words like *Costa Rica* and *coffee exports* and *rainforests*.

"You haven't stabbed me in the neck with a fork even once tonight."

"The night's still young."

"HAMISH!" Marie squeals, giving him a huge hug as she discovers him. "How was the photo shoot?"

He blinks hard, unsure what to do with a fifty-something yoga instructor hanging around his neck like a menopausal rosary. "Good," he says, looking down at her.

"Naked, huh?" she chirps, peeling her hands off his neck. "I've seen that edition of *Sports Illustrated* before. Loved the guy on the Zamboni. What do they have *you* riding?"

*Wink.*

Before poor Hamish can continue breathing, Marie adds, "Can I get an autographed copy when they hit the newsstands?"

"Uh, sure," he says, frowning.

"Just don't sign on top of anything important!"

Hamish's face turns to flames. He catches my eye.

*Crazy*, we mouth together.

"Shot?" I ask, pointing to the whisky.

"Hell, yes," he mutters. "I'm supposed to send her a naked photo of myself, signed? Aren't we basically related? She's old enough to be me mam!"

"Welcome to America!" Amanda says.

"Welcome to Marie," I add.

We all do shots and the whisky goes down smooth. I think about the walk-in closet in Dec's bedroom. Wonder if Amanda will—

"How are the bee sessions going?" Hamish asks me.

Bee sessions. BEE SESSIONS?

He gives me a wicked grin. "Vince is my trainer, too, when I'm in Boston. Remember? He asked if the bee allergy runs in the family."

Damn it. I would fire Vince in a heartbeat if he weren't so good.

The whole room goes quiet. Even Dad stops talking to Pam and gives me an appraising look. Every single person in the room is staring at me, so I take the only reasonable action and pour three fingers of whisky, neat, and chug.

Then I pour again.

"Bee sessions?" Amanda asks quietly, as if I'm not under a microscope.

"Wasp," I grunt under my breath. Not that the difference matters to any of them. Bees, wasps, whatever. They're not allergic. Except for Shannon. The difference between a bee and a wasp sting only matters when you're allergic. Oh, man, this whisky is good.

Too good. I must have another.

"Aye! Andrew's going outside on a regular basis and getting used to being in the sun around the bees," Hamish helpfully explains. "He's working with a personal trainer to get used to it."

"Wasp," Amanda says, correcting him.

Dec and Terry have eyebrows buried in their hair.

Dad pulls away from Pam and turns his back to me, pouring another glass of wine for himself.

"That's wonderful," Marie says. "Overcoming your fear."

"It's not fear," I scoff. "I'm working with allergists. Medical science is catching up to anaphylaxis. Being outdoors is part of a careful, medically-supervised plan to reduce risk."

"You're using a personal trainer known for tying shamanic crystals to his sac to gain strength for *that*?" Hamish asks, genuinely confused. "How is that medical?"

Anger rushes to the edge of my skin, digging its way through my pores. I have just enough alcohol in me to start saying words I'll regret, but not enough to stop giving a shit.

I am firmly in the danger zone.

"Did you know that when a male bee mates, his penis explodes inside the queen bee and falls off? Gone forever!" Pam announces, raising her glass of wine as if in a toast.

A toast to male bee castration.

I'm not so sure she's mother-in-law material, after all.

"Wasps, Mom," Amanda pipes up. "Andrew's not allergic to bees." Like that matters. The woman is talking about insect penises. I don't think we need to split hairs.

Or, uh...penises.

"You always entertain me, Pam," Dad says, raising his glass to her. "Any other strange male penis behaviors you know about?" Dad winks at her.

Pam takes him seriously, screwing up her face in concentration. "The male octopus has a detachable penis. When he wants to mate, he rips it off—"

Every guy in the room just tightened his core and bent in a little, as if we're all Venus flytraps and Pam stuck her finger inside us.

"—and she has sex with the detached penis. He regrows a new one."

"I had a girlfriend I wish I could have done that with," Hamish announces. "Would have made life easier."

Amy looks at him with disgust. "Don't you strain under the weight of carrying that ego around?"

"What?" he says, one corner of his mouth curling up with mischief. "Imagine the convenience of a detachable penis. T'would make the morning so much easier."

All the men in the room nod.

All the women frown in confusion.

"And if you want to talk about carrying heavy objects around, if I had a detachable penis, t'would—"

She shuts him up by walking away.

"At least the octopus can just regrow his penis. The male drone bee dies shortly after. Sexual suicide," Pam muses. "I wonder if that behavior is found elsewhere in the animal world."

All the men in the room flinch except for me.

"Want to give it a try?" I ask Amanda.

"Which one?" she asks in mock horror. "Detachable penis or exploding penis?"

This conversation is making me a little sick.

"Male drone bee."

"You're willing to have sex with me until it falls off?"

"For the sake of science." I nuzzle her ear, a deep warmth filling me, pants getting tight, blood pumping hard.

"For the good of mankind," she says, rubbing her ass slowly against me.

"Walk-in closet? One minute? I'll go first, you come second."

She tenses. "That's not the order we usually go in."

"I meant sneaking out of the room."

"Oh."

A diffuse feeling of love for every person in the room should consume me, given the amount of alcohol in my blood, but lust takes over, and thank *God*. Because that was close.

I grab Amanda just as Marie calls everyone to gather around. Shannon smiles at us.

"Don't make eye contact. It just encourages them," I tell Amanda. "We're three seconds away from freedom."

"Can't wait to open your gift!" Shannon says to Amanda, reaching for her as I stare longingly at Dec's bedroom door.

And we're snagged.

Cockblocked by a wedding registry.

"What on earth are all these file boxes?" Marie asks my dad, who gives her a *Who, me?* look.

"How should I know?" Dad growls.

"Mom, those are all the cards we received. Anterdec staffers organized all the wedding gifts for us." Shannon's explanation doesn't go over well with Marie.

"Staffers? What? Those are all cards? Oh, my goodness!" Marie starts rifling through a box and plucks out a fistful, looking alarmed. "But they've been opened already!" she wails.

Declan and Shannon share one of those looks. The kind people who have been together for a while share.

The *I told you so* look.

"I knew she'd complain—"

"I told you it wasn't normal—"

"Who stole all the money?" Marie shouts, flipping through the file boxes, pulling out brightly colored cards with calligraphy on the front and opening them pell-mell.

"Stole?" Shannon asks, moving to Marie's side.

"There's no cash in any of these cards!"

Dec, Terry and I share uncomfortable looks. What is Marie talking about? Cash?

"Mom, the staffers at Anterdec opened everything. Any money in there was accounted for. But there wasn't much."

"Why would staffers open my daughter's wedding gifts?" Marie huffs. "And what do you mean, not much? Look at all these cards! There must be hundreds of them!"

Carol slowly makes her way across the room, fresh glass of wine in hand, and gives it to Marie. She and Shannon share a look I know.

Dec and I have exchanged the Parental Management Glance. Generally in Anterdec board meetings and not at social gatherings, but...

"Mom," Carol says gently. She looks like a younger version of Marie, but with a calmer face and a lower pitch of voice. None of Marie's frantic energy inhabits her. "The way people like the McCormicks handle weddings is different than the way we do."

"What does *that* mean?" Dad interjects, giving Carol a glare. "There's nothing wrong with how the wedding was conducted."

"Other than Declan and Shannon disappearing on a thousand guests and lying to me about the president!" Marie crows.

Every single person in the room rolls their eyes and drinks.

Including Jason.

"I never said *wrong*," Carol protests. "But different, definitely."

"It means," Terry says, that damn voice making Spritzy bark. I can feel Terry in the soles of my feet. "Dad, it means you threw a high society wedding and never bothered to explain how it all operates."

"Why is the burden on me? It should be on Declan," Dad

protests.

"Who has no idea what the hell you're all talking about," Declan says with an angry half-smirk. "A wedding is a wedding. You hire a planner, they handle the details, you have the gifts opened and your admin manages a thank-you note service, you return gifts you don't need, and most of what you receive goes to charity." He looks to me for backup.

"Right."

Shannon, Carol, Marie, Amy, Jason, Amanda, Pam, and Hamish all look at me like I just started spontaneously speaking Navajo.

"That's not how a wedding works!" Marie squeals. "That's not how any of this works!"

"And a cat as a flower girl 'works'?" Shannon says, turning to her, using Finger Quotes of Doom.

All hope of escaping this wedding gift party is dying as the fight unfolds.

A fight over what, exactly?

"You didn't even have a dollar dance at your reception!" Marie cries out.

"I married a billionaire," Shannon snaps back. "I don't exactly need a dollar dance, Mom! And besides, you were the one who broke protocol and turned into a Momzilla!"

Amanda's standing next to Shannon, offering moral support. I wonder if I can maneuver Amy into Amanda's position and steal my girlfriend away for that closet sex we were talking about a minute ago. Shannon just needs a woman she's close to for support, right? It doesn't really matter *which* woman.

"What the hell is a dollar dance?" Dec asks.

Marie's eyes light up.

We're never getting out of here.

"First, you give the bride a special white silk purse," she explains in a didactic tone that reminds me of the strange substitute teacher who filled in for health class one year at Milton Academy. She was later found to have hoarded more than sixty cats and was part of an underground child-bride ring for a cult.

I give Shannon, Amy, and Carol a second look. Jason as a cult leader? Nah. He strikes me as the guy who mixes the Kool-Aid, not the one who convinces everyone to drink it.

"And then, the men at the wedding approach the bride while she's on the dance floor. They slip a dollar—or, at least, the generous ones put in a ten or twenty—for a dance with the bride."

I start laughing. "Good one, Marie."

"Good one, what?"

"Why would you tip a *bride*?" Declan asks.

"Like a stripper?" I add, laughing. What are they talking about? I've never seen a dance like this at any wedding I've attended.

Shannon blinks hard, looking at Declan with a slow evaluation. "It's not a *tip*. It's a fun ritual."

"You're lining up every man in the room to come with small bills and tip the bride to be able to hold her in your arms and press up against her, if I'm hearing this correctly," Declan says, clearing his throat and looking around the room like we're at a negotiation table for a buyout and he's establishing dominance.

"You're making it sound so lewd!" Marie exclaims.

"*I'm* making it lewd? You're telling us the men pay for access to the bride's body."

Shannon's face turns beet red. "That's not what the dollar dance is!" she says hotly to Declan.

"Even the name—Dollar Dance—sounds like something you'd find in a topless bar on the Strip in Vegas," I add, thoroughly amused by the topic.

Until I look at Amanda for reinforcement.

And find her glaring at me.

"What?" I throw my hands up. "Don't you find this insane?"

"I find your reaction insane."

Uh oh.

"Have you really never been to a wedding with a dollar dance?"

Dec and I shake our heads.

"Not since I was a kid," Dad huffs.

"If you slip a hundred in that purse, will the bride give you a lap dance?" Hamish asks, clearly intrigued by this topic, leaning in as he pops back another shot, a hopeful grin on his face.

Amy smacks his shoulder. "You're disgusting."

"Oh, *I'm* disgusting? You're the ones talking about hooring out the bride for a purse full of cash at her own wedding!"

"WHORING!" Amy shouts. "It's not whoring! It's a lovely ceremonial dance that's part of any normal wedding reception."

Declan bristles. "Normal?"

"As if you can talk," Amy shoots back. "Your wedding was anything *but*."

"How would you know? You didn't even attend," Declan says.

Dude. Just...no.

"I, unlike you, attended *all* of your first wedding!" Amy shoots back.

Dec opens his mouth to say something, but Carol steps between them.

"Awwww, you did not just say that," she says, her jaw tight. "You can't pull that card on her. She had to work. You know—work. That annoying habit people in our class have."

"Your class?" Dad snorts.

Eyes darting all over the room, Amanda looks like she's about to throw up. I wend my way through the arguing throng and grab her hand, tugging lightly.

"Let's get out of here," I whisper.

"You're saying that to my boobs."

"That's who I'm addressing."

"WAIT A MINUTE!" Marie shouts. As Dad and Carol and Amy and Declan and God knows who else all argue over the ceremonial rituals of cash and brides, Marie's managed to sit in a pile of wedding cards, and has opened a bunch of them. "So far, I count ten sheep and three cows as wedding presents to Shannon and Declan."

"I really don't want to listen to this," I whisper. "We've gone from paying the bride for men to touch her to sheep, all in one minute. Do I have to pick you up and carry you into the other room?"

JULIA KENT

Amanda's hand squeezes mine. "You couldn't."

"Couldn't, or wouldn't? Because yes, I can, and yes, I will." I give her a very lewd once-over.

Excited terror fills her eyes. She chugs her drink and grabs my ass.

"You need to slip a dollar in my pocket every time you do that," I inform her.

Her hand slides into my front pocket. I inhale sharply.

"Like this?"

"*Exactly* like that."

"What if I don't have any money?"

"I'll take an IOU."

"Can *I* get a lap dance if I give you an IOU for a hundred?"

"I'll give you one hell of a pole dance for free."

"I assume *you're* the pole?"

I wink at her. "You're quick. I knew there was a reason I fell in love with you." I pull her close, grinding our hips together, her softness in contrast to my hard self. "Brains and beauty, all in one delicious package."

"You've got quite some package, too," she whispers, rubbing against me, hot breath on my ear.

"Want to unwrap it?"

Her kiss is a promise that rolls out like an introduction to the rest of my life.

"Get a room," Terry says, his voice making us both startle. I look over to see him holding Spritzy in one hand, a shot glass in the other.

"How about a closet?" I whisper, as Amanda takes my hand and we slowly peel off from the edge of the crowd, most of whom now bicker about the finer details of social class and wedding traditions in twenty-first-century America.

We're eloping.

Whenever she lets me marry her.

All that alcohol must have soaked into my bones, because by the time we find Declan and Shannon's bedroom, all I can think about is sinking into Amanda. I push her against the wall next to the door and kiss her, hands sliding up under her skirt, pushing the fabric up to nirvana, where I find her bare as can be, smooth as silk.

"What a lovely surprise," I say, with meaning.

"Great minds think alike."

"You planned for us to sneak off and have sex in the walk-in closet?"

"I'm a fixer."

"Fix this." I take her hand and put it where I need a handy-woman most.

"Declan is going to kill us if he finds out we actually came back and had sex in his closet," she whispers as her hands work my belt, unleashing me. "Remember how angry he was at the rehearsal dinner when he caught us in here?"

"I don't care." She's made this so easy I almost groan as I pull her down to the ground and she balances herself over me, her hair a wall of fire blocking out the light. All I see are her eyes, all I feel is her soft silk above me, mouth on mine, sweet wetness and warmth enveloping me as we reinterpret the very notion of a pole dance.

I like my version best.

Neither of us has any illusions about what we're doing. This is a quickie. A check mark on a list of wrongs to be righted. A few months ago we were in here, on shaky ground, trying to figure out what we were to each other. As Amanda and I move in perfect rhythm with each other, my hands pulling down the neckline of her wrap dress, her body arching and curling in so my mouth can take one nipple in and give her just enough attention for her sex tell to emerge, I realize we're being about as authentic as you can get, amidst Declan's suits and Shannon's shoes, the rumble-tumble of their domestic life surrounding us, witnessing the silly playfulness of a very serious lovemaking session that has one singular purpose.

To reclaim.

The familiar tightening, the thready leap of blood in a vein on her neck, and the sudden silence that comes as she holds her breath give me permission to release, to give, to give in and give up and give over as we ride each other into a fit of loose giggles and clandestine raunchiness.

"You're the first person I've ever had sex in a closet with, Andrew."

"I thought you had a gay boyfriend."

"*He* was in the closet. Not me."

We dress quickly, Amanda making little sounds of worry about her sex head, the cock-eyed angle of her dress, the need to rush to a bathroom and straighten up.

"Did we really just do that?" She holds up her palm and I meet it with mine, our fingers cascading down into a grown-up version of a kid's game, entwining.

"Yes." I sigh, pleased and relieved, loose and happy.

"We're a little kinky."

"No. If we were kinky, we'd have used one of Shannon's high heels."

"You'd look good in them."

"That's not what I meant," I growl, tickling her.

"I think I heard voices back here," Pam says from just outside the door. Spritzy barks. Amanda pulls back from me, lips pressed together, eyes wide.

"We smell like sex! If someone catches us, it's so obvious," she whispers in my ear. "The closet reeks of us!"

Pam's voice fades out, followed by a man's rumble. Sounds like Dad.

I carefully turn the doorknob, not making even a click, and we slip out, tiptoeing, grateful for the carpeted bedroom. As we enter the hallway, Terry greets us with a very excited Spritzy and a lecherous grin.

"Checking out Andrew's etchings?" he asks.

Amanda blushes.

"Just, um, getting some fresh air," she babbles.

"In a hermetically-sealed high rise condo bedroom?"

"Right!"

Terry just laughs, nudging Amanda with his elbow as she passes. "Have to get rid of the taste of Jessica in your mouth somehow."

"Hey," I bark. Spritzy joins me.

"You might want to go give Dec some support. He's out there fighting with his mother-in-law."

"Over the gifts?"

"No. They've moved on to her preference for a grandchild."

"You think I want to wade into that toxic sludge of a conversation?"

Amanda practically sprints down the hallway, muttering, "Poor Shannon."

"Poor Shannon?" Terry and I say in unison.

"He married her. Marie was part of the bargain," I say.

"What's wrong with Marie? I think she's hilarious."

I stare at him.

"You have a really unique perspective on the world, Terry."

"No. I have a normal perspective. You, Dec and Dad are the outliers. You just don't realize it."

"You grew up in the same family."

"And I broke away from it."

"We still haven't talked about that. Jessica interrupted us, remember?"

"Now is not the time. Not with Dad here. Not when I have to play nice."

He walks away.

Play nice?

The glow from sex fades as I watch him walk toward the chattering crowd. I can't see anyone because of the angle of the apartment's layout, but I can hear them, feminine voices a mix of pleasant and terse, some high with anger and some low and casual. The men's voices banter and spar, the resulting blend of sounds just a social signal, one that comes with gatherings like this.

It means everything, and it means nothing.

Straightening my tie, pulling my cuffs down, I center my shirt at my belt buckle and take a few deep breaths.

Closet sex achieved.

Family mystery still unsolved.

Chapter Fifteen

Vince drives a yellow Hummer that has a huge logo on the side that says, "ELECTRIC HUMMERS FEEL BETTER."

How do I know? Because he pulls into the parking spot next to my Tesla as we meet here at the soccer field.

Yeah, soccer field.

We're managing my risk aversion with a logical, rational plan designed to increase quality of life. Our outdoor session has been rescheduled for this fine Monday morning.

"Ready for your Wasp Session?" Vince barks out as he leaps down from his yellow perch, clutching a bottle of MCT oil.

"Nice ride." Like I do at the beginning of every outdoor session, I hand him two EpiPens. He shoves them in pockets on his running vest without comment.

"Thanks."

"I was being sarcastic."

"I ignored that."

"Why would you drive that thing?"

He points to the Tesla. "Why you driving *that*?"

"Because it gets nearly two hundred miles to the charge."

"No, you drive it because Teslas indicate status. It's like an electric dick."

I give his Hummer a skeptical look. Pot calling kettle black.

"And a day-glo yellow representation of gluttony converted to electric isn't a symbol?"

"My car says *Fuck the Man*. Your car says *Bend Over*."

I start to argue, but he shoves the bottle in my hand and says, "Drink."

"Drink...oil?"

"Yes."

"From the bottle?" I recoil.

"What? I don't have cooties. This isn't third grade. Chug some. We're running an eleven-mile trail along the river. You'll need it."

"I need electrolytes, not petroleum."

He snorts. "It's coconut and palm based." He hands me a backpack. "And here're your electrolytes." It's a hydration backpack with a drinking hose that comes out of the back, behind the neck.

"Eleven miles, huh?"

"We'll run so fast the wasps can't catch up, Andrew."

I give him a sour look. "That's not the point, Vince."

"The point is to get you outside, moving. Everything else is window dressing."

"I don't need a trainer to do that."

"Then why am I here?"

Because I'm scared shitless. The minute we leave the relative safely of the paved parking lot, we're on nothing but grass and path, weaving between potential death and certain humiliation.

Not that I'm admitting any of that to Vince.

"You're here to help me train."

"For what?"

"Life."

He nods, corners of his mouth turning down in an evaluative look, hair off his face with a combination headband and ponytail holder that would look extremely effeminate on any other guy, but on Vince it looks downright *300*. I half expect Gerard Butler to come crashing through the bushes screaming "Spartans! What is your profession?!"

"Water on?"

I adjust the backpack hydration system. "Yes."

"Go."

For the first mile, I'm Frankenstein's monster, an assemblage of parts stuck together with nothing but adrenaline and testosterone. The combination sucks.

Mile two, the first dive-bomber appears. I twist out of the way of a big, black drone of death and trip, skinning the hell out of my knees, covering half the front of me with regurgitated electrolyte solution from the hydropack.

"Get up," Vince huffs from ahead of me. "Keep running."

I do. As I stand, the damn wasp lands on a small puddle of the liquid I've spilled, pausing on the water.

I hold my breath and stare at it. Knives jab my exposed skin from a thousand angles. My breathing takes on an even more labored quality, like my throat is closed by a boulder in an Indiana Jones movie, my will squeezing through in those final few inches that allow for escape.

I catch up to Vince.

"You still married?"

I show him my bare hand. "No." Talking helps. Talking makes about half the knives stand down.

"But you love her."

I give him a look of disgust. "You want to talk about love now?"

"No better time."

"We're not here for love. We're here to burn."

"Same thing. Just a different kind of pain."

He has a point.

"Hey, man. You're a risk taker. You always know what you want, and go for it. Why should this be different?"

"Because the stakes are higher."

"Are they really?"

"It's my entire life."

"And business isn't?"

I hate when he's right.

But when he is, my life improves.

"Business is different. It's calculated risk based on known and unknown variables, and—"

"I know a variable."

"What?"

"You wore that wedding ring for days longer than you needed to."

"Not this again."

"The fact that it's 'this again' is exactly why that fact is a variable, Andrew."

"You're ascribing too much meaning to it."

"I think you need to think that."

"Why would I?"

"Because you're scared shitless."

"Scared of what?"

"Wasps."

I shrug.

"And scared to admit you know she's your woman. Forever. Done. You're scared because it's too easy."

I would scoff, but my heart is stuck in my throat, along with a frightening amount of bile. Vince must be running at a four-minute mile pace. The greenery is a blur and my calves are threatening to turn to butter.

"When did you become so wise?"

"Since I cut out carbs and started the green coffee bean enemas."

"Jesus, Vince."

He shrugs. "I don't really do that shit, but I thought this conversation was veering into *Fuller House* territory."

"DJ grew up and got hot, didn't she?"

Vince's face splits into an evil grin. "I knew you were a closet pervert, Andrew."

Closets. If only he knew....

"Why would you think otherwise?"

"You know what I do with pervert clients?"

Gina's comment from the other day flits through my memory. "What?" I ask, with great caution.

"I make 'em row until their lats peel off one by one so I can make human jerky out of them."

"Are you related to Amanda Warrick?" She made the same joke. This is getting creepy.

"Who?"

"Never mind."

He shrugs. "And just for you, I'm queueing up the first episode of *Fuller House* in front of the rowing machine next time we train. In public, at a gym. That's your penance."

"Dude, I was joking. Don't make me actually watch that shit."

Evil grin.

That's what I get for changing the topic.

Wait.

*He* changed the topic.

I think I've been had.

"Can your limo dude drive us back here and get our cars?" Vince asks. He's not even panting. His voice is as even as if we were lounging by a pool.

"Sure. Why?"

"A little adjustment and we can just run back to your office. You care about being seen all sweaty and pussified?"

"Don't care about sweat, and the other won't happen."

"If it doesn't happen, I'm not doing my job."

"You use a lot of offensive language."

"Maybe you're just a sensitive pussy."

"Jesus, Vince."

"What?"

"Why are you knocking pussies? Of all the parts of the body you could use for an insult, I don't get it." Never got it.

"Right about now, the comparison fits. You're hot, soaking wet, pink, and you have buttons I can push that make you scream."

I'm glad my lungs have turned into flopping salmon on a rock by the river, because I have no response to that. Finally, I croak out, "You have a way with words."

"That's why you pay me the big bucks. Notice how you

haven't scanned the horizon for the past five minutes, and you're not flinching every time a mosquito zips past?"

He's right.

"You're doing this, man."

"Shut up, Vince."

His only response is to pick up the pace and shout over his shoulder, "You're a walking vagina, man."

I've been called worse.

"And this is my last wasp session with you. You've graduated," he declares.

And then that asshole takes off at a sprint, and keeps the ridiculous pace for the final seven miles.

*Ridiculous.*

* * *

Vince and I make it back to my building. That last mile nearly killed me, but I can't admit it. We take the front elevators at Vince's insistence. He says my employees need to see me being a strong leader.

I think he wants to parade me around like a Derby winner, sweat-soaked and foaming.

"Oh, gross. You're dripping sweat all over my desk!" Gina exclaims, as we walk past her station toward my office door. Her wrinkled nose makes her look even more like a timid little rabbit.

"That's not sweat. Those are Andrew's tears." Wink.

Before I can smack him down, Gina mutters, "Maybe you should use lube next time," and walks away briskly, her Bluetooth turned on, arms full of files.

With Vince staring after her, gaping.

Maybe I've underestimated Gina.

"Wow," Vince finally says.

"I know," I snort, pulling at my soaked shirt, greedy for the cool air that slaps my abs. "Because you'd be the catcher if we were together."

Vince turns and stares at me as if he's an eighteenth-century hangman evaluating my neck.

167

"You're a dead man."

"Dead men can't cry." I make a fake pouty face.

"But they can spin. See you Friday. Get those chicken legs ready." He stares at my calves, then punches my arm and walks down the hall, chest so big and wide his forearms graze against the hallway walls. Turning sideways, he lets someone walk down the hallway, coming from the other direction.

Amanda.

"What was that about?" she asks, eyes wide and open, mouth pressed in a prim line. She's wearing a green wrap dress that makes her eyes extra sultry, and all I want to do is get sweaty with her in my office again. She looks just enough like Christina Hendricks in *Mad Men* to drive me wild. My pants tighten and threaten to cut off circulation to everything below the navel. I want to turn the glass desktop into a Slip 'n Slide.

"We were talking about Vince and I having sex."

"So your usual 2 p.m. meeting?"

There's only one way to respond to that.

I kiss her.

Hard.

She squirms in my arms, hands flat against my sweaty chest.

"It's like you swam in sweat!"

"Pretty close. Vince had me run eleven miles on the trails."

Her whole body pauses. "Outside?"

A swell of pride fills me. "Yes."

"Andrew!" she squeals, pulling me in for a wet hug. "Congratulations! That's wonderful!"

"I don't need praise for being a human being. It's not like I climbed Mount Everest. " But her sweet softness isn't a bad prize.

"You need recognition for being brave."

"I went outside, Amanda. That's second to respiration. No one needs an *I Did It!* ribbon for that."

"How about a celebration at your place? Tonight? I'll give you a major award." Wink.

I don't know why, but I blurt out, "Pack a bag. I'll clear out a drawer."

She frowns. "A drawer?"

"You can start keeping some stuff at my place."

"Some stuff?"

"Clothes. Toothbrush. Stuff. So you can spend the night more."

"You mean—what—huh?"

"I want you to spend more time at my place. With me." A single drop of sweat chooses that moment to dangle from the end of one curled-up piece of my hair onto my cheekbone, making me feel like I'm crying.

I'm not.

"Are you asking me to—" Amanda can't say the words, so she just narrows her eyes and waits me out.

"To bring some of your stuff over. Keep it in my apartment. For convenience."

"Convenience."

"Right."

"How much stuff?"

"As much as you want."

"For a man whose entire company functions as a result of his painstaking clarity, you really suck at this conversation, Andrew."

"If I asked you to move in with me, would that help clarify?"

"You're asking me to move in with you?"

I guess I am.

I shrug.

"We were practically married. I'd marry you if I thought you'd bite."

"I was closer to being married to Chuckles than you, Andrew. Or should I say, *Ayndrough*." She's using a light tone, but I can tell she's covering for deep feelings that I've stirred up.

Mine are churning, too.

"If it's too much, just start with an outfit. A toothbrush. Some makeup."

"I get my own drawer?"

"And a hook. I'll install a single hook in the closet for you."

"So generous!"

"Hey, you can have the entire closet if you want. I don't want to scare you off." I know not to say it, but I can't help myself.

"You're not scaring me. You're just...this is fast." She's skeptical.

"Fast?"

"We never really dated."

"Of course we dated! We went to Consuela's, and..." I snap off in mid sentence. We also went to... My mind goes blank.

"See? You can't even—"

"Fenway Park!" I snap my fingers. "We went to a game."

"And that day turned out so well."

I pinch the bridge of my nose. That was a terrible day. Trapped between business associates and Amanda's obvious distress as she unraveled from something I didn't understand, I failed her. Fear (fine, I admit it) of going outside and following made me a prisoner of my own failure.

"I found you at home."

"You did."

"And as I recall, we did just fine after that."

"Until you dumped me."

"I didn't—" The truth hits me, like a foul ball gone funky.

"You did." The finality of her words feels like a shattered baseball bat.

"I did." I accept the truth of how much I hurt her that day. I know it hurt, because it pierced me to do it. When you trap yourself inside a double bind in your own mind, an irrational emotion can lock you up forever, because it's self-justifying. All the reasons you're wrong are overridden by this perfectly reasonable, absolutely rational set of rules that make sense.

Only in a closed system.

When you turn your heart into a fortress, you can defend it against anything.

Including love.

"And I was wrong," I choke out. "I've lived a life so closed off from any hint of openness. You felt expansive, like I would be carried off in the wind, floating out of control, carried by the whims of Mother Nature, exposed. That's how loving you feels, Amanda. Like every part of me can't quite catch its breath because I'm dissolving, becoming part of everything else."

She reaches for my hand. I thread my fingers in hers. Our eyes meet.

"I'm going to screw this up," I confess.

"Say it anyway."

I nod.

"It's barely been a week."

"It feels like a month."

"Like eternity."

"We're not competing for a Hyperbole Prize here, Andrew."

"No. The stakes are higher."

"Much higher."

"Stratospherically higher."

She punches me.

"Is your only objection that we haven't dated long enough?" I press. Because if that's it—really, truly the only problem here— then there is no real conflict. No true doubts. If Amanda's hesitation comes from a sense of disbelief that I can feel great certainty in the face of being together for a short time frame, then this is a done deal.

I am the master of persuasion.

I need to apply my boardroom skills to the bedroom.

Convincing her that I am sincere and sure will be a pleasure.

"I don't know."

Shit.

*I don't know* is the cockblocker of all negotiations.

"You don't know whether we've dated long enough, or you don't know whether your only objection is that we haven't dated long enough?"

She blinks, her face changing expressions, trying a few on for size, her inner state written all over her face. I love that she's comfortable enough to drop her masks more and more with me. Meanwhile, my inner state is a war zone, complete with bombers on an air raid and artillery exploding all over the place as I try to keep my emotions in check and figure out the lay of the land here.

"I can't wrap my head around the fact that you pushed me

away less than a month ago and now you're certain you want to spend the rest of your life with me."

Oh.

*That.*

"Clarity."

"You've achieved emotional clarity like *that*?" She snaps her fingers.

"Yes."

"And you expect me to be so clear, too."

"Of course."

"Of course?"

"I'm not fooling around here, Amanda. You have nothing to worry about. This is it. You're the person I want to be with forever. All I need now is your buy-in, and we're good to go."

"Buy-in?"

"Your agreement."

She peers at me with such incredible concentration that I feel something loosen, an internal *aha!* that tells me I'm finally getting traction.

This is a done deal.

"You make it sound like a detail in a business negotiation."

"Marriage is a merger."

The incredulous look she gives me makes my confidence falter. "Whatever happened to the guy who quoted Dickinson on our first date?"

I point to myself. "Same guy."

"And now you're describing the biggest emotional commitment of my life as a buy-in?"

"When you know, you know."

"Maybe I don't know."

Blood pounds through my body like a clock, measuring time by my pulse, each second profound and painful, achingly slow and ponderous. *I don't know* chimes over and over.

"You don't have to know," is all I can croak out. I'm dying. This is how it feels to have blood pump through a heart that is collapsing, cell by cell. Slow motion makes it all so much worse.

And then our eyes meet.

"I propose a traditional courting," she says, as if a light bulb just went on inside her head.

"A *what*?" Don't mind me. I'm just pretending to be alive.

"Court me."

"*Court* you? Is that a new sex thing?"

"No, Andrew. It's a very old-fashioned love thing."

"Courting? Like something from a Jane Austen novel? You want me to turn into some Regency-era duke with rules and calling cards?"

"And breves. If you're going to go to the trouble to get calling cards, make sure your liveryman brings me breves, too."

"I highly doubt the Darcy and Bennet families drank breves during calling hours."

She arches one eyebrow. "Your knowledge of Austen and Dickinson is so hot." She fans herself.

"You and the breves. They're like tiramisu to most women."

She gives me a coy smile.

Oh, no.

She's *serious*.

"Amanda. I don't have time to play games. Either we're dating, or we're not." *Either you love me, or you don't.*

"And if I said 'not'?"

My entire body turns into a bundle of frozen meat filled with icebergs in my blood. The Titanic crashes on one of them.

"Is that what you want? To not date? To not—" I can't say it. *Not be together.*

"No."

"No, you don't want to date, or no, you—"

"I want to be with you."

I breathe again.

"But with courting," she adds brightly, giving me an amused grin, eyes flashing.

"What does that mean?"

"It means I need clarity, too. You already have it. I don't. Figure it out, Mr. CEO." She gives me that damn finger-shoot Declan uses when he's being extra sarcastic. "You're a sharp guy."

And with that, she walks out of my office, the view of her sashaying ass turning the ice in my blood up to a boil.

Courting? *Courting*?

"How do you court someone you've already been almost-married to?" I mutter to myself.

"I guess we'll find out," she calls back through the door.

*Bzzzz.*

"Mr. McCormick? An official from the FCC is on your line? He says you're ten minutes late for a conference call?" Gina's voice startles me back to reality.

"Gina. I want you to research courting and have a report for me in my inbox by EOB."

"Courting?"

"Yes."

"Is that a new sport?"

"No. An old one."

"Courting?" I hear the tap of keys. "Do you mean courting, as in wooing a woman for marriage?"

"Yes."

"And you want me to research this for you?"

There's a distinct tone of sarcasm in Gina's voice. That's new.

"Yes."

"You realize this is something most women want the man to do on his own. Having your admin research how to court a woman is kind of impersonal, Mr. McCormick."

Huh. That did not sound like a question. Gina's marked change in vocal patterns troubles me.

But not enough to do anything about it.

"And make sure none of the courting ideas involve being outdoors during the day."

"But Mr. Mc—"

*Click.*

I've never looked forward to an FCC conference call with so much relief.

Way easier than dealing with women.

# Chapter Sixteen

Gina's report is on *regency-era* courting. Reading through the seventeen-page report, which is meticulously organized by subsections such as "How to Give Your Daughter a Season," "Proper Chaperone Techniques," and "Elopement to Gretna Green," I realize the entire file is nothing but bits and bytes of sarcasm designed to meet my exact request within the letter of the law.

Or, to put it another way, she's being maliciously obedient.

"Gina."

"Yes?"

"Great report. Make it happen. If we were near Scotland, I'd take the Gretna Green option, but we'll have to settle for the rest."

"Make it happen?" she squeaks. "Make *what* happen?"

"All of it. The outfit, the carriage, the whole bit. No budget. Just do it."

"No budget? But Mr. McCormick, I—"

*Click.*

Twenty-five minutes later, Gina buzzes me.

"Professor Victoria Kensley-Wentingham from Boston University on the line for you, Mr. McCormick?"

"Professor who?"

The line changes over. A sweet, chortling older woman's voice fills my ear.

"Mr. McCormick! I understand you have a grave costume emergency. I am a historical costumer and here to help. I understand you need a bespoke 1809 duke's costume and carriage with liveryman?"

I've underestimated Gina.

*Gravely.*

"Yes. I have been asked to court my partner, and—"

"Court your partner? Impossible!"

"Excuse me?"

"One cannot court one's partner. If one already has a partner, then the courting is redundant."

"Exactly! That's what I said."

"If you wish to marry, however, then courting is essential."

*Wife.*

The professor rattles off a list of clothing, accessories, horse and carriage requirements, and names a price tag that doesn't even register.

*Wife.*

"Yes."

"Yes to all of it?" The professor's elation pours out of the phone like a honey factory exploded in my ear.

"Yes." I'm too distracted to sort through the details. It's easier to just agree and make this master plan work.

"Can you come to the university costuming department for a fitting? We'll need your exact measurements, your inseam, which way you dress—"

My schedule is insane.

"I'd prefer you come to my office. I'm very busy, and—"

She instantly quotes a higher price.

"Fine."

She clears her throat as if the act is a form of supplication. "Your attention to historical accuracy is admirable," she declares.

I'm sure my wallet is, too.

"I must say, Mr. McCormick, I haven't had an assignment

like this since the Sultan of Al-Massi asked for a re-creation of *Pride and Prejudice* in Dubai."

I perk up. "He *what*?"

"I suppose I shouldn't mention it, but I'm not violating confidentiality. The Sultan is an enormous Jane Austen fan. He has an entire wing of his palace devoted to an exquisite—and exact—replica of Pemberley."

Tucking *that* detail away for later, I give the good professor over to Gina to make arrangements.

In exactly one hour, there's a knock at my door, and then Hyacinth Bucket enters the room.

Mom's favorite show, when we were kids, was this crazy British comedy, *Keeping Up Appearances*. I do a double take as a matronly, confident, curvy woman with a slightly pinched face but bright, cunning eyes marches into my office carrying a sewing basket, trailed by a frail, terrified teenager with long, blonde dreadlocks who is dressed like H.G. Wells has a clothing line at Hot Topic.

"Mr. McCormick! Victoria Kensley-Wentingham. So good to finally meet you."

I stand and approach her, Professor Kensley-Wentingham taking both of my hands in hers and giving such good eye contact I feel like a lab specimen.

"Finally? We only spoke for the first time an hour ago, Ms. Kensley-Wentingham. Or is it *Dr.* Kensley-Wentingham?" I shake her hand and mentally reprimand Gina for letting this woman in.

"Oh, and this is Patience Overton," she says, waving blithely at the waif behind her. "She is my intern."

Patience gives me a wan smile and zero eye contact.

"Nice to meet you," I lie.

"I said *finally* with great intent, sir," the professor announces, "for any man ruled by such traditionally romantic passions must have his needs quenched in a timely manner." She grins broadly. "And it is, in fact, Dr. Kensley-Wentingham. Thank you for your attention to detail with the honorific. So few people understand true respect." *Sniff.*

I'm going to kill Gina.

"But please, call me Victoria."

"And I am Andrew."

She nods, half in indication that my words are appreciated. "Let us begin your extraordinary transformation into the external manifestation of the greatest man—a true man, if ever there was one, even if he is fictional. Mr. Fitzwilliam Darcy."

"Excuse me?"

"You asked for a duke's costume, but you do realize Mr. Darcy was no duke."

"I—"

"With *no* expense spared, I've taken the liberty of bringing only the finest period replicas, made with cloth that is as close as possible to the original. Your need for authenticity drives you to new heights of boldness in your attempt to woo, does it not?" Her eyes comb over me, from shoe tips to forehead cowlick. I can't tell whether she's calculating revenue, taking measurements, or eyeing me for her secret Red Room of Pain.

Or all three.

She continues. "I am, of course, most flattered that you would choose me for your costumer. I've taken the liberty of ordering a barouche for you—"

"A what?"

"A carriage. A horse-drawn barouche is difficult to find this time of year, but I have one on hold. The owner is awaiting the date, time, and location for his arrival to be at your service."

"Were horse-drawn carriages part of courting?" I explicitly told Gina that none of this should take place outside. A muscle in my jaw starts twitching.

"Of course! Your administrative assistant is printing your calling cards, as we speak, unless you would prefer hand-drawn calligraphy. As you said that time was of the essence..."

"That is fine."

"Rise!" she shrieks, looking at my crotch like Marie looks at my cousin Hamish. "You have a freakishly long rise!" The satisfied chuckle that erupts from her makes Patience twitch as the intern hands over two pairs of pants.

I stand tall. That's right. I sure do. Too bad Vince isn't present to hear *that*.

"This will take some adjusting, Mr. McCormick."

I repress the bizarre urge to mutter, *That's what she said*.

"Call me Andrew."

"Andrew," she purrs, putting on a set of tiny glasses, peering at my package. "I'm afraid all of our existing costumes are for men considerably shorter than you, but we can do a fitting with my samples. This will require made-to-order trousers after we find your exact measurements."

Meanwhile, little Emo Patience is taking notes suddenly while chewing on a fingernail until it bleeds.

"Fine. My tailor in Milan can give you my measurements."

The woman titters. "Oh, dear, no, that won't do at all. You see, Regency-era trousers are quite different from any bespoke modern day suit."

She's holding that tape measure like a dominatrix with a whip. "Or shall we fit you with breeches?" Her eyes narrow as she circles around me, taking in my body, the tip of her pink tongue poking out to lick her lips.

"Breeches?"

"Pantaloons?"

"I want whatever's in Gina's report." What started out as a silly joke to call Amanda's bluff has turned into something more annoying. I should call this off.

"She calls for the full Mr. Darcy treatment."

"Fine." I widen my stance. "Let's get my measurements and just do it."

Ten minutes later, the professor has recorded all my inches along with whatever last vestiges of innocence I used to possess. I feel like I should offer her a cigarette. I've had less intimate sexual encounters at frat parties.

"Did you have to be that...thorough?" I ask, resisting the urge to adjust everything.

"Nothing but the best for you, Andrew." She hands me one of the pairs of pants she's brought. "Please change into these. They are made of a fine wool and while the length is unacceptable, I believe the rise will be a near-perfect fit. We will recreate the design."

I sigh and walk into my bathroom like I'm on Death Row, then repeat the walk two minutes later to show her the result.

Only this time, my stride is about six inches. I walk like a nineteenth-century upper-class Chinese woman with bound feet.

"These are—"

"Perfect!" the professor squeals.

"—cutting off blood supply."

"One must suffer for historical authenticity. Men in Regency England were unashamed of their stallion-like figures." She gives me a long look, eyes hooded. A long sigh ripples out of her. "And yet, we do have an issue with the front flap buttons."

"Flap?"

She drops to her knees in front of me and pulls out a small measuring tape and a magnifying glass. "One moment," she declares with a sigh, holding up a flap of fabric with buttons on it.

Just then, the door to my office opens. I look up.

And in walks Vince.

"I am having a hard time finding it," Professor Kensley-Wentingham announces in a breathy voice. "I might need to get my tweezers."

Vince crosses his arms over his chest and leans one hip against a chair near my desk.

"When dealing with a freakish rise like yours, Andrew, I am forced to be creative."

"Freakish?" Vince asks.

"Freakishly *long*," I clarify.

"The magnifying lens in her hand tells me everything I need to know, Andrew. No need to elaborate." His tone tells me I'm never, ever living this down. At least he's not Declan.

Professor Kensley-Wentingham looks up. "Oh, my goodness! You're not the person he's proposing to, now, are you? Because fitting a body like yours into breeches will require a crowbar!" she chortles.

"Proposing?" Vince asks, eyebrows up.

"Oh, dear. Have I ruined the surprise? Were you going to pop the question to your boyfriend? You used the term 'partner' and I—"

"Girlfriend," I say tersely. It's hard to be angry when a woman has a pincushion millimeters from parts of me that should poke, not *be* poked.

Professor Kensley-Wentingham stops what she's doing, hand in mid-air, and slowly drops every implement, including the thimble perched on the tip of her tongue. She stands and gives Vince an aggressive visual inventory, taking in the broad muscles, the long black hair. It takes her a while. It should. He's the size of a small mountain.

"You," she finally says, "are a biological female?"

"No."

"Then by *girlfriend*, Andrew's referring to...?"

"Not me."

"I am quite confused."

"We noticed," Vince and I say together.

"You're not a couple?"

Gina walks in at that exact moment, eyes twinkling, pinging between me and Vince before settling on the professor. She punctuates that question with a shrug.

"Isn't it obvious?" she asks the professor. "You see it too?"

Vince glowers.

"I'm preparing to propose to Amanda. My girlfriend."

"Amanda Warrick?" Gina peeps. "The woman from Consolidated Evalu-shop who has all those two-hour meetings with you three days a week? Ohhhhhhh." Her face twists with disgust. "Meetings?" she asks, using finger quotes. "I need more Lysol in my desk drawer," she says out of earshot.

Except she's not.

"And my sexuality is none of your business," Vince declares. "But Andrew's not my type."

"I could be your type," I insist, a little offended.

He gives me a funny look.

"Not that I want to be," I quickly add.

Professor Kensley-Wentingham claps her hands twice and

shouts, "Boys! Boys! As lovely as this sweet argument is, we have more important issues to attend to, such as your leggings."

"Leggings?" I keep my voice nice and low. Masculine.

"Yes. In theater, the men wear thick pantyhose—"

Vince snorts.

"But for this custom fit, I suggest thigh highs."

Gina snorts.

"Thigh what?"

"Thigh highs. Long leggings much like dress socks for men of your stature. They need to go far above the knee to fit the look. The fine wool we'll use for the pants will be dry-clean only. Wouldn't want to wash it and have it shrink!" she adds, with a laugh that sounds like a happy teakettle. Not that I would know, because I've tuned her out. The only sound I really hear is the mocking laughter radiating off of Vince.

"You are literally a walking vagina, Andrew," Vince mutters.

"Why are you here?"

"To torment you."

"That's it? This isn't our regular time."

"Your Human Resources department hired me to do a wellness program."

"On what? How to kill people through spin?"

"Reiki."

"Reiki?"

"Yeah. Reiki. I'm a master."

"You believe in that shit?"

"You don't? You're the one paying for it, Andrew. Anterdec's writing me a big fat check."

And with that, he walks out, leaving plenty of life force energy in the room.

"What a fine, strapping young man," Professor Kensley-Wentingham says, craning her neck to watch Vince as he exits. "If he is ever interested in performing in a production of *Beauty and the Beast*, I would love to stay in touch." At the word *touch*, she flutters her fingers on my forearm.

"How soon can the courting materials be ready?" I snap.

"During our earlier call, you said you needed this in three days. That was your request."

"And?"

"I can do this in one week, exactly. I do need your girlfriend's measurements."

I mull this over. One week works. "Gina!"

"Yes?"

"Get the tailor from my brother's wedding on the line and ask for Amanda Warrick's measurements. Give them to the professor."

"Oh, she will look delightful in a sheer bonnet! Or shall we do a capote? You are breathtakingly efficient, Andrew!"

So efficient that I escort her to the door—and make her Gina's problem.

*Jessica's at it again*, a text from Amanda declares as I read through my phone.

Sighing, I check out the Twitter stream. Jessica's posting pictures from the Turkish restaurant and my hashtag:

#mccormickmendipitincrazy

"Ugh." I click on the hashtag and find thousands of retweets, comments about Amanda and Shannon, links to the YouTube video of Amanda rescuing that dog from the hawk, and pictures from Dec and Shannon's failed Boston wedding.

*See?* Amanda's next text reads. *She has more power than you think.*

*No, she does not*, I text back.

I'm ending this. Now.

"Gina!"

"Yes, sir?"

"Call me Andrew, damn it."

"Uh....yes, Andrew?"

"Get the local media buyer on the line."

"The media buyer for all of Anterdec?"

"Yes."

This is simple. Jessica's power comes from being an influencer. If you want to cut an influencer off at the knees, you take away their ability to influence. Local restaurants, public relations firms, marketing specialists and more all feed Jessica a steady stream of information and magnify her importance by referring to her on Twitter, re-tweeting, and elevating her importance in social media.

Remove all that and she's the peak of a pyramid of cheerleaders without a base.

And comes tumbling down.

"Cassandra Horning, Mr. McCormick. I do most of Anterdec's Boston-area media purchases," says a confident woman. I close my eyes and conjure up an image of a woman about my age, short brown hair, smart eyes behind glasses.

"Cassandra, I have a project for you."

Within thirty minutes, we've banged out the details.

Amanda's about to see exactly how powerless Jessica really is.

# Chapter Seventeen

In the time since Declan and Shannon's wedding, I haven't gotten a haircut. The professor comes to my apartment this afternoon, exactly one week after our first encounter, for the final fitting and proclaims, "Your countenance suits the character! Dark, angelic hair with a touch of curl about your face. Pity you couldn't grow out your sideburns enough to give yourself more authenticity."

I think I paid her too much.

She insists on having me tuck my shirt into the breeches, and uses needle and thread to tighten the waistband, adding a few stitches at the back.

"Is that necessary?" I ask.

She seems offended. "I wouldn't do it if it weren't necessary."

She sounds just like Dad.

By the time I evacuate her from my apartment and take a good look in the mirror, I realize she was right:

I could be a movie actor.

Amanda's empire-waist dress, a dark beige on top and a billowy white skirt on the bottom, is slung over my arm, with a bonnet on the hanger. If I'm going to court her, she has to play the part, too.

Like it or not.

I arrive at the agreed-upon corner around the block from

Amanda's duplex just as the horse-drawn carriage makes its entrance. I drove here myself, in full costume, and I park the Tesla on the side of the road, hoping Newton is a decent town with low crime.

"Mr. McCormick? Will Sawyers." The carriage driver is dressed in similar fashion to my own sartorial flair, though Professor Kensley-Wentingham was quite clear that my 1809 suit replica was one that an aristocrat would wear, while the livery-man's suit was "for one of his station."

*Sniff.*

I shake Will's hand and look at the carriage. A throng of kids stands across the street, gawking. A few adults come out onto their front stoops and curiosity makes a few pull out their phones, snapping pics.

"We need to move fast, before social media beats us to Amanda."

He doffs his hat and opens the carriage door. It's an open-air barouche, with a single horse pulling the entire load. Lightweight and made of thick black material with huge metal wheels, it reminds me of a spider in carriage form. Amanda and I will sit next to each other, facing front.

Riding in a horse-drawn carriage along the streets of Newton, Massachusetts is a surprisingly uneventful process until you reach a stoplight. We're stuck behind two cars, unable to make the quick right turn to go three houses down to find Amanda's driveway.

"Filming a movie?" someone shouts from a group to our right.

I ignore them.

"Are there zombies? I loved that historical zombie movie!" a kid in a baseball cap screams.

"ZOMBIES!" a little girl shrieks. "I hate zombies!"

She bursts into tears just as the light changes.

"I hate zombies, too!" I call back, fist in the air. "Don't worry."

Her startled expression makes me laugh.

At least I don't have to worry about the pictures finding their way to Jessica's toxic stream of hatred in 140-character chunks.

A crowd follows, mostly full of pale kids who still have enough curiosity left in them to be peeled away from their video games, and by the time I climb out of the carriage, Will holding the door for me, Amanda and Pam are at their front door. Pam's laughing as Spritzy barks.

Amanda is blushing, wearing a tight tank top and shorts that are about as long as my breeches.

And far looser.

"Mr. Darcy!" Pam calls out. "Does this make me Mrs. Bennet? Please tell me your per annum income."

"I see you've read Austen."

"Who do you think introduced Amanda to *Pride and Prejudice*?"

"Then I can blame all of this on you, Mrs. Bennet," I say, as she comes in for a quick hug, pulling back and touching the lapel of my tailcoat, eyes wide.

I see the resemblance to Amanda when Pam smiles.

"Blame all of this on what? Because I think you've gone half mad, Andrew," Amanda says. "Or you've been drinking. Maybe both. Did Lüq send Declan and Shannon another bottle of entheogenic wine?"

I ignore that. "You told me we haven't dated long enough for me to think long term," I say, making Pam's smile freeze as if she just bit into a live lizard. "And that I needed to court you."

"I meant go out on a few more dates before asking me to move in with you!" she contests hotly. "Not....this!"

I shrug. "I took you at your word. I am a man of mine."

"Oh, brother."

"Neither of them had anything to do with this, I assure you."

Will approaches with the dress and bonnet Professor Kensley-Wentingham made for Amanda.

"What's this?" she squeaks.

"Your dress and bonnet."

"Bonnet? I'm not wearing that!"

"Let me go get my iPad so I can take pictures," Pam says, clapping her hands with glee. Never seen the woman run like that.

"You brought an actual horse-drawn carriage from the Seaport District? It must have taken you hours to get here." Her sense of marvel is not, I realize, because she's impressed with my fine attention to detail.

It's at the idea that I would actually spend hours doing this.

"No. My Tesla's around the corner."

She chortles. "The idea of you tootling around town in this —" she points to the carriage—"is absurd."

"It's still a better vehicle than your Turdmobile."

The damn horse picks that exact moment to produce a giant pile of steaming manure.

"Looks like you've got a turdmobile of your own, Mr. Darcy."

"Quit stalling." I nudge her. "Go get dressed."

"Get dressed? You're serious?"

"I take my courting very seriously."

"Andrew."

"Amanda."

"Mr. McCormick."

"Ms. Warrick."

Her eyes narrow and she throws her hands in the air. "Most guys would take my request for more courting and put a modern spin on it. You know. Dinner and a show. A Boston Harbor Cruise. A weekend in the Cape. Stand outside my bedroom window with a boom box playing Boston's "Amanda.""

"I'm not most guys." I make a note to get her that Boston album on vinyl, though. Nice touch.

"You're really going to make me do this?"

"I'm not making you do anything, Ms. Bennet."

She groans, but she does take the dress and bonnet with her.

Pam appears carrying an iPad and with the look I imagine most mothers have on their face when their kid goes to prom.

I wouldn't know, because my mom died before I went to mine.

"I assume there is quite the backstory on this, Andrew."

Pam's face lights up, her eyes smart and savvy, even if the way she carries herself is meek. Spritzy pants at me, beady little eyes blinking like he expects an answer, too.

"There is. It's all Amanda's fault."

"Do tell." Pam walks over to a cheap white plastic chair that's on her porch and gently lowers herself, careful not to dump Spritzy out of the crook of her arm. Amanda mentioned her mom has fibromyalgia, and Dad's mentioned Pam needing to rest more than most people, but I've never really noticed it.

I've never really been alone with Pam, either.

A jumble of thoughts race through my mind as I realize that needs to be rectified. If I want to spend the rest of my life with Amanda, Pam's part of the deal.

Just like my dad is for Amanda.

I think Amanda gets the short end of the stick in this deal.

The expectant look on Pam's face turns to mild concern as seconds tick by and I don't answer. Damn. Need to come up with something other than, *I want to marry your daughter after that mess in Vegas but she doesn't believe me.*

Pretty sure that would be a mistake to blurt out.

"Amanda has informed me that she requires a proper courting."

"She has? You mean, practically marrying a cat after drinking entheogenic wine in Vegas wasn't enough?"

"Apparently, she requires more."

"She always was a demanding child," Pam says. "Ice cream was never enough. Had to have her jimmies on top, too."

I see where Amanda gets her dry wit.

I've never talked to the mother of someone I've dated, much less bantered with one, so this conversation feels about as comfortable as my breeches right now.

"Courting is a tradition done in preparation for marriage," she says softly.

"Yes."

"Is that...are you two planning for this?"

One of us is.

"Mom!" Amanda calls out. "Can you help me with these buttons?"

Saved by the costume.

Pam starts to stand, her body achingly slow as she rises up. It's like watching the Tin Man stand before having his hinges oiled.

"Coming!" Pam calls out.

I break out into a sweat instantly.

Damned thick clothing.

A minute later, Elizabeth Bennet walks through the front door, Amanda's hair tucked up in the bonnet, her face framed by a three-quarter-circle hat with ruffles.

She looks, well...

Ridiculous.

"Charming. Shall we?" I hand her two EpiPens. She tucks both in her purse.

"Where are we going?"

"Courting."

"I meant, where specifically?"

"I thought we'd visit Louisa May Alcott, then Henry David Thoreau."

"How about Shakespeare?"

"Wrong century. And continent."

"Where are you really taking me?"

"'I hoped to obtain your forgiveness, to lessen your ill opinion, by letting you see that your reproofs had been attended to,'" I declare, pulling out the first of about five lines from *Pride and Prejudice* that I've memorized.

She looks at me like I just answered her in Mandarin Chinese.

"Excuse me?"

"Say 'Darcy'!" Pam announces, holding the iPad up.

"Crazy!" Amanda gasps.

"Close enough," I mutter, taking her hand and placing it on my forearm in a formal style, giving the camera a closed-mouth smile. I'm doing my best to look like Colin Firth, which means pretending to look constipated.

These pants have about an hour of life left in them. It's not that hard to pretend.

"You kids have fun!" Pam says, chuckling. "I'll email your dad a photo."

"Why?"

She seems genuinely perplexed. "Because you two look cute."

"I don't understand."

"And because he's your father. He must like seeing you enjoying yourself."

"Still don't understand."

Pam's shoulders lower and the look she gives me deepens. "Don't you—"

"Mom. It's fine. Go ahead and send the picture to James." She peers down the road. "At the rate the neighbors are recording us, the pictures will be all over social media in a half hour anyhow. James can just log in to one of his accounts and download whenever he wants. Jessica Coffin's going to have us all over her Twitter stream within the hour."

Not if I have anything to say about it. I wonder if Cassandra's completed our little project yet. If not, soon.

Amanda squeezes my forearm with a sigh of recognition. "How about we just go on to whatever the next crazy stage of this set-up involves."

"You asked for it."

"I asked for courting. Not *nineteenth-century* courting."

"Blame Gina."

"Gina? What does your admin have to do with this?"

Shit.

"You look so beautiful in that dress."

"*Gina* arranged this?"

"The sunlight makes your eyes look like honey."

"Honey made by *bees*," she says savagely. I start to correct her. Shannon's allergic to bees, not me, but I'm not stupid. Don't correct a woman when she's angry.

Especially when she's angry at *you*.

"Gina arranged this? You handed over your courting plans to your administrative assistant?"

Will reaches for Amanda's hand and helps her up into the carriage, where I hastily get us settled and shut the door.

"Busted," she mutters, turning away from me. "Let me guess. I told you I wanted to be courted and you buzzed Gina and told her to arrange the whole thing."

Shit.

"No! No, not...not really."

"But close."

"If it's any consolation, I got felt up by Hyacinth Bucket's identical twin."

She screws up her face in confusion, opens her mouth to start to ask a question, then slumps in resignation. "I can't believe this. I just wanted a few dates at Legal Sea Foods and some Netflix and Chill."

Hold on.

"But noooooo. Mr. Let-Me-Get-You-A-Six-Foot Anima-tronic-Bear-and-an-Array-of-Solar-Panels-at-a-Fair-Trade-Coffee-Plantation has to turn himself into Fitzwilliam Darcy."

"You wanted the seven-foot bear? Because I can get you the—"

"Andrew!"

I frown. It makes me look even more like Colin Firth. "You really would have been happy with some lobster tails and binge-watching series television while having sex?"

"Not the 'while' part, but yes."

"You said you wanted to be courted!"

"Wooed! Not turned into a Jane Austen novel cosplay!"

"Then why the hell are we wearing these costumes and riding in a carriage drawn by a horse who needs to cut down on fiber in his diet?"

"I don't know! Why don't you ask *Gina*?"

How did this turn into a fight?

The diamond ring is in my front left pocket, burning a hole against my thigh.

A hole of hellfire and damnation.

"You do this," she says slowly, contemplatively, with the air of someone mulling over a topic they've struggled with for a while.

"You hand off complicated issues to your people. And most of the time, that works. Really. It's why you're on top of the business world. You know how to make snap decisions and how to delegate. I've seen it in action, in meetings, and it's astounding. You're brilliant."

I really like the turn this conversation has taken.

"Go on," I urge.

"But."

Uh oh.

"But I am not a task to be managed. That doesn't work in relationships. Or maybe it does, but it doesn't work in a relationship with *me*."

Shit.

The *clop clop clop* of the horse's shoes on pavement comes to a halt, right in front of my shining Tesla. The incongruity would be amusing if my intestines weren't doing an impression of a state fair pretzel.

"Let's talk in the car."

"The car?"

"You thought we were taking this carriage all the way to Walden Pond?"

"Walden Pond? You weren't kidding about visiting Henry Thoreau?"

"I never kid about literature."

"You are such a geek."

"No. I'm not. James McCormick would never allow it."

That's meant to be a joke, but her eyes soften with sympathy. "I'll bet he wouldn't."

"Besides, with a body like this, I could never be a geek." I primp, tightening my arms. I hear seams pop in my tailcoat.

"Geekdom has nothing to do with the body. It's a state of mind. And any guy who would basically turn *Pride and Prejudice* into a LARP is a geek, hot or not."

"LARP? Live-action role-play game? This is an historical re-enactment!" A damn expensive one. One that might cost me my balls, in more ways than one. I re-adjust. There's no room. I really understand why Colin Firth pursed his mouth so much.

"Same thing."

"No, Amanda, they are not the same thing! You think we're playing a *game*?"

"Of course we are. It's just not the game *you* think we're playing."

I didn't think I could fall in love any deeper with her, and then she says *that*.

"I did this because I couldn't think of any other way to make it clear to you that I love you and want to be with you forever."

"Oh." She swivels toward me, eyes wide with surprise. "Oh."

I shrug. Or at least, I try. The coat is so fitted I think I know what it's like for Amanda when she wears a sports bra.

And now all I can think about is her breasts.

Because...breasts.

"You keep saying that you're not good at this whole sharing emotions thing. But you're better than you think."

I don't know what to say.

"And you can become better. With me." Her eyes move down, her focus on me but not piercing, the difference between eye contact and being the center of her attention enough to give me the space to actually share.

"Thank you."

"We can become better, Andrew. Together. That's how this is supposed to work. You share your story with me, and I share my story with you, and over time we have a third story that is ours."

"A better story than the other two."

"It's not a competition." She kisses the tip of my nose. It tickles.

"Everything is a competition, Amanda."

"If that's how you view life, then I can see why you think you're bad at revealing your feelings."

"Explain."

"You can't compete with someone and be authentic at the same time. It's impossible, like trying to orgasm and pee at the same time."

Can't argue with that logic. *Again*.

"You're comparing my difficulties talking about feelings with...that?"

"I suck at analogies. It's a weakness." She shrugs.

No kidding.

But she has a point, in her weird way. Being competitive means using analysis and risk assessment to determine the best approach for gaining the upper hand. Sometimes, it involves subterfuge. Half-truths. Holding cards and revealing information only when it's to your strategic advantage.

As Amanda watches me and her expression deepens with concern, I wonder how much my innate competitiveness has cost me.

And how innate it really is. Was I like this before Dad got ahold of me and turned me into his replacement for Terry? Who is the real Andrew—the guy I am now, or the guy I would have been if Mom had lived?

No.

I can't think this way.

Not the time, not the place.

Especially when I have to drive.

"I'm impressed," she says, as we drive away from the curb, leaving Will with the carriage and a fat tip.

"By all this?"

"By you. All the time you're spending outside. Found the cure for vampirism, eh?"

"I did. It's between your legs."

"Mr. Darcy!" she says viciously.

"And ears! Between your ears, too," I add, but it's obviously an afterthought.

"Why, though? Really."

"What? You can't believe you're really the cure?"

"It's not just me."

It is.

"You are so raunchy." A bubbly laugh, deep and smoky, pours out of her. "Between my legs." She shakes her head, giving me an up-and-down look. "Do you know how porny that sounds, coming from you in that get-up?"

"Is that arousing?"

She whacks me.

"I'm driving!"

"You're vulgar!"

"I'm honest. Damned if I do, damned if I don't."

"What?"

"You want me to tell you how I feel. Just did. And I get hit for it."

"You told me the cure for your fear was my...you know..."

"Vagina."

"How in the hell is a vagina a cure for anything?"

Women really are from another planet. I let out a long sigh and just drive.

I did my research on Mr. Darcy, thank you very much. Aside from having been forced to read Jane Austen's *Pride and Prejudice* five different times in various classes throughout high school and college, I read an executive summary on it this week, and watched the pivotal pond scene on YouTube.

I am practically a scholar at this point.

Walden Pond is the perfect location for an idyllic re-creation of the Colin Firth scene. As we stroll along the shoreline at dusk, I begin to loosen my cravat.

"Is the temperature a touch too warm for you, Mr. Darcy?" Amanda jokes as I slide out of my tailcoat and hand it to her, along with my cravat.

I begin pulling off my boots, tugging just hard enough on the strings below the knees to make the entire assemblage of breeches pull on items further north. My eyes water.

Could these pants be any tighter?

"I, Ms. Bennet, strive for historical accuracy."

She eyes the water, her bonnet framing her face and making those eyes seem impossibly larger. Amanda becomes a historical re-enactor of a Regency-era Powerpuff Girl.

"You are not!"

"I am."

And with that, I race toward the water and do a shallow dive, the long tails of my shirt pulling out of my pants, causing drag but giving me a little breathing room in my waistband.

In the water, I am me. Technically, I am supposed to be Mr. Darcy, but right now, as I do the butterfly stroke that made me a conference champion for my college swim team, I'm Andrew McCormick. Within minutes, I'm a quarter mile into the clear, otherwise-placid lake, the water revitalizing, welcoming me home.

Swimming wasn't my first sport. It welcomed me when I learned about my wasp allergy, taking my football-honed body and turning it into a sleek water baby. I hated making the change at first, but in time I learned to love it. Being here in the water, using rhythm and muscle memory to come back to Amanda with a push and a roar, makes me break surface and stand, laughing in the waning sun, watching her watch me as she claps and giggles.

Courting.

Turns out she was right.

"Mr. Darcy, I can't keep my eyes off your wet chest underneath that soaked shirt," she says in a sultry voice that is about as close to Elizabeth Bennet as Marie is to the Queen of England. "But I never took you for a show-off!"

I'm standing in waist-deep water, watching her on the shore as she laughs.

"'Where there is a real superiority of mind, pride will be always under good regulation.'"

"Oh, God, you're quoting the book again, aren't you?"

"Just substitute 'swimming' for 'mind' and it's correct."

She closes her eyes and quietly says in a slow, halting voice, "'Nothing is more deceitful than the appearance of humility. It is often only carelessness of opinion, and sometimes an indirect boast.'"

"That's my line!" In fact, it's one of the five I memorized. Damn.

"'I could easily forgive your pride, if you had not mortified mine.'"

I've gravely underestimated Amanda's knowledge of this book.

I am starting to think I gravely underestimate *everyone*.

"'I have been meditating on the very great pleasure which a pair of fine eyes in the face of a pretty woman can bestow,'" I counter. Hah. Take *that*.

Her expression is one of approval.

I walk slowly out of the water, suddenly stripped of the desire to continue the charade, wanting only her. Now. Here.

The masquerade has been fun and silly, but it is just that: a mask. A shell, a suit of armor designed to call her bluff in a memorable manner, but the bluff's been called. We're done with the cute ritual, and while I know Amanda didn't want—or expect—any of this, it's symbolic.

We don't need this.

We just need each other.

The water brushes against my bare ankles and I emerge, watching her as she stands on shore, still in the silly bonnet, mouth open with a belly laugh, a single curl escaped and flowing over her eyebrow. She's in my arms, squirming as my wet body presses against hers, the dress made for costume and thinner than an authentic Regency-era frock would be, and I'm thankful as my thighs capture the warm swell of hers, my belly against hers, those sweet breasts smashed against my wet shirt.

My pants tighten.

"Ever had sex outdoors, Mr. Darcy?" she whispers while biting my earlobe.

"No." Not a fantasy. Not even close.

Her hands are on my breeches flap, trying to unbutton me.

I can be flexible. The patch of greenery behind that bush on the shoreline has potential.

"Did you glue these on?" she asks with a grunt, both hands on the left-side button of the weird flap that passes for a "fly" on my pants. I pivot, because the ring is in the other pocket.

"What do you mean?"

"I can't unbutton it."

My erection's making the pants tighten horribly. I reach down and try.

I fail.

"As enticing as outdoor sex is, how about we settle for good old-fashioned bedroom sex with a wine chaser?"

"Done." Her laugh has the promise of a lush few hours buried in her and my blood rushes through me, ready for it all.

I pat my front pocket, ready to reach in for the ring, because now is the time.

Now.

I'm ready to propose.

"In vain have I struggled. It will not do. My feelings will not be repressed. You must allow me to tell you how ardently I admire and love you,'" I call out, using Darcy's most famous line.

"You can stop with the quotes, Andrew! I'm a sure thing!" she calls back, already a few yards ahead of me.

I pat my front breeches pocket again.

Hmmm.

Maybe it's in the other pocket.

No. Just touched that when I was fiddling with the buttons. It's flat, too.

Must be in my coat, which is hanging on a branch a few feet to Amanda's left. I zag as I approach her and grab the coat, putting it on casually, grinning at her as she tilts her head, slightly off kilter.

I pat myself down like a TSA agent searching a patchouli-oil-coated guy after Burning Man.

Nothing.

Where the hell is the ring? I know I had it. It was in the front pocket of my breeches when I got out of the Tesla. No question.

None.

# Chapter Eighteen

"The mosquitoes are coming out in full force," she says, smacking her arm. "Open the car door!"

I smash my palms against my breeches pockets, then rifle through the coat again.

Losing the ring is bad. Bad bad bad.

But where is the key ring for my car?

"You don't have the keys?" I call out, knowing it's a hopeless question, but trying anyhow. We all have our verbal Hail Marys.

"Why would I have your key fob? You drove." She reaches in her purse. "All I have are two EpiPens and a tampon."

"Right." Can't start the car with those. Those tampon commercials say you can swim with them, horseback ride with them, drive with them...

They *lie*.

"What's wrong? Can't find the key?"

"No."

"Maybe you dropped it? On shore?" There's still enough light as the sun starts to set. We both sweep the bare-ground shoreline. It shouldn't be hard to spot the key fob, a bright red leather object with the logo on it. Unlike a standard car key, the key fob is designed to let me unlock and start the car as long as I have it on me.

I clearly don't have it on me, and neither does Amanda.

"It has to be somewhere!" she says, exasperated.

We both turn slowly, in tandem, and stare at the water.

"No," I groan. "Oh, no."

"Oh, God." Me and my swimming, showing off my fly stroke, powerful kicks and strokes churning the water.

These damn pants and their buttons. Weird pockets. My key fob.

But worse—

*The engagement ring.*

I can't let her know about the velvet box. Losing the keys to the Tesla is bad enough.

Losing her engagement ring? Talk about a major screw-up. Teasing Declan for the ring in the tiramisu mistake is pure gold. I can't give him leverage with my own proposal catastrophe.

My pride is at stake here.

Amanda wades into the water in her costume and bends at the waist, her arms pumping up and down in a pattern.

"What are you doing?"

"Searching for the key fob."

"Amanda, there's no way we can find them. Look at the size of this pond. It could be anywhere." And I had to show off and swim a quarter mile sprint into the middle, then back. On the other hand, my butterfly skills are still quite impressive almost a decade out of college.

I still got it.

"You lost the keys! How will we get home?"

"We'll call."

"With *what*? Our phones are locked in the car, Mr. Leave-the-Technology-Behind-for-Authenticity."

Shit.

Wading in, I give it a try, replicating her hand motions. Searching for a set of car keys and a jeweler's box in a giant pond is like having sex for the first time and trying to find the clitoris. You know it's there, and you know that finding it will change your life forever, but you also have a sinking suspicion that the search is futile.

Yet desperation drives you to continue.

As dusk settles over the placid waters, another similarity hits me.

We'll be searching in the dark soon.

"I can fix this," Amanda mutters to herself. "How hard can it be to find a set of keys?" I look past her. The pond is pretty big. They should call it Walden *Lake*. I had to do a quarter mile, didn't I? And back.

The Tesla key fob could be anywhere. If I had my smartphone, I could use the keyless-entry app. If I had my key fob, I could access my phone.

I am in a double bind of my own creation.

Which means we have only one option.

"Stop," I say, making my way slowly through the water to Amanda, who is starting to shiver. I pull her to me, my heart slamming in my chest. I'd pumped myself up for this moment, a grand pronouncement after even grander gestures, all the hope in my heart poured into a diamond ring that symbolized a promise.

A promise that is being eaten by fishes right now.

Aside from losing a mid-five-figure ring and my car keys, which is bad enough, I've lost the potential for this evening.

I feel like a ten-thousand pound millstone.

And I can't say a thing about the ring.

She's not shivering. The shaking I'm feeling is laughter. It's the raw, bony laughter that comes from bitterness and surrender.

"The phones are in the car. The keys are in the water," she says.

The engagement ring is at the bottom of the pond.

"And we were about to have sex in the bushes," she adds.

I groan.

A long sigh, and then she adds, "We have to accept the facts. Let's start walking."

I look down at my historically-accurate shoes, which are about as comfortable as a pair of drag-queen stilettos.

She's right, though. As dusk settles in, the mosquitoes kick up. My pants are soaked through, though my coat's still dry, hanging on a bush branch. I ease my wet shirt into it and shake like a wet dog.

"I can't believe you did something so impulsive. So ridiculous."

*Ridiculous.*

That damn word.

"You're never going to live this one down, Andrew."

She's right.

And then she kisses me.

Costumes be damned. I'm half wet, have lost my keys and the carefully-chosen engagement ring that was handmade and inscribed with the words, *There's a pair of us* on the inside. We are stuck in the middle of nowhere, looking like historical re-enactors from a film set, and it's at least a mile to walk to Route 2, where we might find a gas station.

And Amanda is *kissing* me.

"This is the most romantic gesture any man has ever made for me."

"It damn well better be!"

Her laugh is almost painful to hear, the melodious chords of her voice strummed by amusement, frustration, disbelief and a charming sense that, for as much as I screwed this up, we're in it together.

Fate.

She's being fatalistic about the next few hours.

I'm being fatalistic about the rest of my life.

I open my mouth, feeling my knee bend just enough, the movement hard to resist. *Propose now*, a part of me hisses, the echo in my chest making my heart vibrate.

And yet I don't. I can't. It needs to be better than this.

I can do better than this.

I sling my arm around her shoulders and we begin the arduous walk up the dirt shore, to the path that takes us to Route 126. I don't know what we face if we head south, and Route 2 is a busy road to the north.

"Route 2?"

"Hopefully someone will give us a ride. Or just let us use a phone before we have to walk that far," I say with a sigh. This is befuddling. I haven't been this—yeah, I'll say it—*helpless* in years.

Not since I woke up in a hospital bed thirteen years ago.

"No phone. No car. No direction."

*No engagement ring.*

"This'll be one hell of a story to tell our kids," she says under her breath as we continue, turning left.

Kids.

My right knee starts to bend again, and my hand drifts to her waist. If I just stop right now and ask, she'll say yes, right? She just mentioned kids. *Our* kids.

Instead, I stall.

"You really want four kids?" I ask, remembering Josh's comment back in Vegas.

"I did."

"You *did*? As in past tense?"

"I'm an only child. I always thought having a big family would be the answer to all my problems."

"You have problems? You're the most with-it person I know."

She quirks an eyebrow. "You must not know many functional people, then."

I mull that one over as I smack a mosquito on my neck. "No. I don't."

A car whizzes by. We wave. The driver ignores us.

"Damn," I shout.

"It's Boston. What do you expect, Andrew? Would you pull over for some guy dressed like Napoleon and a woman with him who looks like she belongs in a Mormon split-off cult?"

I give her a long look.

She's right.

The sepia-toned daylight peeks through the woods, giving dusk an eerie look. We walk on the pavement, next to each other, footsteps smaller than normal because of our strange shoes.

This is not going well.

"What about you?"

"I'm pretty with-it."

She bumps me with her elbow. "I meant kids."

"I want them. Not yet, but some day."

"How many?"

"Nine."

She begins coughing uncontrollably.

"Nine?"

"That's right. I like my women barefoot and pregnant."

"You can't even say that with a straight face."

"I'm not smiling. That's me grimacing from these tight breeches."

She takes a peek behind me, pulling up the tails of my coat. "Damn fine breeches they are, too."

"For someone who doesn't want nine kids, don't make comments like that."

"Good thing kids come out one at a time. Mostly."

This conversation makes me want to pull her into the bushes and have sex.

"Amanda, I—" We stop and I reach for her left hand, rubbing her knuckles, worrying the finger that was supposed to have my ring on it by now. We should be back on shore, kissing and whispering words of love and commitment. We should be on the phone, telling our families and friends, making plans for celebration, racing back to my apartment in my car and making love with wild abandon on my bed.

Or couch.

Or kitchen counter.

I'm not picky.

Instead, we're walking in the worst shoes ever on a messily-paved state route, hoping for a good samaritan or cop to come along and rescue us from my courting madness.

"You what?" she asks, picking up where I began.

"I think I'm losing feeling in my testicles."

Her face scrunches with dismay and disbelief. "So...no kids, then?"

"Not if we don't get help soon."

Moment blown. Again.

A car flies by. This time, I jump out in front of it, hoping to force the person to stop. Instead, they swerve, grazing the thick bushes along the berm, and lay on the horn. Two sets of glaring eyes meet mine and go blurry as they accelerate.

"Asshole," I mutter.

"You're going to get yourself run over," Amanda tasks.

Who cares? The night might improve if we could get an ambulance out here for a ride back to civilization.

Ten minutes later, we're closer to Route 2, and no additional cars have passed. I assume it's been ten minutes. Maybe it's only been three. Maybe it's been an hour. We don't talk, focused entirely on walking, and my clothes feel like I'm wearing a giant body-sized wet cotton condom.

That is slowly drying and adhering to my body.

A low buzz comes from behind me and I duck, flinching, mind splintering.

The sound disappears.

My jaw tightens, all the muscles in my face turning to lead. Picking up the pace, I realize this is what it feels like to have everything fall apart. It's insane. This doesn't happen to me. To people like me.

Another buzz fills me, a low-grade hum that makes me walk faster, painful shoes be damned.

A red Mazda Miata, driven by a guy who's wearing a fraternity shirt, flies by.

"HEY! HEY, MAN! STOP!" I bellow, moving out into the road. His companion is a young blonde, her hair whipping behind her like a veil as the guy turns into a lead foot and throws a lit cigarette at me.

In fury, I grab a rock and throw it.

Something dings.

"Andrew!" Amanda gasps. "You can't do that!"

The convertible keeps going, disappearing around a corner.

"AAARRRRGGHH!" I scream, knowing my shout is half frustration, half pain, and half karma.

"Route 2! It's close!" Amanda says, catching up to me. A few more steps and I see the traffic light. "Forget about that asshole."

"What do we do once we're there?" I ask, rage pounding my skin.

"Hitchhike. Hope a cop car comes along."

"Hope?"

"We have to get home somehow."

"Why don't we just knock on someone's door and ask for help?" My voice drips with sarcasm.

It flies over her head. "There aren't any houses here. Look." To the right, cars whiz by on the multi-lane highway, a huge solar farm taking over a stretch of land. Up ahead, if we can safely cross without a sidewalk, is the town of Concord, where surely someone can lend us a phone.

Or a crowbar for my pants.

We reach the light. No cars appear on our side, so we move twenty feet to the right, contemplating what to do.

Someone honks. Another person honks. We ignore them. Masshole drivers are a way of life here.

The light changes and the honking resumes, a few beeps followed by one long push as a car carrying a brown canoe on top slows down and turns on its blinkers, pulling up to us.

Wait.

That's not a canoe.

It's a piece of shit.

Being driven by a very familiar Masshole.

# Chapter Nineteen

"Need a lift?" Declan's peering at me through Shannon's open window in the Turdmobile.

"No, thanks. We're fine walking," I say, turning away.

Amanda lets out an exasperated sigh, unties her bonnet, pulls it off and hits me with it. "Get in."

"Yeah, Mr. Darcy. Get in," Declan says. "This is going to be one hell of a story."

If only he knew.

"I'm fine. I'll just wait to catch a ride from someone. If I'm lucky, the Zodiac Killer will come along any minute."

"He dresses better than you. Get in." Dec's snapping command makes me just stand there, weighing out my options, which boil down to one:

Get in the Turdmobile.

I hate when he's right.

"What are you doing here in this part of town?" I ask as Amanda opens the back door to the tiny compact, folding her glorious ass into the tiny backseat. I'm not sure my limbs bend that much. I'm not sure I won't split my ass seam if I try to get in.

"I think that's the question we should be asking you." Shannon can't stop laughing. "We were scouting out future locations for Grind It Fresh! coffee shops in the suburbs. What the hell happened to you two?"

"What? Haven't you seen two people out on a simple date before?" I come two inches short of needing a shoe horn to sit behind Shannon. My balls feel like they're in the trunk.

"Where's your car?"

"Back at Walden Pond."

"What happened?"

"Mr. Darcy went for a swim and lost the key fob to the Tesla," Amanda says bitterly.

"In the water?" Shannon exclaims, laughing.

"Probably. Maybe in the bushes. I don't know," I grumble. "But we looked. It's gone."

"Why didn't you call someone for help?"

"Phones are locked in the car."

"And you walked all the way to Route 2 in those outfits?" Declan hoots. "How embarrassing."

"Oh, no," I grouse. "The embarrassing part is happening right now."

"Telling the story?" Shannon asks.

"Riding in this piece of shit."

Declan snickers. "Thanks. We're testing out a new logo— notice the Grind It Fresh! wrap on it?"

"All I see is a pile of metal excrement."

"This was my car for nearly two years!" Amanda says, patting the door's armrest like it's a cat. "Nothing wrong with it." She frowns. "Now that I think about it, you never rode in it with me."

Coincidence.

"You are so status conscious!"

Amanda says that like it's a bad thing.

I hunch down as Declan merges into traffic. No one says a word, though Shannon and Declan are giving each other looks like they are stars in a Mexican telenovela performed by mimes.

We cross the Lexington line. Getting closer.

"We need gas. Shannon, can you find us a gas station?"

She pulls out her smartphone and uses an app, programming the GPS to re-route.

"Can't it wait?" I ask. This car is a tin can.

JULIA KENT

"No. The car's on empty and we need to stop."

Three minutes later, he's pulling off the highway and into a gas station bay.

"No full serve," Declan says with a sigh.

Shannon opens her door.

"Why are *you* getting out?" Amanda asks.

"Because Declan doesn't know how to pump gas."

Amanda snorts. "What?"

"Why is that funny?" I ask.

Dec cocks an eyebrow and gives Shannon a pointed look. "See?"

"You can't pump gas, either?" Shannon asks me, incredulous.

"It's not that I can't. It's just—why would I? That's what Gerald and Lance are for. They keep the gas tanks full on all our cars. And now I have a Tesla."

"This is what I have to look forward to?" Amanda mutters, opening her car door with a sigh. "I'll help Shannon."

"It takes two people to fill a gas tank?" I whisper to Declan.

He shrugs. "Guess so. I don't know how it works. Once, I was in the limo when Gerald had to stop and refill it at a regular gas station and not at the Anterdec pump in the building garage. He did it alone."

"But he's a professional. It's his job. I guess Shannon needs help."

We shrug.

Declan twists in his seat and shakes his head, obviously enjoying my predicament. "What happened back there? Were you about to propose?"

I jolt. "How'd you guess?"

"Andrew, why the hell else would you be dressed like something out of a Masterpiece Theatre presentation?"

"Fine. Yes."

"And?"

Damn. Better to get it out now while the women aren't here.

"Don't say anything to Amanda."

"She said no?"

"I couldn't ask her."

"Lost your nerve?"

"No. Lost the ring and my key fob."

"You *what*?" His eyes comb over me. "Holy shit. You re-created the pond scene from *Pride and Prejudice*? Complete with the Mr. Darcy swimming scene?"

"How do you know that?"

"You're getting my backseat all wet, and because I've seen that stupid miniseries about ten times since Shannon and I got together. It's on the Top 10 Period Weekend movie list." He snorts. "You lost the ring? *Lost* it? Thank God you didn't have Mom's engagement ring after all."

"Dec, you set the bar for proposals in this family pretty damn low. I have to thank you for that. I may have lost my car keys and my engagement ring in Walden Pond, but my woman didn't end up in the Emergency Room."

"Yet."

"You're such an optimist."

"Realist."

"Pessimist."

"CEO."

"So am I."

He looks at my crotch and frowns. "Is something bad going on in your pants?"

"You're stooping to penis jokes?" But he has a point. Walking has become increasingly painful. Sitting in this backseat is even worse. Professor Kensley-Wentingham's warning dings in the back of my mind. Something about the pants being made in such a way that they should never, ever get wet.

Tears fill my eyes and I flinch as some short and curlies get caught in a seam while I try to get comfortable in this shitmobile.

"Dealing with some shrinkage?"

I give him a sharp look.

"I meant the fabric. It looks like it's molding to your body. You're a human papier-mâché."

"Let me borrow your phone." I don't give him a choice, snatching it off the dash. "What's Gina's number?" I snap.

"How the hell would I know your admin's—"

"Never mind." One tap and Grace answers.

"Grace! Can you connect me to Gina?"

"Mr. McCormick? This is Denesh, from the temp agency. I am sorry, but Grace has left me with firm instructions that I am never to contact her for any reason, even if you offer me five-figure bribes."

"Connect me to Gina San Giotti. She's Andrew McCormick's admin." I'm talking about myself in the third person. Desperate times call for desperate measures.

"Yes, sir."

One minute later.

"Yes?"

"Gina, it's Andrew."

"Yes, Mr. McCormick?"

"Get the theater professor on the phone for me."

"Professor Kensley-Wentingham?"

"Yes."

"May I ask the reason?"

"He's about to lose reproductive abilities," Declan calls out.

If I could stretch forward, I'd hit him, but self-preservation is a stronger instinct than anger.

So far.

"I'm experiencing a wardrobe malfunction," I explain.

"Wardrobe malfunction? Like Janet Jackson at the Super Bowl?" Gina gasps.

"*Exactly* like that."

"Are you with Justin Timberlake?" she squeals. "Can you get me his autograph? You meet lots of famous people, don't you? Could you get him to sign my *NSYNC poster from when I was a kid?"

Gina can be a touch too literal.

"No. Get the professor on the phone."

"Yes, sir?" She sounds like she's about to cry.

Silence, then:

"Andrew!" Professor Kensley-Wentingham chirps. "How is your marriage proposal?"

"I have a problem. The pants got wet."

She clears her throat softly, twice, in rapid-fire succession, like a '57 Chevy revving the engine. "Oh, dear. Well, it happens to every man some time. Don't believe the ones who say it doesn't. You get overly excited, and when sexually aroused, the cannon can fire a bit early—"

"Not *that*!" I shout in horror. "Water. I went swimming in the costume. In a pond."

"WHAT? Why on earth would you ruin my beautiful costume with such an atrocious, impulsive act?"

"*My* costume. I paid for it. And I can't feel my legs. The button holes have shrunk to the point where I cannot unbutton the front flap. I am trapped in my own breeches."

"Circulation will be an issue," she says tersely. "You need to take the breeches off."

"Take them *off*?"

Declan's booming laugh is so close to Terry's that I jump.

"Immediately. As the fibers shrink, you will find yourself in an increasingly uncomfortable situation."

I look at the car. "Already happened."

"If you are able, remove the breeches. Where are you? I am happy to come to your location and help."

I'll bet you are.

"No, thank you. I'm perfectly capable of taking my own pants off, Professor."

Amanda climbs in the car and whirls on me. "Who are you talking to?"

"The costumer."

"But Andrew, you have been *sewn into* the pants, remember? You wanted authenticity," Professor Kensley-Wentingham declares.

*Sniff.*

"At this point, screw authenticity. I'd like to hold onto some surviving sperm. I want children someday."

I hang up on her.

And with that, I reach behind me and rip the seam.

"Thank God," Amanda and I say in unison, for completely different reasons. The seam in the back was a long one, so the pants are completely useless. The cold feel of cheap vinyl is a relief as I peel the front panel of the breeches off me, wincing.

"It's like you're getting a free waxing," Amanda marvels.

Dec won't stop laughing.

*Tap tap tap.*

I look up and out my window to see a uniformed police officer looking right back at me.

Then at my hands in my undressed lap. I scurry to pull my shirttails over my open pants.

"This just gets better and better," Declan gasps.

"Excuse me, sir? Please roll down the window slowly." The cop is wearing a hat and I can't see his eyes.

"Officer? Is there a problem?"

"Your junk is resting on my backseat, Andrew. Of course there's a problem," Declan hisses. "You're paying to steam clean the car when this is over."

"Shut up, Declan!"

"I need you to roll down the window, sir. We had a series of reports about a man and woman in period costume harassing people at Walden Pond, and you fit the description. Did you throw a rock at a red convertible on Route 126?"

"Oh, God."

"I'm going to have to ask you to step out of the car, sir."

Amanda's mouth is open, eyes the size of globes, and she lets out a shaky breath.

"Dec?" I ask, pinching the bridge of my nose as I prepare for the inevitable.

"Yeah?"

"Get Grace to call the family lawyer."

"Will do."

"Sir." The cop's voice has gone firm. "You need to step out here."

"I can't."

"You *can't*?" I can hear the felony charge in his voice.

"I'm not wearing any pants."

He frowns. "You realize I could charge you with public indecency if that's true."

Dec is holding back laughter so hard he's crying.

"Technically, I have pants on. But I had to rip them off."

"Rip them off?"

"I was losing circulation to my stones." When confronted with possible arrest, my Scottish roots emerge.

"Stones?"

Amanda leans over my lap, looks up, and says, "Al?"

"Amanda?"

"You set this up?" I sit up in shock so fast my head bangs against the car ceiling.

"No! This is a true coincidence!" she says to me. "Hey, Al! Sorry to cause trouble. We were just doing a re-enactment of parts of *Pride and Prejudice*. You know, Jane Austen?"

"You two are into that?"

Amanda gives him a sweet smile that goes all the way to double dimples. "You know."

His eyes go to my lap, then her face. "Right. But the pants...?"

"These old costumes." She plants a possessive hand on my thigh, moving the cloth just enough that I really am in danger of public indecency. Her hand right *there* is like pouring Miracle-Gro on a tomato plant. "They tear. Andrew was in the middle of a sword battle when they split."

"Sword battle!" Al's estimation of me goes up while his eyes remain glued to her hand. "Good for you."

"I learned from the best," I say. "My brother's really good at digging in the knife."

Al slaps the car once. "Well, then, if it's just you two playing around, you're good to go. I'd recommend a spare set of pants, though, for you there, uh..."

"Andrew."

"Right. Andrew."

Dec turns on the car.

"Are we free to go?" Shannon asks nicely.

"Sure."

Amanda waves to Al as Declan pulls back onto the road and follows the GPS.

"That did not happen," I grunt. "You tell Dad, I will kill you."

"I won't tell Dad."

"I mean it, Dec."

"Jessica Coffin already has pictures of you two on her Twitter stream," Shannon says sadly. She holds up her phone and hands it to Amanda.

"'Andrew McCormick takes his zombies seriously,'" she reads. "What does that even mean?"

"See?" I grumble, holding my junk carefully. The shocks on this piece-of-shit car are terrible, and my boys are pretty blue. "She's losing her touch."

"Wait a minute," Amanda says, tapping the screen. "Her account—just now! Where'd it go?"

"Where'd it go?" Shannon repeats. "What do you mean? It's right there."

"I hit refresh. It's gone."

"Gone?" Shannon's face lifts with a triumphant smile. "Good riddance to bad rubbish."

My project has been fulfilled. I just unplugged Jessica Coffin's influence.

At least something went right today.

# Chapter Twenty

Saturdays like this are rare in Massachusetts. The wide, open sky is a shade of blue you only find in a jeweler's shop, and the light wind is a relief from the sweltering late-summer air. After a string of muggy days where breathing feels like drowning, the change is welcome.

And today is a day for nothing but change.

The path away from the giant patch of grass where the town has carved out fifteen regulation-sized soccer fields is well marked, but my eyes can't seem to find it. The sign is right there: "Honeysuckle Path," with the piece of wood carved into the shape of an arrow, the words burned into the wood in a quaint, quasi-colonial font designed to add prestige to the town, one of the oldest in the state. I read the words, but my brain doesn't process them, and then—like a bird of prey with telescopic sight—it all clicks.

I take my first step on the bare-dirt line in the center of wild weeds. This park land was set aside for families and school children to use as a nature preserve, for sports, for picnics and hikes.

And this is where my mother died.

Her grave is not here. Elena Montgomery McCormick's final resting place is in a cemetery a few towns away. But this is where she took her last breath.

A breath I never saw.

I come here when I want to torture myself. Always at night,

and always in the cooler seasons. Cross-country skiers burrow tracks in the winter and I follow them, head down, always pausing right by the bridge where she died.

Where I almost died.

Where, for years, I wished I'd died.

Declan's never been back here, as far as I know, and I can't blame him.

Knowing what I know now from Terry about Dad's treatment of Declan, I need to come here. After she died, Grace set up therapists for Declan and me, but the sessions were short. We were fine. Trauma? What trauma? It was a freak accident.

I was the freak.

My skin itches, the bright sun pouring down on me, my body uncovered, a short-sleeved polo, shorts, and sneakers all I chose to wear. Vince is right: I take greater risks every day just driving to work.

But living a life hidden in darkness and cold was never about logical risk assessment and playing the odds.

I almost invited Amanda to join me here, today. Almost.

As I walk, I hear the rumble of car engines behind me, a flurry of activity, then shouts and screams of kids unbound. Music from an ice cream truck jingles in the background, blending with the muted cacophony of childhood fun. That day, thirteen years ago, when I was a forward on my team and taking a break between games to go for a hike with Dec and Mom, I remember Dec asking if we could grab an ice cream bar.

And I said, "Coach doesn't want us loading our stomachs with junk."

Those were some of the last words my mother ever heard from me.

What if I'd said yes? What if we'd gone to the parking lot instead and had Mom chide us for eating too much sugar, had Dec buy us each two chocolate-coated bars, had shoveled them in like the growing teens we were? What if I'd paused and what if, what if, what if?

Thirteen years of *what ifs*.

Except none of those comes even close to the *what if* Declan carries inside him.

It's the question I can't ask him.

It's the question he asks himself every day.

As I reach the split in the path, another *what if* assaults me, the Y in the road a dimension splicer, my dead mother down one path, my living mother down the other. We picked the right-hand path out of sheer randomness, a decision that meant nothing in the moment, yet everything three minutes later.

When Amanda jumped in the water to rescue the animals at Dec and Shannon's wedding, she made one of those instinctual decisions, the kind that makes sense at the time.

Everything makes sense at the time.

Until it doesn't.

Fresh air assaults my lungs, the scent of freshly-mowed grass nauseating. It takes me back thirteen years ago, my legs shorter, tighter, body all elbows and knees, getting used to my newfound height. It was the very end of sophomore year and I just got my driver's license. Mom let me drive. Declan mocked me endlessly from the backseat, calling me "Grandma" at every intersection.

But I drove, proudly.

I'm here as an exercise in futility, an attempt to inoculate myself against memories of evil in quarter-ounce doses. The dose makes the poison, right? That's the saying.

What if Mom had only been stung once?

What if I'd been stung before and we'd known about my allergy?

What if. That's what I want on my grave.

*What if.*

I don't want to put Amanda through a life of *what if*. Our fight that day, two months ago, at the wedding fittings wasn't about fear. Not the kind of fear everyone thinks.

It was about love.

The kind of love so strong you'll push it aside for the sake of preserving the other.

A chipmunk chatters at me as it leaps over a cluster of rocks, pausing to stand on hind legs and stare. Deeming me too inconsequential for more of its precious time, it skitters off into the woods, the rustling of leaves my only way to track it. Concentrating on minutiae like that is easier than thinking about the fact that I tried. I tried to push Amanda away, and I tried to save her from all the what ifs that come in the baggage I carry with me.

The god-damned ocean liner I pull through life via a yoke around my neck.

But I failed to account for an important variable.

Turns out, she loves me enough to push back. To stay. To accept the *what ifs* as part of the equation that says if—and only if—love can be so profound that a mother would sacrifice herself for her son, then maybe he should find someone to love that much.

To pass on the legacy.

To live out my mother's greatest wish.

That I live.

"What am I supposed to do, Mom?" I say, as if she can hear me. As if she's here, right now, with that intense look of listening that you only got out of her when you changed the timbre of your voice to cut through the busyness of being James McCormick's wife. Mom did that. Stopped everything for us when we needed her most.

Nothing else was more important.

This is the part where I stop at that damned spot by the bridge and exorcise my demons. Talk to Mom and tell her how great Amanda is and how I wish she were alive to know her. That's all a given. I don't do that.

Instead, I pick up a handful of rocks and start throwing them, one by one, in rhythm to slow, deep breaths.

This is where I should have died.

This is where I didn't die.

And this is where a single wasp could kill me.

"Fuck wasps," I whisper, using Vince's mantra. "Fuck wasps." I bend down and pull out the hem of my shirt, turning it into a holding place for more rocks, mindless and stupid, just a guy gathering rocks to throw in the water.

And then I throw.

Each stretch of my arm takes about ten seconds, and as I calculate the value of my time spent collecting and throwing rocks, I say, Vince's mantra over and over.

Vince is right.

It's surprisingly cathartic.

Until a little voice behind me chimes in and echoes me.

"Fuck wasps. Auntie Shannon, what does 'fuck wasps' mean?"

I whip around, dropping the end of my shirt, the rocks spilling down my shins, the *plunk plunk plunk* of a hundred stones the backdrop for a wholly unexpected sight.

Shannon and her nephews, Jeffrey and Tyler.

"Why do you want to fuck wasps?" Jeffrey asks.

"Jeffrey!" Shannon scolds him. "Don't say that word."

"What word? 'Wasps'? What's wrong with the word 'wasps'?"

"Jeffrey," she says in a low voice of warning.

Tyler peers up at me, shielding his eyes from the blazing sun. "How do you fuck a wasp?"

"Very carefully," Jeffrey whispers, laughing at his own joke.

Tyler doesn't get it.

He damn well shouldn't. The kid's what—seven? Eight?

"You say that word again and no ice cream," Shannon threatens.

Jeffrey's smart. He shuts up instantly.

"*Andrew?*" Shannon asks, her tone changing. "What are you doing here?"

"Reliving old times."

She frowns, then beneath her furrowed brow, her eyes fly open. Taking in the bridge, the water, the soccer fields far off in the distance, she morphs, the realization of where we are sinking in layer by layer.

"Here?" she gasps, then shakes her head very slowly. "I guess I always knew, but didn't think about it when I brought the boys here."

I shrug. My ability to speak is rapidly fading.

"Is Amanda with you?"

I shake my head.

"We're here because of Tyler's soccer game." The soft melody of an ice cream truck grows louder in the distance.

I look down. The kid's wearing shin guards and tall soccer socks, with a sports team shirt for a team sponsored by a local plumbing company. Team colors are the same as mine from thirteen years ago, green and white.

My stomach feels like it's been mowed.

By a flamethrower.

I reach in my back pocket and pull out my wallet, peeling off a twenty. "Here," I say, handing it to Jeffrey. "You and Tyler go get yourselves some ice cream."

He takes the bill but waits, giving Shannon a look of deference that I would find admirable if I weren't half out of my mind right now.

"Can we?"

Her smile is shaky, body language tight and on guard. She can tell I'm upset and she's frantically trying to read the situation. Meanwhile, every inch of my skin is on fire and I'm trapped in tenth grade.

"Sure. Just stay close to Tyler."

The boys run off with hoots and shouts of "thanks!"

"What is wrong?" Shannon's on me in under a second, her face twisted with fear. Small, breathy gasps come out of her. Fresh-faced, no make-up, and with her hair in a messy ponytail, she looks ten years younger, especially in a softball shirt and yoga pants.

"Are you following me?" I joke, only to say something that will override the sound of a hurricane between my ears.

"Andrew." Compassion radiates off her, the fear dissolving like a swarm of emotion broken by some force no one has yet discovered. "What's going on? Did you and Amanda have a fight?"

"Hah. No. The opposite."

"The opposite?"

Two opposing forces square off inside my chest while my mind plays the role of whirling dervish, complete with turban and nausea, but minus the poverty. Declan's groused about the whole "talk about your feelings" bullshit that Shannon and her family engage in.

Maybe there's something to it.

"She doesn't believe me," I confess. Someone is using a jack-hammer in my solar plexus.

"Believe you?"

"That I want to marry her."

Shannon cranes her neck forward in disbelief. "You do?"

"I want to marry her. Really marry her. Propose and the whole bit." I kick the haphazard pile of rocks at my feet off the edge of the bridge.

"Why haven't you?"

"Because I lost the ring in Walden Pond," I mutter under my breath.

"Come again?"

"Because she really doesn't believe me."

"It's a lot of believe."

"I know."

She gives me a sad smile. "Congratulations."

"That is the weakest version of congratulations I have ever experienced."

"Not for realizing you love Amanda and want to be her husband, Andrew. Congratulations for sitting outside with me and joining the human race."

"The vampire thing got old."

She studies me. "Why?"

"Even immortality has its limits."

She punches my shoulder. "C'mon."

I look around, my head tipped up to take in the bright blue sky. Some flying insect buzzes by, high near the leaves of the big oak trees at the edge of the path, and I freeze.

"Because thirteen years is long enough for me to torture myself. It's time to live the life my mother saved." I look at her, catching her eyes, and she's blurry. She needs to work on that. How can the edges of her body become so diffuse? "The life

Declan saved. Mom paid the ultimate price—with her life. But he paid the biggest price of all of us."

Her hand is warm and smooth as she covers the back of mine. "You *all* paid the biggest price. No one's suffering is more or less than anyone else."

"Dec had to choose, though. I was out cold. Mom gave him an impossible choice."

"No. She didn't."

"Right. I know. Mom made him pick me." I huff. "But he didn't have to, and Dad eviscerated him for it."

"James can be a hard man."

"There's more to it, Shannon."

She quickens, eyes darting to the field where the boys went. "More?"

"Do you know why Terry stepped down from Anterdec?"

She blinks hard. "No."

"But you know something."

"Only Declan's comment that Terry and James had a standoff after your mom died, and he and James didn't speak for over a year."

I swallow, as if the bile can ever go down. "That's about all I know, too. My dad is at the center of so much anger. So many secrets. When Mom died, she took all the glue that held us together with her and we just turned into a pile of loose, splintered sticks."

"Your mother raised good sons. Good men."

"So did my father." Defending Dad is reflexive. I've done it for years without thinking, because Terry faded out and Dec and Dad have such a contentious relationship. At some point, I named myself peacekeeper.

No one asked me to do that.

"Yes," she says softly. "He did." She bends down and picks up a handful of rocks, tossing them one by one into the water, staring at the ripples. "When did life become so complex? I thought once I was an adult, it would all be easier."

"Really?" It dawns on me that I've never been alone with

Shannon. We've worked together and been at family events together, but a conversation like this is new.

"You know how when you're a little kid, you think that life is one big series of rules you don't know exist? And you come across them whenever you're trying to do something really exciting and neat?"

"No. We always knew the rules in advance."

"How did you learn to take risks? Break the rules sometimes?"

"In school. Work. But not in life. And after the wasp sting, risk was unacceptable. Another rule of Dad's."

"Is that why it's been so easy for you to be outside again?"

"What do you mean?" If this is easy, I'd hate to see hard.

"Once you realized you were living out a rule you didn't make for yourself, you could drop it."

A slim, green leaf flutters onto the surface of the water, right at the edge near the bank, and floats on one of the ripples caused by the rocks Shannon tosses into the stream. It catches in an eddy, twirling in a circle over and over until the current is so fast in that little whirlpool that it becomes a solid green circle, all the edges blurred into something new.

"You're saying I've been living life as a vampire not because I'm afraid to die, but because I'm afraid I'll disappoint my dad."

She just shrugs and tosses another rock in the water.

It lands right on the leaf, which breaks free from the eddy and wanders downstream, swept away by forces bigger than it can fathom.

"Disappoint him by being the victim of some random wasp, a one in a billion chance, but one with dire consequences." And the consequences aren't death. Look at Declan. Look at what he's had to bear because of that randomness.

And Terry.

And me.

"See? Complex." She gives me a sad smile, her eyes open and searching.

I see why Declan loves her so much.

"Why doesn't Amanda believe me?"

"I think she does."

"Then, when I told her I knew she was the only one for me—when I said I wished we had turned out to be married in Las Vegas—and she dismissed the idea...why?"

"Have you asked her to marry you?"

"No. Not yet."

"Why not?"

An image of the velvet jeweler's box being eaten by a beaver at the bottom of Walden Pond clutters my mind.

"I meant to. Long story."

"The *Pride and Prejudice* stunt?"

"Right."

"Did you say earlier that you *lost* the ring in Walden Pond?" Her eyes crinkle in amusement.

I nod.

"At least she didn't swallow it." Shannon's hand goes to her throat, fingers fluttering at the hollow.

I laugh.

"That's cute—the *Pride and Prejudice* thing—but did she want that?"

"Did she want *what*?"

"All that? The pageantry, the silliness, the finery?"

"She wanted to be courted." My voice lifts on the last word, like a sarcasm breeze blew it into the clouds.

"Did you ask her what she meant by that? What she was really asking for?"

My shoulders drop and I look up at a lone cloud in the sky, a white puff against the bright blue.

"No."

"Why don't you find out what she really wants?"

"And then what?"

"Then give it to her."

I sigh. "When did being an adult become so complex?"

Just as Shannon laughs, Jeffrey and Tyler come running down the path, Jeffrey's shirt pulled out and turned into a holding case for a pile of ice cream bars.

"What's this?" Shannon demands. "Where did you get all this?"

"Andrew gave me a twenty," Jeffrey explains. "So?" He shrugs, as if he's not responsible for the sudden appearance of three bomb pops, two SpongeBob Squarepants ice cream bars, and three Reese's Cup ice cream bars.

"So you bring back change!" she sputters.

Jeffrey gives me an even stare that reminds me of Declan as a kid. "Andrew didn't *say* to bring back the change. You and Mom and Aunt Amy and Grandpa and Grandma always say it."

"JEFFREY!" Shannon explodes, taking in a deep breath, clearly ready to unleash a parental lecture.

"It's fine."

I subvert her.

Jeffrey looks at me like I am a god. Declan told me that little boys are easy—just joke about poop with them. I've got him one-upped.

Buying them lots of ice cream is even better.

"What?" Shannon gasps, all that energy in her lungs ready to do indignant damage.

"It's fine. He's right, even if he's being cunning and using semantics to test out the world."

Jeffrey's eyes narrow. I narrow mine right back as we stare at each other.

That's right, kid. I've got your number.

And in ten years, come work for me.

"But—"

Jeffrey reveals his wares to me, like a dog rolling over and showing his belly in submission. "Pick your poison, Andrew." He glances at Shannon, turns back to me, and says in a very pronounced, stilted voice, "Thank you very much for the treat."

"Thank you!" Tyler says to himself, staring at the googly eyes of his Spongebob popsicle.

Then he eats them, cackling.

"How are we going to eat eight ice creams!" Shannon bursts out.

"Two each," Tyler says.

"Good math." I ruffle his hair and give them each a look I can't quite describe, just as a bee makes a lazy path toward Tyler's ice cream. It's not a wasp, but still...

Shannon starts herding her nephews off the path and back to the relative safety of the asphalted parking lot. There's no panic in her movements. Just a calm, centered aversion to risk. She moves quietly, but with purpose.

I grab an ice cream bar from Jeffrey and rip it open, sinking my teeth through the hard chocolate outer shell, tasting peanut butter and ice as we walk away from the bee.

And walk toward my future.

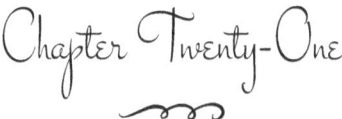

Chapter Twenty-One

I didn't have to ask Amanda what she wanted. I just knew. It's been a month since the Walden Pond fiasco, and we've both been busy. I was gone for nine days, then she was gone for four, and in between has been glorious.

Divine.

And I want so much more.

Arranging dinner tonight, here at Consuela's, is perfect. The exclusive rooftop-garden restaurant owned by my dad's celebrity-chef friend was the site of my first date with Amanda. This place holds meaning for us. Aside from being beautiful and intimate, the expansive view of the ocean gives it a carefree feeling of potential, as if the world were limitless.

I now know that love certainly is.

First, we'll have dinner by candlelight. Then, a special dessert (not tiramisu) and go straight to the proposal. Finally, Dad and Pam and all our family and friends will show up for a big surprise party.

See? Perfect.

And I didn't delegate one bit of it to Gina.

It's seven p.m. and I've cleared the entire restaurant, paid for the night, and Consuela's brought me a fine bottle of red wine, which is airing nicely as I wait for Amanda.

The ring is in my front pants pocket, safe and deep in modern, bespoke trousers. Fool me once, shame on Walden Pond.

Fool me twice, shame on me.

Ten minutes pass and my mind races through all the ways I'll ask her. Imagining her face lighting up the minute the words are out of my mouth has become an endless movie reel in my mind, the flickering images like watching your life pass before your eyes.

Except instead of preceding death, it precedes pure joy.

A lifetime of it.

Now Amanda is twenty minutes late and the server pours my glass of wine. Might as well have a drink to loosen up. I'm sure she's late, caught up with some last-minute task at work.

Nothing to worry about.

By seven thirty I break down and text her.

Five minutes of staring at the screen does not magically result in a reply.

"Andrew?" It's Consuela, looking at me with an expression only older European women can manage, a mix between *So delighted to spend time with you* and *I am so sorry your cat got run over.*

"She's running a bit late. Just texted her," I say with confidence.

Feigned confidence.

Consuela bends and pours me another glass, smiling. "You have the ring?"

I pat my pocket for the umpteenth time. "Yes."

"I knew when you brought her here for that first date, you know. That you would marry her."

"You did?"

"Any woman you brought here who also likes cilantro had to be a good match."

I groan.

"And I could tell by the way you looked at her."

I'm halfway through this second glass of wine and I halt, our eyes locked. I set the glass down. "You could."

"I could. And I was so relieved!" Her voice picks up volume

and she sits in Amanda's chair, pouring a mouthful of wine for herself, swallowing it. Animated eyes look back at me. "My God, child, you of all people need a wife!"

"Excuse me?"

"Andrew, you are the kind of man who cannot be alone."

I frown. "What?"

"Most men are children, content to play with toy after toy, never happy with one that they can use their imagination to turn into a million different playthings."

"But I'm not that guy."

"No. You need one toy to open you to the richness of your inner world."

"One toy."

"One woman."

"Amanda."

"Yes?" The word comes from behind me, low and pleasant, curious and amused.

I jump in my seat, the hand holding the wine glass almost tipping, as Consuela looks up and gives Amanda a grin, standing with her arms open, welcoming my future wife with the kind of gentle openness and sophisticated grace that my mother would have extended to Amanda.

My shirt collar suddenly got tight.

"And now we can start dinner!" Consuela says, giving me a pointed look. "Something other than grapes." She pours the rest of the bottle of wine into my glass and a fresh one for Amanda, and quietly leaves.

I stand and wrap my arms around Amanda, pulling her in to my chest, inhaling the sweet smell of her hair. She's wearing a tight cream-colored dress and a lilac jacket, pearls and high heels, and she's sweet and soft and warm and *everything*.

"I like this welcome," she says to my chest. "I thought you'd be angry I'm so late. I had a work meeting with one of those people who wouldn't stop asking questions that were just about them, and that the other forty of us on the call didn't need to hear, and—"

I cut her off with a kiss. We kiss until she's moaning in my arms, pressing against me to the point where I have to pivot so she can't feel the very hard thing in my pants.

No. Not that.

The ring.

"I *really* like this welcome!' she gasps, looking up at me with smiling eyes. "And this is nostalgic. Our first real date."

"But not our first real kiss."

"No," she says, looking out at the cityscape. "That came more than two years ago."

"Too much time wasted."

A server delivers a breadbasket and oil, explaining the lavender and sage infusion origins as if I care. A strange chatter fills my mind, as if I'm simultaneously listening to an announcer do a play-by-play of every second of my life while living it.

I'm not nervous.

This isn't anxiety.

I'm just hyperaware. It's a skill.

"How was your day? Did the meeting with the Sultan go well?"

I crack a smile and watch her eat the bread. She has this cute way, breaking off tiny pieces, dabbing them in the oil until the piece is completely soaked, then sprinkling salt on it before eating.

I just drink my wine and polish off the bottle.

"Hey there, cowboy. Slow down."

"Why? Gerald's driving."

"I haven't seen you for nearly a week. I want you functional tonight."

"Define functional."

Her leer is all the answer I need.

"The Sultan? I know you were hoping for a win on that."

"Actually, I have to thank Jessica for her help on that."

Amanda drops the piece of bread between her fingers. It plops in the oil with a tiny drop of backsplash that lands in the web of her hand.

"Jessica?"

"Funny story. Her Twitter feed—the one I killed—may have helped me close a nine-figure deal."

Amanda resumes her oil-soaked-bread lovefest. "Explain."

Every move she makes is enchanting. Every word that comes out of her is intriguing. Has she always been so alluring, or are my senses heightened by the presence of the ring in my pocket? I felt like this at Walden Pond for a split second, but it was tempered by the silly pageantry of the *Pride and Prejudice* scene.

This is pure. Unalloyed.

"Andrew?" She nudges me. "Eat some bread. You look like you're already a little drunk."

*Drunk on you.*

Without thought, I imitate her, pulling a tiny piece of bread from my larger chunk and dipping it in the oil. I never do this. She laughs.

The laughter carries on the wind, over the water, and around the earth in full circumference to find its way back to me.

Maybe I am a little drunk.

"The Sultan saw Jessica making nasty tweets about my Pride and Prejudice stunt. She got pictures from God knows who. Turns out, he has a wing of his palace in Dubai that is an exact replica of Pemberley. He called for a video chat and because I am practically an Austen scholar—"

Amanda snorts.

"—we had an extensive conversation, then an intense negotiation, and now Anterdec is the official developer for their new resorts."

"How wonderful!" she claps. "But how did you shut down Jessica? You were the one who killed her Twitter stream? Was this your wedding present to Shannon and Declan?"

"No, but that would have been a great idea." I chuckle as the server brings another bottle of wine and pours. This time, I sip. "No, I had Anterdec's local media buyer contact every single outlet where we advertise and gently inform them Anterdec's ad money would go elsewhere if they didn't stop retweeting her."

"But that wouldn't shut down her account."

"And I called my former husband, Josh—"

She starts choking on her bread.

"—who is an accomplished hacker. Gave him a video. He uploaded a link on her Twitter account. She killed her own account all by herself."

"What was the video?"

"Can we talk about something else?" The server brings two ramekins filled with some kind of dip and a pile of fist-sized shrimp. The video is a secret I'd like to hang onto for a little longer. No need to air out *everything* in my past just yet. "I'd like a dinner out that doesn't involve Jessica."

"Or videos of transvestites who look like her, kissing you."

"Or images in my mind of you *actually* kissing her," I add in an acid tone.

She giggles and digs in. I eat, but my stomach is battery acid poured on top of a hundred pounds of feathers.

A sudden breeze lifts Amanda's hair from behind just as she's raising her glass to drink, the ethereal glow of the string of lights behind her adding to the mystique. She's a wild spirit, a witchy woman in that second, and my heart beats for her, like a planet revolving around a heavenly body only because it knows no other option.

"Nine figures, huh?" She smiles, then sighs. "I guess I'll need to figure out the time difference between here and Dubai. You'll be there for the next two years."

"No. Declan will...oh." She's right. Declan's got his own company and this will fall on the new VP of Marketing in the long run, but for now, it's me.

"Let's not talk about work," she says. "Even if I do work for you now."

"Let's mix business with pleasure."

"If it involves going to Dubai and dressing like Elizabeth Bennet, no way."

"How about going to my bedroom and dressing up as Miss Bennet?"

"Pervert."

I laugh as my heart slams against my breastbone like a calypso drum.

Consuela herself delivers the main course.

"Lobster and steak?"Amanda asks, delighted.

"Simple yet elegant," Consuela explains. "And no cilantro." She tosses me a mock-angry look and leaves without fanfare.

We eat.

Rather, Amanda eats. I push food around on my plate and feel like time collapsed into three molecules on a steeplechase in my brain.

"Are you okay?" she asks as she finishes her food, pushing the plate away with a little groan of satisfaction.

"Yeah. Fine. Why?"

"You seem weird."

"It's been a long day."

"No. Not tired. *Weird*. Are we okay?

I pat my front pocket with the ring. "We are great."

"Good." She gives me a shy look, then reaches down to a bag next to her, on the ground. "Because I packed an overnight bag."

"Even better."

"With a whole change of clothes for work to leave at your place." The words come out in a rush, as if she thinks saying them quickly will make them less powerful.

"You're moving in?"

"If leaving a single change of clothing is your definition of 'moving in,' then yes."

I just smile.

"It's a first step," she says.

I touch the ring.

And the server appears with orange balls.

Yes.

Orange balls.

"Dessert!" the server says, leaving two ramekins of hot chocolate sauce next to a series of cheese puffs with fondue skewers.

"What's this?" Amanda asks.

Consuela appears, frowning. "Andrew asked me to make you

a special dessert. It was made to his exact specifications. Butter. Marshmallows." She winces like she's swallowed a bug. "Cheetos." She sighs. "The chocolate sauce was my own doing. How do you eat these monstrosities without chocolate?"

Amanda laughs, pokes a ball, dips it, and eats. "Oh, Consuela! Chocolate sauce on balls is divine."

I wisely keep my mouth shut. Consuela departs.

"Try one, Andrew!"

"I'm good."

"C'mon! Live a little."

"Those are for you."

"They should be for us. Share with me. I want you to enjoy this, too."

I follow her lead and try one.

They're surprisingly good.

And the taste is familiar. I'm remembering Vegas. Orange stains.

"What a lovely night," Amanda says with a sigh. The wind's picking up, and the sound of people walking on the streets below filters up, the conversation boisterous.

And then the conversation gets louder.

And *louder*.

"I think he said up here," Dad says, loud and clear.

"I've had dinner plenty of times at Consuela's, Dad. She'll greet us and tell us where to go." That's Declan.

"Andrew said he rented the entire rooftop." And Terry.

Amanda gives me a confused look. "Is that Declan I hear? And you rented the entire rooftop? Why?"

I stand quickly and pull the damn ring out of my pocket.

I told them all to come at 8:30, and Amanda was late, so—

"CONGRATULATIONS!" Dad booms as he explodes through the main door, followed quickly by Declan and Shannon, then Pam carrying Spritzy in a new red leather handbag that matches her red dress. Terry's in the mix, and is that Josh?

"Andrew? What is going on?" Amanda asks, taking in the sudden rush of all these people we know.

People who just interrupted the most important moment of my life.

*Our* life.

"James!" Consuela appears, giving Dad a hug and a double kiss on the cheeks. "So good to see you, but your timing is lousy. Andrew has not yet completed his task."

"Task? He hasn't asked her yet?"

Amanda grabs my hand. "Asked me...what?"

I open my palm. The glow of the lights makes the purple velvet glitter in the night.

"Oh!"

I guess I'm doing this with an audience.

"I brought you here tonight because I love you."

I bend down on one knee and look up into her lovely, captivating face.

"You are everything to me. I spent two years fighting it, punctuated by two stupid kisses in closets that were driven by a part of me that couldn't stay away from you."

"*Stupid* kisses?" One corner of her mouth turns up in a smile, her eyes on me, so big the irises don't touch her eyelids, and I could lose myself in her. Isn't that the point? To do so with intention.

And a ring.

"Yes. Stupid. None of your kisses are stupid in and of themselves. I made them stupid. I knew, more than two years ago, when you pulled me into my office closet to hide from Shannon that I was hopelessly falling for someone who would challenge me. And I was weak."

She gasps.

"That's right—weak. I was too weak to let myself admit I wanted you from the first moment I laid eyes on you in that meeting. The one where my stupid brother met the love of his life. Turns out I do copy my big brother—at least in one way."

She smiles.

"We both met the love of our life in that boardroom meeting that day."

"Oh, Andrew," she says with a sigh. Her voice trembles,

wobbling like my heart, which is flopping in my chest like a poorly-programmed Mars Rover robot in a cyclone, screaming *Please say yes please say yes please say yes.*

I've stacked the deck. Like walking into an intense negotiation with a great deal at stake, I've done my homework. My plans are airtight. I'm pretty certain this deal is going my way, and that the terms and conditions will be satisfactory to both parties.

Mergers are delicate business situations.

But heart and soul mergers are another animal entirely.

And then there's the body...

I've accounted for every contingency I can think of, save one.

If she says no, I don't know what to do.

*Please say yes.*

"This is my ring for you. I hope it's my penultimate ring, and that the final one will be our wedding band."

She gasps again, one hand splayed across her collarbone, the other reaching for my shoulder, stretching down. All my earlier nervousness fades. Memories of Vegas, of awakening to the rings on our hands, of the insane search for the truth, the exhalations of relief that we weren't married, all come barreling into my stream of consciousness.

Unnecessary panic and worry. Wasted anxiety. Childish agonizing.

It's all *gone.*

I have never been more sure of any choice in my life.

And now I hope she feels the same certainty. *Please*, I think. Please.

Looking up at her, the stars suspended in the dark sky above her, framing her as if she's a celestial body, I don't see Amanda.

I see my future. She is the love of my life, but even more—she is love itself.

Life would not be the same without that love.

"Please," I say, struggling to keep my voice steady. I open the box, the hinge like a heart valve. "We were practically married already."

Her laugh combines with a funny sniffling sound, and the hand on my shoulder digs in.

"But this is a first for me," I continue, determined to get this right. "I've never proposed to anyone before." Our eyes meet. She sends a charged signal through me, the words easier and harder, the struggle to take infinite emotion and distill it down to a few paltry sentences too brutal.

"Me, too," she murmurs, her smile adorable. "My first. So show me how this is done. You're the CEO. You take the lead."

I laugh, the sound more a pressure valve than true amusement, and startle to find we're surrounded by an audience that laughs along with me. I'd invited Dec and Shannon, Dad and Pam, and Terry, Josh and Grace to come to dinner after our engagement, to celebrate with joy, but all the crazy delays meant that I was proposing too late.

Time kept us apart.

I won't make that mistake again.

"I met you more than two years ago in a business meeting. You weren't Toilet Girl. I wasn't Hot Guy."

"You are so Hot Guy," she protests.

"But not *Hot Guy* Hot Guy."

My dad clears his throat. "Andrew is the only man who could get into an argument during a marriage proposal," he says in *sotto voce*, though not *sotto* enough. I should never have invited anyone.

"Dad, shut up," Terry says in a friendly voice. He's the only one of us who can get away with that.

"Fine," Dad mumbles.

"You brought an audience for your proposal?" Amanda asks, her voice shaking. "What else? Is Jessica Coffin behind the chef's herb garden, on Instagram now?"

"Oh, God, she isn't, is she?" Shannon asks with a gasp.

"But," I say in an exaggeratedly loud voice, my eyes matched to Amanda's, everyone else shoved away by the hand of love, "all I saw at that table was you."

"More like her breasts," Declan mutters.

"OUT!" I shout. "Consuela! Get them all a round of drinks or tiramisu or—"

"Check the tiramisu for engagement rings, though," Dad whispers.

"This was a mistake," I say to Amanda. "Not the proposal, but them." Why the hell did I invite them in the first place?

"Nothing about any of this is a mistake, Andrew." She reaches for my hand and pulls me away from the crowd to a small door next to Consuela's herb garden. Amanda opens it, peers in, and yanks my arm, then closes the door.

"Ask me here." The tiny space smells like soil and clay, metal shavings and aging wood. It's the scent of work, of art, of nature.

The crowd outside laughs.

"Here? In a—" What she's doing hits me.

"Closet." I can't even see her face, but she reaches for me, fingertips brushing against a bare spot on my neck, and all the emotion roars to the surface, as if my heart dances on my skin.

"You're it. You're everything. You keep asking me how I know, and Amanda, I can't keep trying to find the right words. I give up. I surrender. I don't know how to say it in a way that makes you understand how I know. You're my bedrock. I live in a world where business is complex and twisty, sabotage and intrigue rife, and where thinking you know something can be the worst form of arrogance. But this I know: you're my person. You're my soul mate. I don't want anyone else but you. And every minute I'm not married to you is like dying a slow, suffocating heart death."

"Oh!" Her warm breath tickles my nose. I smell her hair, a coconut-lime scent from the shampoo at my apartment.

"You fit. You're the puzzle piece that makes the whole picture of my life fall into place. We can spend years trying to justify what we already know, or we can just do it. Please." She still hasn't said *yes*.

"Andrew, I—"

I reach into the velvet box, going entirely on touch, and pull out the ring. "Please. Amanda—" I frown and blink hard. Shit. What's her middle name? She's told me this, right?

"It's Hortense."

"What?"

"My middle name."

"Your middle name is Hortense?" I can't keep the incredulity out of my voice.

"That's a deal breaker, isn't it? Sorry. Family name. Some great-great-grandmother from France."

I can't stop laughing. "*Hortense?*"

"You have a fabulous middle name. James is easy. I got stuck with Hortense."

"Is that why I didn't know your middle name?"

"If you were stuck with Hortense, would you run around sharing it?"

Can't stop laughing.

"It sounds better when you say it in French!" she protests.

Enough. I take a deep breath and start over.

"As long as you don't stick one of our kids with that name, I'm fine."

"Trust me, Andrew. No problem." She laughs, the sound fading into a breathy anticipation.

"Amanda *Hortense* Warrick, will you marry me? Will you let me finish what we started back in Vegas? Will you let me love you for the rest of my life? And give me a lifetime to make up for denying you the right to love me? Because I was—"

Her mouth is on mine and I almost lose my grasp on the ring, fumbling at the last second and feeling the cool metal in my palm, fingers folding over it into a fist. Damned if I'm losing another ring.

"Yes. Oh, God, Andrew, yes! Of course. I love you so much. And it took you long enough."

"What?"

"I couldn't believe you. Couldn't. Not that I didn't trust you, but I couldn't believe you felt the same stone-cold certainty inside that I felt."

I am stunned. "You felt it, too? All this time? Then what was with all the 'ridiculous' comments?"

"I was terrified. I figured you didn't feel this. I had to cover up my own feelings."

"I can't believe this."

"We really are a pair, aren't we?" she says with a tiny sound of joy.

"We are now." I pull my phone out of my pocket and turn on the flashlight app.

"What are you doing?"

I show her the ring. The inscription.

"'There's a pair of us,'" she reads slowly. I tuck the phone in my back pocket, find her left hand, and slowly slip the ring on her finger.

It feels exactly like the moment I slide into her when we're making love.

Magnified by infinity.

"I never have to wonder again," she whispers, her tone filled with the same marvel that overflows from my blood.

"Me neither."

"I knew, you know," she says into the darkness. "I knew the day you kissed me in your office."

"Me, too."

"We're nobody. There's a pair of us," she gasps.

"Shhhh," I say, "Don't tell." And then we silence each other with a kiss that seals the deal. Forever. It's done. I asked, she answered, and the search is over. It's been over for two years.

I just didn't know it until I almost accidentally married her in Vegas.

This time is no accident.

*Tap tap tap.*

"Andrew? Amanda?" It's Consuela. "I know the rooftop is a bit small for a large party like this, but Andrew has already tested my patience with his cilantro ban. I refuse to serve you in a garden closet as well. I have standards."

I grab the doorknob and slowly crack the door open to find an audience of faces we know and love surrounding us.

And Declan's there, too.

Behind the crowd, the white string of holiday lights provides a warm glow against the panoramic view of the city by the port, the moon's glow infused with a happiness I don't remember noticing before.

"Where's the ring?" someone shouts, and Amanda holds up her left hand, diamond facing out. My eyes catch the glitter of light on metal.

Two months ago, I saw sunshine dancing on a different ring on her hand in bed in a hotel room in Las Vegas.

I like Boston moonlight on this ring even more.

## Chapter Twenty-Two

The engagement party is over. Everyone enjoyed a night of food and wine, and at some point, Consuela hired a piano player to come and we even danced, Dad twirling Pam, Amanda awkward in my arms. "I've never actually *dance* danced with a guy!" she protested, as the piano player pounded out some old dance hall tunes. All the dance lessons Mom forced me to attend came to fruition, Amanda's body light and fine in my arms, even as she stepped on my feet. Shannon giggled as Declan led her through their own clumsy steps, while Josh turned Terry's offer down with a blush and a stammer that made Terry's sonic boom laugh appear.

And then Terry hogged our women, proving just who really is the best dancer out of all the McCormick brothers.

Dad showed him up, though.

Yes, we're a competitive bunch, but I'm the winner tonight.

The true winner.

My fiancée and I are home now, exhausted and exhilarated. My place. I have to stop calling it that. Now it is *our* place.

Amanda's work outfit hangs in the closet. Her toothbrush is on the counter in my bathroom, along with hair-styling crap and a bunch of creams that smell good but that she doesn't need. She's beautiful and perfect right out of the shower, no artifice, no adaptation.

Just as she is.

Naked and real.

Like right now.

Amanda and I are in that space that you learn exists only when it finds you. No amount of searching helps you to locate it. This space appears at the intersection of awareness and volition, of love and permission.

Where the wiser mind waits patiently, waiting for you to visit.

We stand at the edge of the bed, the slider door open, the ocean air tickling our bodies. The same air that welcomed Amanda's *yes* at Consuela's rooftop restaurant just hours ago is joining us in this deeper *yes* here in my bedroom.

*Our* bedroom.

Her hair falls in straight lines, ending with a slight curl at her shoulder, framing a face with eyes that look at me from galaxies afar. I stare openly, my own eyes eager to take her in, watching my hand as it cups her jaw, feeling the enormity that comes from knowing my skin touches hers, and that we are bonded forever.

Such a revelation seems both impossible and inevitable, a paradox I only reconcile when she kisses me, standing on tiptoe, the press of nude flesh against nude flesh a startling reminder that this is really in the moment. It unfolds before me like an hourglass clock, each grain a kiss, a sigh, a breath.

Moonlight shines on her ring. Soon I will wear one, too. My thumb finds the soft spot at the base of my left ring finger and worries it. Not much longer, I tell myself.

Soon.

"You proposed," she whispers, her smile a universe of its own. "We're getting married."

"Yes."

"I'll be your wife."

"Yes."

"Amanda McCormick," she says, as if trying on the name like a dress in a store.

I relax. "Sounds perfect." My body moves closer to hers, seeking the softness, but without urgency.

"You want kids."

"Yes. 6.5," I joke as I just watch her.

"Split the difference between four and nine?"

I shrug.

"Maybe we should start practicing now."

"You told me *maybe* isn't part of my vocabulary." I move her back against the bed so she drops, sitting on the edge, and we love in long, languid shifts until we're lying parallel to each other. Her breasts drop to the bed cover, gravity pulling them the way Amanda pulls me to her, making me change shape. We're open and on display for each other, hiding nothing, baring all.

We are real.

"When you touch me," she says in a low, strong voice, "all the pieces of me that hum throughout the day go silent. All the chatter in my mind halts. You ground me, Andrew. You fix me."

"Fine praise coming from a true fixer."

"I'm not broken, though." Her palms start at my wrists and slide up my forearms, caressing the outer edge of my arms, coming up my shoulders and making goosebumps ripple across me like fire and ice in one stroke. "You fix me in ways that enhance."

"Good."

"You potentiate."

"And you exponentiate."

She laughs. "This isn't a contest."

"I'm not joking. And I'm not competing." I trace the outer edge of the circle of her nipple on the breast that falls against the other. Her skin tightens, and so do I.

"We're greater than each other when we're together," she says before she kisses me.

She is every fantasy in front of me, a fusion of hot flesh and intelligence and maternal promise and a life's journey I don't have the script for but want to live anyhow.

Amanda is mine.

And she wants me right back.

Her ring shines as she reaches up and slides her hand against the back of my neck.

"Then competing is foolish. We need to collaborate." I kiss her shoulder.

"Work together," she gasps as I move down, taking that same nipple in my mouth. The vibration of that noise she makes in the back of her throat drives me crazy.

"Find a rhythm," I growl, mouth still on her, talking around the pink delight.

"Oh, yes," she sighs, fingers threading in my hair. "Most definitely that."

I revel in the perverse pleasure of knowing this body that moves beneath me, that responds to my touch and tease, is the only body I'll know intimately until my dying day. Perverse because I should be horrified, mortified and sad to reduce my pool of female flesh down to a single woman.

And yet it's the depth of the water that makes the swim so divine.

She comes with a cry of my name like she's drowning and only I can save her, yet I'm the one who's sent her into this helpless state, floating and gasping, and as I come up for air she grabs me with such fiery need our mouths crash into each other, her strength so arousing we become damn near violent, the kiss desperate and drawing. Amanda's body changes after climax, turning warmer and looser, more expansive and distilled into a pink heat that covers her like a magnetic force field drawing me through, captured and captivated.

I'm drawn to it, invited to come into a world where no one else gains entry. A world that only exists when we're this close.

Her hand runs from my neck down over my pecs, the touch lightening at my abs, fingers tickling the thick hair trail that leads to an even thicker destination. As her hand traces lines on a map that lives only in her mind, I close my eyes, inhaling deeply, tasting and smelling her.

The cool metal on her ring finger warms from my body heat. This ring is permanent. I'll pair it with a wedding band, one that matches a thicker one on my own left hand, and we'll be bonded forever.

We'll make formal what we already know.

A deep tingle pulses through me at the thought, at knowing the search is over, and as Amanda reaches for me and wraps her hand, stroking with her palm, sending a roar of desire shooting through my bloodstream at the speed of light, I open my eyes and look out the open balcony door to find the cityscape staring back, blinking in color and white, the dull hush of wind outside a whisper that chants approval.

And then I grab her, pulling her on top of me, the jumble of legs and arms and moans and gasps settling as she straddles me, then envelops with a welcoming warmth and a pensive smile, her face hovering over me, hair spilling onto my forehead.

"You're mine," she says, moving until I groan.

"That's my line."

"It can be mine, too. We can both feel it."

"I'm feeling it." I move up until she arches back, her control tenuous. I love how her body looks in the moonlight, the landscape full and round, uninhibited. She's a goddess.

We quicken, the emotion urging us forward, need replacing love at some point, all of the emotions converging until lust takes over our pulses, time becoming meaningless, pushing us to an explosive release, all pretense of the polite shells we wear in public shed like old skin.

Coming together has new meaning now, and as she relaxes on me, her cheek buried in my shoulder, her ass in the air, my hips tight and my hands and feet half numb, the wind pushes the curtains into the bedroom again, the edge brushing against my toes.

"It might rain again," she says, dazed and slow. A kiss on my ear makes me smile.

"Let it rain."

I look at the clock with an exaggerated head move.

"What are you doing?"

"That took thirty-nine minutes," I say, stretching my neck like a rooster strutting.

She smacks my breastbone. "It's not a competition!"

But it is.

For the record: I am not making the next part up.

Fireworks explode outside the window, the high-pitched whine of a bomb on its trajectory piercing our hearing in the split second before the firework explodes.

Amanda moves and looks out the window as a shower of red and white light dots fills the night sky.

"I knew I was good in bed, but *damn*," I say.

She laughs as she moves next to me, hip to toe touching me as she cuddles against my chest and we watch whatever show was long-ago scheduled, timed serendipitously for our engagement night.

Our coming together.

Our declaration of dependence.

## TWO MONTHS LATER...

"Mr. McCormick? Your brother is on the line? He wants you to stop ignoring his texts and talk to him?" Gina's standing in the doorway, waving at me.

I look up from my computer, where I've just ended an online meeting with the very happy Sultan of Al-Massi. A nine-figure meeting that will leave our board of directors very happy as well. Amanda and I have been invited to attend a sprawling gala on the grounds of his estate. Professor Kensley-Wentingham will be there as well, as historical consultant.

I think I'll have my tailor do my own pants this time.

"What does Declan want?"

"Something about the local news? How you're on it?"

"What?"

She shrugs. "Pickup the phone and ask him?"

I do.

"Did Amanda freak out yet?" Dec asks, dispensing with the preliminaries.

"Freak out over what?"

"Turn on New England Cable News. The Walden Pond story."

"The *what*?"

"Just watch."

"Why should I watch a—" I click on the television in my

office, rattle through channels filled with nothing but bad daytime soaps and old movies, and then:

LOCAL WOMAN FINDS THREE-CARAT DIAMOND RING IN WALDEN POND

*Bzzz.*

Texts start pouring in.

"Lucky you, Amanda's in Chicago on business. You're never living this down," Declan says. "Shannon's laughing her ass off."

"Amanda won't care," I lie. We've been engaged for two months, just starting to make wedding plans for next year. I wondered if anyone would ever find that ring.

He snorts. "You really don't understand women, do you?"

*Click.*

"Gina!"

"Yes, sir?"

"If a guy went to propose to you but lost the ring before he had a chance to propose, then bought another ring and proposed later, but never told you about ring number one, would you be upset if you later learned about it?"

She just blinks.

"And if the story made the local news, would that be upsetting?"

"Mr. McCormick?"

"Yes."

"You are the weirdest boss I have ever had. And I worked in academia as a temp, which is the very definition of workplace dysfunction."

That's two declarative sentences in a row. I'm on Gina's shit list now.

"But I'm never boring."

She laughs and walks out of my office.

*Ring!*

An actual phone call. It's Amanda.

"Funny how some woman found a three carat engagement ring in Walden Pond. Wonder if she found the Tesla key fob, too."

She has picked up the rude habit of starting conversations midstream from my brother.

"What are you talking about?" I lie.

"Don't play that game." Her voice goes soft. "Declan told Shannon who told me."

The modern equivalent of the party line.

"You think I have something to do with this?" I put the television on closed captioning.

"Andrew."

"You have a ring, right?"

"Yes. It's beautiful."

"Then why do you care about some crazy story about some stupid guy who lost a ring in Walden Pond?"

"He isn't stupid."

"You know him?"

"I might."

"Sounds stupid to me if he decided to jump in the pond and re-enact a classic scene from nineteenth-century British literature and wound up unable to finish the job by proposing."

"Loose pockets?"

"Something like that."

Her breath catches. "News reports say the ring has an inscription. You can guess what it says."

Damn.

"You were going to propose then?"

"Yes."

"Why didn't you tell me?"

"Have you met my ego? He's the size of Vince, and doesn't exactly run around admitting to monumental mistakes."

"I was so mean to you about losing your keys."

"Yes, you were."

"And your pants."

"The hair on my thighs is starting to grow back in." And it itches. I don't get how women wax everything.

"And it turns out you were freaking out because you'd lost so much more."

"It was just a ring. What I couldn't bear to lose was you."

"You have me now."

"Yes."

"Forever."

"Soon."

"We need to set a date."

"How about next week? When you come home. We'll just go to the courthouse, get the license, and quietly run off."

"My mom would kill me."

I think of Pam, who would be devastated if we eloped. My dad, on the other hand, would just be angry that we deprived him of a public relations boost.

"Fine. But I draw the line at cats acting as flower girls."

"My mother would never do that!"

"Good."

"She would use Spritzy."

"That's supposed to be better?"

"Spritzy is a dog. Not a cat. A cat as a flower girl is crazy. A dog is just silly."

"You have a spectrum stored in your mind that is calibrated in ways I cannot fathom."

She ignores that and says, "Montelcini Flowers is *not* doing our wedding."

"Agreed."

"This is really happening, Andrew? You're sure?"

"You keep asking me that. I'm going to stop answering. I'll have Gina make a big sign that says *Yes, I'm sure* and I'll just hold it up whenever you ask." I wish she were here so I could look her in the eye. "I wouldn't have asked you if I weren't sure."

"No, you wouldn't have. I know that. And I'm not uncertain. I think I'm just reeling."

"Me, too."

She laughs. "Can we have the wedding at Consuela's?"

I grin. "Perfect. When you come home, we'll pick a date."

"I can't believe you lost a three-carat ring while trying to court me."

"I can't believe you made me court you."

"It worked, didn't it? We're engaged."

My office door flies open and there's Amanda, on her cell, dragging a carry-on bag.

"Surprise!" she says in stereo, in person and on the phone.

"What's this?"

She hangs up. "Client meeting ended fast."

"For good or bad reasons?" I give her a peck on the cheek. She pulls me in for a long, slow, wet welcome kiss that makes me wonder how quickly Gina can clear my next meeting.

Or ten.

"I'm a fixer, right? We closed already."

"C'mere, fiancée."

"You c'mere, fiancé."

The kiss. The taste of her after spending a week apart. It's like taking that first breath when you break the surface after swimming underwater until your lungs are about to burst.

Like a male drone's penis during sex.

Great. It's official.

Amanda's bad analogies are contagious.

"Why are you laughing while kissing me?"

"Because I love you."

"And that makes you laugh?"

"Yes."

"What are you laughing about?"

"Exploding penises."

"Was my mom just here?"

I laugh harder. I kiss harder.

Everything gets harder.

But life just got easier.

And so did love.


:)


*A note from Julia*: Thank you so much for reading Andrew and Amanda's crazy Vegas fun. I am often asked, since I introduced the idea of Cheeto-marshmallow treats back in early 2015, whether people really eat them.

Yes! Amanda's crazy fixation is real. <u>Here's a recipe</u>.

The next book in the series, *Shopping for an Heir*, is a bit of a departure, but no less fun! This time, we get the story of Declan's chauffeur/sculptor, Gerald:

Gerald Wright *works* for billionaires. He never imagined he'd *become* one.

The former Navy Seal is a chauffeur by day, artist by night, so when hotter-than-ever ex-fiancée Suzanne Dayton interrupts his nude model sculpting class to serve him with inheritance paperwork from a man he's never heard of, he assumes it's a joke.

Turns out the joke's on him. There's just one catch. A big one.

And it might be Suzanne—in more ways than he ever dreamed.

Read the first chapter of *Shopping for an Heir* now! Keep flipping the page.

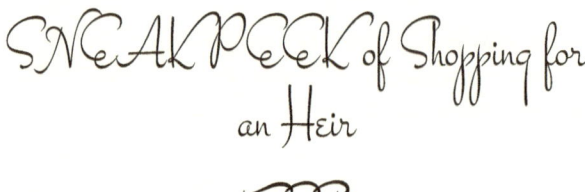

SNEAK PEEK of Shopping for an Heir

## Chapter One

"You promised me a naked hot young man, and you'd better deliver on that promise, Mr. Clean."

Gerald Wright wasn't quite sure he'd really heard that. Did the sweet old lady who wore sequined white tennis shoes that matched her pink cardigan really say—

"I didn't pay $149 for this art class to play with pears and apples and make ashtrays out of clay. I want some man candy to ogle."

Oh yeah. Heard it loud and clear.

Gerald Wright looked up slowly from his clipboard, eyelids in place, eyeballs doing the work as he met the steely glare of a woman old enough to have voted for Roosevelt.

Maybe even *Theodore* Roosevelt.

"Class doesn't start for five minutes, ma'am. Cool your jets." He took a good look at her. He'd seen holy men in Afghanistan with fewer wrinkles. Eyes sunken deep into weathered flesh, she had a twisted, puckered mouth, moved with slow intent, and wore a pink t-shirt with white lettering across the chest that said, "My Breasts Used To Be This High."

Without thinking, he looked down and saw that along the hemline the shirt said, "Ha! Made You Look."

He cringed.

"I haven't had to cool my jets in forty years. My jet hormones left along with all my tight skin," she said, jiggling her arms. The woman had *batwings*.

Gerald nearly ducked.

"Agnes!" Another older woman appeared behind the old lady, hobbling on a metallic walker with yellow tennis balls covering the front two posts. She wore a blonde wig with feathered hair. Gerald tried not to do a double take, because the wig looked exactly like hair from that old '70s show, *Charlie's Angels*. Bright red lipstick completed the look.

"Quit pestering the nice young man." She stopped and gave Gerald a once over. "You look like Kojak."

Agnes blinked hard. With no eyelashes, she looked like a baby bird. A very wrinkled, ornery baby bird with a mouth like a sailor. "He doesn't look like Kojak! Get with the program, Corrine. Kojak sucked on a lollipop. This one looks like that other bald actor."

Gerald ran a palm against his shaved head and tried not to groan. He searched the class list. Yup. There they were: Agnes Duchamp and Corrine Morris.

And the magic words: Paid. In. Full.

It was going to be a long eight weeks.

"What other bald actor?" Corrine asked, squinting. She flashed Gerald a great big flirty smile, so full of life he couldn't help but smile back.

"You know. The one in that movie about the boy who saw dead people."

"Casper?"

"No."

"The two of them at the pottery wheel, having sex?"

"No."

"The one who was the captain of that new *Star Trek* show?"

"No."

"Agnes, I don't have all day to sit here playing Celebrity

Alzheimer's with you. Which bald actor does this art teacher—what's your name?" Corrine pursed her lips as she asked the unexpected question, making Gerald sigh.

"Gerald. Gerald Wright."

"Gerald!" Agnes laughed. "What kind of name is that for a bald sculptor? Sounds like an accountant."

"Don't blame me, ma'am. My parents picked it."

"They must be wildcats. What'd they name your sister? Iphigenia?"

He opened his mouth to defend Victoria, his BASE-jumping, outdoor-survivalist-instructor little sis, but stopped himself.

"Like you should talk, *Agnes*," Corrine snapped, pointing at her friend. "People with old lady names shouldn't cast stones."

Agnes scowled, layers of skin folding in on each other, like origami. "What actor does he look like?" Agnes demanded of her friend, who reached up to her ear and fiddled with her earring, giving Gerald another bright smile he couldn't help but return.

"What?" Corrine asked Agnes sweetly.

"What actor does Gerald the Accountant look like?"

"What?" Corrine began moving like a turtle on speed toward the front of the room. A bumper sticker wrapped around one of the posts of her walker said, *I Brake for Naked Hitchhikers with Guitars.*

"Damn it, Corrine, you turned off your hearing aid again, didn't you?"

"What?" Corrine winked at him.

He was starting to like her.

"You're lucky you're still recovering from that surgery, Corrine, or I'd punch you."

"You punch me, and I won't share my lorazepam with you for those long weekends when your son-in-law comes to visit. You know. The one who wants to put you in a home?"

Agnes shut up.

As the two old ladies took their places in the front row, at the table directly before the model's platform, Gerald greeted incoming students. So many new faces. He was lucky to get eight students per class, but tonight's roster showed twenty-seven.

The new marketing intern in the office was doing a bang-up job.

Woman after woman, most of them over fifty, began to assemble, buzzing with excitement, taking their places at the carefully spaced tables in the room.

"Gerald!" Stacy, one of the other interns in the art center's office, waved to him from the doorway. "You need more chairs? We have some walk-ins."

"Walk-ins? We never have walk-ins." Gerald strode across the room as the women in the front row hissed at each other under their breath, some kind of argument brewing.

"We do today!" Stacy had a high, squeaky voice when she was excited, a mouth full of braces, and more freckles than common sense. She was a good kid, twirling her blonde ponytail, eyes wide with an eagerness to please. "I think the total will come close to thirty."

"Then we need more sculpting clay."

"Want me to check the inventory?" she begged, eager for responsibility.

He grinned. "Of course. Couldn't pull this off without your help." The dazzling smile she returned cut quickly as she pivoted and sprinted down the hall to the supply room.

Thirty students. He hadn't taught thirty students all year, across four different sessions, for this Nude Sculpting class. What was going on?

Puzzled, he walked back into the room, a short line forming before him as people registered, by turns nervous and calm, some in pairs with a buddy, most of them seeming to know old Agnes and Corrine up there in front.

He narrowed his eyes and strode with purpose to the two of them, catching the end of a fevered conversation between Agnes and a fifty-something brunette.

"I've seen his ass before. Touched it, even," Agnes insisted.

"Class was supposed to start two minutes ago, and no Declan McCormick, Agnes. If I gave up my Tuesday night Wine and Whine Book Club because of you and there's no cute butt guy, you're toast."

"What are you going to threaten me with, Pauline? I'm ninety-three. Nothing scares me."

Corrine whispered, "Your son-in-law. Nursing home." She rolled her eyes. "And you're ninety-two, Agnes. For God's sake, can't you keep track?"

Agnes turned the color of a sheet.

"I'm not sure which one pisses me off more. My son-in-law or realizing I've been telling the world I'm a year older than I really am."

Corrine just shook her head and began making what looked like a penis out of the lump of modeling clay in front of her.

"Declan's coming. Don't worry," Agnes insisted, standing her ground, eyeing Corrine's sculpture with interest.

Gerald sighed, crossing his arms over his chest, clipboard bouncing in one hand as he tapped it against his biceps.

"You're quite the maven, aren't you, Agnes?"

"Maven?"

"Someone who spreads the word. Information broker."

"Been called worse," she cackled.

"You told all these women to come because of Declan McCormick's naked body?"

"Yes." She stared at him like the female version of Clint Eastwood in a *Dirty Harry* movie. Gerald stared back. A grudging respect began to grow in him. She was hard core.

"The Westside Center for the Arts thanks you," he replied, not breaking steely eye contact. "We've been trying to grow our classes."

"Get some hot nude models, then."

"That's not the purpose of these classes, ma'am."

"Purpose, schmurpose. You want more people like me, with disposable income and nothing more exciting at home than reruns of *To Catch a Predator* and videos on how to make gluten-free cauliflower pizza crusts on cable television to come to these classes, you spice them up."

"This is nude-model sculpting, designed to teach basic artistic anatomy. We're not here to titillate."

She reached into her purse and pulled out a flask. "Call it

what you want, Gerald the Accountant. This is like the bache-
lorette party I never had."

And with that, Agnes sucked down a shot of whatever was in
that flask.

Corrine reached for it. "Give me a nip."

"What?"

"I said, give me a nip."

Agnes' mouth twisted with a grin. "What?" She pointed to
her ear and said, "Two can play that game, Corrine." She guzzled
the rest of whatever liquid joy was in there.

It was going to be a *glacial* eight weeks.

Stacy jogged into the classroom, carrying a massive tub of
modeling clay, face flushed, the hair around her scalp damp with
sweat. "Here you go."

"Hey." The rumble of a man's baritone made all the sopranos
and altos come to a halt. Gerald looked up.

Declan McCormick was finally here.

"I am late because I don't have a chauffeur anymore," he said
pointedly, making a face. That was as close to an apology as the
class would get out of the man. "Do you know how time-
consuming parking in one of those garages can be? They make
you walk to a pay station and walk back to your car with the tick-
et." He let out an exasperated sigh. "I don't know how people live
like this. What a waste of time."

The room broke out in spontaneous applause.

Agnes got to her feet and turned around, facing her class-
mates, arms in the air like Rocky after defeating Apollo Creed.
"See? Told you he'd be here."

Declan's eyes darted to the old lady, then rolled so high they
might as well be cherry pickers. "Oh, God. Are you sure we're not
in Salem? Because I see a witch."

"I see you've met Agnes," Gerald said, smothering a grin. He
reached out to give Declan's hand a shake, the two pumping arms
madly, women in the room sighing loudly.

"We're *intimately* acquainted," Agnes crowed proudly, then
hiccuped. The crowd erupted into titters.

JULIA KENT

Declan pulled him in for a half hug. "Watch the fingers," he whispered. "She's more nimble than you think."

"Is that why enrollment's triple the norm? Word got out you're the model?"

Dec shakes his head. "Marie."

"Your mother-in-law is crazy."

"Tell me something I don't know."

"I know a lot about your family that *you* don't know." Because Declan no longer worked for Anterdec, their relationship had changed. He wasn't Gerald's boss anymore. Two months ago, he married Shannon and bought his own chain of coffee shops. Gerald still worked for Declan's brother, CEO Andrew, and their father, James, who founded Anterdec more than thirty years ago.

"If you've got good dirt on my brother, I need to know."

"Non-disclosure agreement." He almost called him *sir*, but caught himself. "Sorry, Declan."

Oblivious to the twenty-seven sets of eyes on him, Declan took stock of Gerald. He knew how the guy worked. This was banter, word play, a man's-man kind of joking around.

"Fight you for it."

See?

"What're the terms?"

"Pool. Two out of three games. You win, you get me as a nude model for every class. I win, you give me one juicy detail about my brother. Something actionable."

Having a set model for every class would make the sessions flow better, and allow Gerald to get into advanced sculpting techniques. On the other hand, he liked having varying models. Light, shadow, contour, and all the finer points of sculpture could be assessed and taught with variation.

"I'll pay extra if he's the class model for all eight weeks!" crowed Agnes.

Murmurs of furious assent filled the room.

"You better be good at billiards, Mr. Clean!" Corrine chimed in.

"Mr. Clean?" Declan's eyebrow went up.

"Keep that face. I want it like that for the entire hour pose."

One side of Declan's mouth twitched, but he kept the perfect arch.

"Ladies! Ladies! Let's get down to business."

"I thought you were!" Agnes gave him a creepy smile. "You'd better be good at stripes and solids, mister. My husband was a pool shark. Too bad he's dead, or he'd teach you a few things."

Declan walked through a small door right behind the instructor's platform.

"Where's he going?" Corrine asked sweetly. All the heads in the class turned to track him. It was like watching sunflowers follow the sun.

"To get ready," Gerald said, setting down his clipboard and looking out at the sea of faces. What a boon.

And as a matter of fact, he was a damn fine pool player.

Shark, even. That's how he made some extra money in high school.

Play stupid and let people underestimate you.

Then you have them at an advantage.

Declan emerged wearing a plain white bathrobe. The room filled with whispers.

"Welcome!" Gerald clapped his hands once, bellowing out the word. The commanding voice got their attention, heads swiveling toward him. They wore smocks and poked at the clay in front of them, uncertain but eager. Half the women looked at Declan like they were here for an appetizer rather than a lesson, but that was his model's problem.

Gerald was here to teach.

"I'm Gerald Wright, your instructor. Before you at each student's place, you'll find the necessary supplies for all eight classes, including a folder. Please take the notecard inside, fold it in half, and write your name on one half, facing it toward the front of class. Normally, we introduce ourselves, but the class is so big that we'd lose an entire session, so let's use name tags and go from there."

For the next two minutes, students shuffled notecards and

pens, writing and folding, until all twenty-seven had little inverted Vs on their tables.

He walked in front of Declan, who now sat on his posing stool, still berobed.

Declan was frowning.

"What's wrong?" Gerald asked.

Following the billionaire's gaze, he quickly got the lay of the land.

Twelve women had written their phone numbers on their cards, instead of their names.

"Fascinating, ladies," Gerald said dryly. "So many of you have the first name 617. Must have been popular sometime in the early 1960s."

The laughter that filled the room was genuine.

One minute later, actual names were on the cards, and Gerald got down to business.

"Unlike most classes, we don't spend our first day learning theory. We dive right in."

Someone in the back whistled.

"This isn't a Pats game," Gerald said.

"Hope not! Don't need to see any deflated balls," Agnes cracked.

Declan's face was stone.

"Or a Red Sox game," Gerald said, trying to change the subject.

"You got a Green Monster under that robe?" Agnes asked Declan, grinning madly.

"What does that even mean?" Declan hissed. He turned to Gerald. "And stop with the sports comments. I don't want to know what she comes up with for hockey."

Agnes chortled.

Gerald had to get his class under control.

"Ladies!"

Someone in the back had just entered the room. Two guys cleared their throats meaningfully.

"And gentlemen," he added with a nod. The two guys took their seats and put on aprons.

"Welcome to Nude Sculpting 101. This is a class for beginners. That said," he continued, his voice growing firmer, "this is a class where respect for the model is Rule #1."

The tittering simmered down.

Gerald mustered his old commanding voice, the one he had eased out of himself for the past ten years. From the gleam in a few eyes, he'd need it more than he did when he was in the Navy.

"You will not make jokes about the model's body. If this were a female model, you would never dare. Why should it be different because it's a man?"

Agnes started to open her mouth. He spun on her, finger pointed, and before she could speak, barked, "That was a rhetorical question."

Her mouth snapped shut.

"We are here to be artists."

Someone sighed. It was a happy sound.

"We are here to learn to connect what the eyes see with what the hands do."

More sighs and a few uncomfortable looks.

"You will learn about shadow and curve, form and realism, and how to find the deeper eye within you that guides the body toward what it knows it can recreate from memory, from stored touch—"

A sound of appreciation between two black women who had been chattering in whispers almost made Gerald smile. They gave him their rapt attention.

"You are artists," he repeated. "Not office workers or retirees or stay-at-home parents or college students. In this class, ninety minutes a week, you are creators. You are visioneers. You are sensual and grounded in the core essence of what it means to be human. Your hands and arms will take what you know, what you see, and give it life through the clay."

Now he had them eating out of his hand. He paced in the space between Declan and the first row, eyes on the students as he walked back and forth, slowly, but with deliberation.

"Let's see what you find within yourselves, ladies and gentlemen. That's what art is—self-exploration through expression.

Connection by touching others through the visual, the tactile. Welcome to the world of art. And our arts center thanks you— your tuition money helps fund arts programs for kids and seniors, so the enthusiastic attendance is a welcome sight."

He stopped and looked at all the faces.

"Let's begin."

As if on cue, Declan dropped the robe.

The class gasped.

Gerald grinned.

***Read the rest of* Shopping for an Heir *wherever you find* books!**

*Acknowledgments*

To Elizabeth, who helped me with the historical costume details in the book, and whose tour of the Vokes Theater in Wayland, Massachusetts and discussion and review of parts of this manuscript helped me greatly. I now know the difference between "rise" and "inseam," and so do Andrew and Vince. ;)

To Kate, whose post on detachable octopus penises in my Facebook group provided a lively little fact in this book.

To my husband, "Clark" Kent, for sparking an exceptionally lively discussion on my Facebook reader group, <u>Laugh Your Way to Love</u>, about MATH. Only you, honey. Only *you* could get a bunch of romance readers arguing over exponential vs. factorial combinations.

And to my maternal grandmother, whose love for the 1990s BBC production of *Pride and Prejudice* was infectious. I attended a very high-tech university at the time, and had early access to good Internet search engines. Printing off the rare fan pages about Colin Firth and Jennifer Ehle became a hobby for me, and Grandma's deep appreciation for those pages, and utter delight at the miniseries, has stayed with me as I wrote portions of this book. The image of those VHS tapes in their boxed set, proudly displayed on her television and lovingly re-watched, resting next to the stacks of printouts about the stars, makes me now realize my grandmother was an eighty-something diehard fangirl.

She's been gone for many, many years, but her love of *Pride and Prejudice* remains in me. I miss you, Grandma. I wish you'd lived to see this book. You were a librarian and instilled a love of reading in me, bringing my five-year-old self with you to alphabetize the library return cards, and letting me re-shelve books, all with an eye toward exposing me to a richer culture through books. You succeeded.

For EFW, who lives on in so many different ways.

# Other Books by Julia Kent

Love You Fiancee

Little Miss Perfect
Fluffy
Perky
Feisty
Hasty
Tasty

Random Acts of Crazy
Random Acts of Trust
Random Acts of Fantasy
Random Acts of Hope
Randomly Acts of Yes
Random Acts of Love
Random Acts of LA
Random Acts of Christmas
Random Acts of Vegas
Random Acts of New Year
Random Acts of Baby

In Your Dreams
Her Billionaires
It's Complicated
Completely Complicated
It's Always Complicated
Eternally Complicated

Maliciously Obedient
Suspiciously Obedient
Deliciously Obedient

Christmasly Obedient

Our Options Have Changed (with Elisa Reed)
Thank You For Holding (with Elisa Reed)

# About the Author

SIGN UP FOR MY NEWSLETTER ->
EEPURL.COM/UXB4R

*New York Times* and *USA Today* bestselling author Julia Kent writes romantic comedy with an edge. Since 2013, she has sold more than 2.5 million books, with 5 *New York Times* bestsellers and more than 23 appearances on the *USA Today* bestseller list. Her books have been translated into French and German, with more languages coming.

From billionaires to BBWs to new adult rock stars, Julia finds a sensual, goofy joy in every contemporary romance she writes. Unlike Shannon from Shopping for a Billionaire, she did not meet her husband after dropping her phone in a men's room toilet (and he isn't a billionaire).

She lives in New England with her husband and three kids in a household where only she has the gene necessary to change toilet paper rolls.

She loves to hear from her readers by email at jkentauthor@gmail.com, on Twitter @jkentauthor, on Facebook at https://www.facebook.com/jkentauthor . Visit her at http://jkentauthor.com

**f** 𝕏

# Join My Substack!

What the heck is a Substack, you ask? It's like a blog/newsletter/podcast, all rolled into one.

You don't just get an email from me saying "Hey, buy my books!"

Instead, you get a richer, more fun experience, with posts/newsletters that are designed to be savored over a long stretch in a comfortable chair, sipping your beverage of choice while you laugh, imagine, and stay entertained.

You can read one (or more) of my posts here, and sign up on the spot to get my "Julia Kent's Writing Cabin" delivered to you at least once a week.

https://juliakent.substack.com

Many posts include an audio conversation between me and my husband, Clark. We talk about my books, ideas about romance, and so much more. Sometimes we're even funny! ;)

I'm having so much fun reliving into topics ranging from wedding romance to one-night stands to cover design to food insecurity and volunteering. Designed to be a free-flowing place for ideas, my little online writing cabin invites you to come on in, take a seat by the fire, and chat with me and other readers in the comments.

Or just read. It's all up to you.

<3